DUKE OF CHARM

Dukes of Distinction

Book 2

Alexa Aston

Text by Alexa Aston
Cover by Wicked Smart Designs

Dragonblade Publishing, Inc. is an imprint of Kathryn Le Veque Novels, Inc.
P.O. Box 7968
La Verne CA 91750
ceo@dragonbladepublishing.com

Produced in the United States of America

First Edition February 2021
Print Edition

ARE YOU SIGNED UP FOR DRAGONBLADE'S BLOG?

You'll get the latest news and information on exclusive giveaways, exclusive excerpts, coming releases, sales, free books, cover reveals and more.

Check out our complete list of authors, too!

No spam, no junk. That's a promise!

Sign Up Here

www.dragonbladepublishing.com

Dearest Reader;

Thank you for your support of a small press. At Dragonblade Publishing, we strive to bring you the highest quality Historical Romance from the some of the best authors in the business. Without your support, there is no 'us', so we sincerely hope you adore these stories and find some new favorite authors along the way.

Happy Reading!

CEO, Dragonblade Publishing

Additional Dragonblade books by Author Alexa Aston

Dukes of Distinction Series

Duke of Renown

Duke of Charm

Medieval Runaway Wives

Song of the Heart

A Promise of Tomorrow

Destined for Love

King's Cousins Series

The Pawn

The Heir

The Bastard

Knights of Honor Series

Word of Honor

Marked by Honor

Code of Honor

Journey to Honor

Heart of Honor

Bold in Honor

Love and Honor

Gift of Honor

Path to Honor

Return to Honor

The St. Clairs Series

Devoted to the Duke

Midnight with the Marquess

Embracing the Earl
Defending the Duke
Suddenly a St. Clair
Starlight Night

Soldiers & Soulmates Series

To Heal an Earl
To Tame a Rogue
To Trust a Duke
To Save a Love
To Win a Widow

The Lyon's Den Connected World

The Lyon's Lady Love

Chapter One

London—June 1808

If George didn't notice her in this dress, then she would never win his heart.

Lady Samantha Wallace stepped back and gazed into the mirror. Her raven hair was piled high atop her head, adding some to her average height. Her aquamarine eyes sparkled. She'd rubbed a tiny bit of rouge onto her lips, giving them a trace of color. Smoothing the skirts of her blush-colored gown, she looked critically at the neckline. It exposed more of her bosom than usual but she needed something to attract George's attention.

She couldn't remember a time when she hadn't been in love with George, the Duke of Colebourne. He'd been her brother's best friend from the cradle, just as their fathers had been best friends all their lives. George was a constant visitor at Treadwell Manor, just as Weston spent many hours at Colebourne Hall. Samantha had toddled after the pair as soon as she could walk and continued to follow them all their years growing up.

It was George who had taught her to ride. To shoot. To skim rocks across a pond. Anytime Weston complained about his sister wanting to be with them, George would stick up for her. He teased her unmercifully and declared her a pest but he was never cruel to her, only kind.

George had ignored her during her come-out, only dancing with her a handful of times that Season while he flirted outrageously with every other debutante. Then tragedy struck. Both the Duke of Colebourne, George's father, and their own father, the Duke of Treadwell, had passed away from a fever going around, making George and Weston the new dukes. It had occurred just before last Season started, so Samantha had gone into mourning. It hadn't mattered. She'd spent all of this Season hoping George would notice she'd grown up.

He hadn't.

While she missed her second Season, both her brother and George returned to their country estates, learning as much as they could about running their various properties. The two men had met frequently and exchanged numerous letters, asking each other's opinions and advice on a plethora of matters that befell becoming a duke. It touched Samantha that George had taken time and written to her twice, asking how she fared after her father's death. Her life hadn't changed much. She'd served as a hostess for her father and ran Treadwell Manor since her mother had died many years ago and her father had never remarried. She continued in her duties regarding the household, waiting to return to London—and have the man she adored finally see her in a new light.

Her hope had been to gain George's notice this Season but it was already halfway over and she seemed no closer than before to having him realize she was an eligible, attractive young woman, one perfectly suited to be his wife. She knew he and Weston were thinking of marriage because she had accidentally overheard them discussing it two nights ago—thus, the dress that showed off more of her ample bosom than usual. She hoped George would ask her to dance tonight and see that the gangly tomboy she'd been had finally turned into a woman.

Samantha collected her reticule and went downstairs. Weston awaited her, handsome in his dark evening clothes.

"There you are. The carriage is waiting. I don't want to be late to George's ball." He took her arm. "My, don't you look pretty tonight, Sam?"

He handed her into the carriage and climbed in after her. "You'll certainly attract your fair share of eligible bachelors this evening." He sighed. "It just means the house will be overrun tomorrow with men calling and bouquets being delivered. I won't have a moment's peace."

"You really like it?" Samantha asked. "It's not . . . too much?"

"I do like it," he assured her. "Maybe you'll land a fiancé tonight." Weston studied her a moment. "Has anyone special attracted your attention yet?"

"Yes, someone has."

"And?" Her brother's eyes twinkled. "What is the name of the man I'll be negotiating marriage settlements with?"

"I don't think I'm ready to share that with you yet," she said mysteriously, wondering how Weston would react if she and George did become engaged.

"Well, I have something to share with you. George and I have been talking it over. We know we're young, only twenty-three, but being dukes now makes us feel the need to become more responsible. We've both decided to take brides so we can start a family."

Samantha's stomach tightened. "Oh?"

She wanted to ask what woman George was considering but knew it would be better to ask about her own brother first.

"Might I ask the name of the woman you're interested in wedding? You've danced with every eligible girl this Season."

"I know. I've made up my mind, though. I find myself hopelessly intrigued by Lady Juniper Radwell."

Her brother couldn't have made a worse choice. Juniper Radwell was Samantha's age. She was beautiful beyond measure and turned down every man who proposed, which only made them flock to her more. She was the kind of female who was all smiles when a man was around. When one wasn't, she became vindictive and hateful. Samantha wanted to tell Weston he was thinking with his cock instead of his head—or heart—but she didn't think her words would be well received.

"Lady Juniper is very pretty," she admitted cautiously.

"Pretty?" Weston scoffed. "She's downright beautiful. I was taken with her looks from the start. She was the measuring stick I've used as I've gotten to know other women on the Marriage Mart. Lady Juniper outshines them all in every way." He took her hand. "I hope that you two will become fast friends. Even as close as sisters."

The last thing that either Samantha or Juniper Radwell would want is to have to pretend to like one another. It would be as if two cats had been tossed into a bag. She thought her brother would be miserable with his choice once a little time had passed but she was going to keep her mouth closed. Wallaces were notoriously stubborn. If she said she disliked Lady Juniper intensely, it would only draw her brother closer to the girl.

"Remember, I won't be living at home forever," she reminded him. "I also would like to wed and move to my own household and have children. Just be sure that Lady Juniper will make you happy, Weston. You deserve that."

"She will," he said with determination. "I'll admit it. I'm smitten with her. Of course, I haven't spoken to her of my intentions but she'll have to say yes when I offer for her." He grinned. "After all, I am a duke. I'm considered quite the catch."

"What about George?" she inquired blandly.

"What about him?

"You said you both were considering taking a wife. Who will George saddle himself with?"

Weston shrugged. "He hasn't said. He did tell me he was making up his mind and would announce his decision at the ball he's hosting tonight."

Butterflies exploded within Samantha. What if he was thinking about her? He knew her better than any woman in society. They got on so well. Oh, please, please, please, let her be George's choice.

They arrived and went through the receiving line. George was his usual charming self and complimented her on her dress. It gave her a small bit of hope. She joined some of her friends as they waited for the *programmes du bal* to be given out so that gentlemen could start vying for dances. As they spoke, it surprised her when Lady Juniper joined them.

"How are you this evening, Lady Samantha?" the newcomer asked.

"I'm quite well, thank you. And you?" she asked politely, eyeing this woman with more interest, knowing her brother would be offering for her soon.

They chatted about the weather and a new milliner on Bond Street as a footman distributed the dance cards. The group started tittering. Samantha glanced up and saw Weston and George heading their way. Weston immediately went to Lady Juniper and led her away, while George spoke to the rest of the women. Finally, he made his way to her.

"Your ballroom looks delightful, George. The decorations are divine."

"Thank you. Andrew's aunt Helen helped in that regard since I have no females to guide me in domestic matters. I wanted everything right for the first event I hosted as the Duke of Colebourne."

"Your mama and papa would be proud. Not just of how the ballroom looks but the man you have become," Samantha said.

"Why, thank you, Pest."

"Don't call me that," she said, frowning.

"Why not? I have for years. Pest. Poppet. I have several nicknames for you."

"Please, George," she said forcefully. "If you haven't noticed, I'm not a child anymore."

He looked at her thoughtfully. "No. You're not." After a moment, he asked, "Would you care to open the ball tonight with me, Sam?"

Her anger vanished. Giddiness swept through her. "Yes. I'd enjoy that."

He signed her card and told her he'd be back to claim her shortly. She glowed as others made their way to her and claimed spots on her programme. It didn't matter who else she danced with. George wanted her to help open his ball. Every eye would be on them. Perhaps he had noticed she'd matured.

Oh, she wanted to be his wife more than anything.

He returned and offered his arm, leading her to the center of the ballroom. She was so proud to be the first to dance with him. He looked splendid in his black evening wear, his tawny mane of hair making him look like the king of the jungle. With a nod to the musicians, they began playing.

Samantha noticed him glancing at her bosom and felt a blush tinge her cheeks. She decided to help nudge the conversation along.

"Weston tells me that you and he have decided it's time to become responsible members of Polite Society and marry."

"Yes, we have. Though we're young, family means a great deal to the two of us. I always hated that I was an only child." He smiled fondly. "At least I had you and Weston as my pretend brother and sister."

No. She did not want him thinking of her in that light. Not at all.

"Well, we aren't truly related."

"No, but you will always hold a special place in my heart, Pest. Sorry. Sam."

His words created doubt in her mind. Would he be calling the woman he was about to ask to marry him *Pest*?

She pressed him, dreading what he would say. "Weston tells me he's going to offer for Lady Juniper Radwell. Have you made your selection?"

"Yes, but you must keep it a secret. You're the only one I would tell." He paused. "Lady Frederica Martin."

Samantha felt as if he'd punched her in the gut as something more than disappointment filled her. She'd made her come-out with Lady Frederica. Her father had passed away close to the time of Samantha's own, causing Frederica to also miss last Season. This year, she'd taken the *ton* by storm and had caught the eye of every bachelor in London. The year away from Polite Society had brought a maturity to her but Samantha hated the fact that the woman was a vicious gossip. She also was close friends with Juniper Radwell.

"She is very pretty but have you really spoken with her, George? She doesn't have much conversation." *Unless she's tearing down other women.*

He looked puzzled. "Why would I want to converse with her? That's what friends such as you and Weston are for. I'm looking for a wife, for goodness' sake, not a companion, Sam."

Now, she was confused. "But . . . don't you think your wife will *be* your companion?"

George shook his head. "Not really. I am looking for a woman of good breeding and family. A beautiful one, for certain. But I expect her to lead her own life. Yes, she'll bear my children and be my hostess, but I doubt I'll have much to do with her beyond that."

His words angered her. "Well, I'm glad you're not considering me for your wife then. When I wed, I *want* to be friends with my husband. I want us to confide in one another. Share our dreams and make them a reality. I want us to have children and raise them together in a loving environment. I want a man who will laugh with me. Challenge me." Samantha shook her head. "You are not who I thought you were, George."

Worry creased his brow. "But . . . you'll still be my friend, won't you, Sam? I look upon you as my sister. We've always been so close."

The music ended and she said sadly, "I am not your sister, George. I never was."

He escorted her back to her friends without a word and bowed. "Lady Samantha," he said brusquely.

As she watched him walk away, hurt filled her heart. She had idolized George from the first time she'd seen him yet he'd only seen her in the role of a younger sister. It didn't matter what she did. She could have paraded naked in front of him and he would never realize she had grown up. The fact he wanted to keep his wife at a distance shouldn't surprise her. His parents had a loveless marriage and his mother had died when George was only ten. He hadn't had a good example of how marriage could be a fulfilling partnership.

The ache continued filling her as the evening wore on. She danced with numerous men and noticed as George was busy every dance. Even though he had disappointed her, she didn't want him to have the power to hurt her any longer. Samantha had waited her entire life for George Moore and she wasn't about to waste the rest of it pining away for him. She'd had a bevy of suitors all Season long and was actually fond of several of them. Two viscounts. An earl. A marquess. Surely, one of them would make for a decent husband. She hadn't really given any of them a fair chance because she'd been so wrapped up in a man who was blind to who she truly was.

In that moment, she decided she would wed one of them. The man who lived the greatest distance away from Colebourne Hall. If she never saw the Duke of Colebourne again, it would be a good thing. She would encourage one of the gentlemen who interested her and treated her with kindness. She would build a new life away from George. The one thing which ruled her life was optimism. She would drink fully from its cup now and move on. She had to. It was that or be miserable the rest of her life. At twenty, she was not willing to accept such a terrible existence. It was time to move on and discover her full potential.

Samantha looked at her current partner, Viscount Haskett, the future Earl of Rockaway. She'd danced with him several times this Season. He'd called upon her four times and taken her driving in Hyde Park once and riding in Rotten Row twice. He was quite handsome if a little bland. A bit bookish and with a tendency to be shy. He had a good heart, though.

Most importantly, he lived in Durham, which was almost to Scotland.

When the song ended, George invited everyone into supper and Haskett escorted her there. They joined friends of his at a table opposite one where George sat with Lady Frederica, Weston, and Lady Juniper. Samantha deliberately kept her focus on the viscount and made an effort to draw him out. She found him a bit boring but very nice. With a little work and encouragement, she thought he would make for a good husband.

Suddenly, George called for the group's attention and the room fell silent, anticipating his announcement. They weren't disappointed, minus Samantha.

"I have wonderful news to share with my guests this evening," George said, his rich voice carrying throughout the room. "I am honored that Lady Frederica Martin had agreed to become my duchess."

Applause broke out across the room. She politely clapped, her heart breaking, but she smiled bravely as the entire room toasted to their health and engagement.

"And my closest friend, the Duke of Treadwell, also would like to share something." George nodded to Weston, who rose.

"Colebourne and I have done everything together since we were boys who toddled about. I couldn't let him get married without doing the same." Weston smiled down at the woman on his left. "I am proud to announce that Lady Juniper Radwell has agreed to become the Duchess of Treadwell."

More enthusiastic applause broke out. Samantha forced herself to maintain the smile on her face, knowing others would be looking at her for her reaction. Weston blew her a kiss and she pretend to catch it.

"Did you know this was coming?" Haskett asked.

"Yes. Weston and I discussed it in the carriage tonight and Colebourne and I talked over his decision while we danced tonight."

Haskett looked at her wistfully. "I saw you dancing with His Grace earlier. I thought . . . that is, I believed . . ." His voice trailed off in embarrassment as his face reddened.

Boldly, Samantha placed a hand over his. "Colebourne is like a brother to me, my lord. I've known him all my life. In fact, he rarely calls me by my name. I usually hear him refer to me as Pest."

The viscount looked aghast.

"Oh, don't worry. It's said with affection. His Grace has teased me as much as my own brother for all my twenty years."

"So . . . you are not . . . what I mean is . . ."

"I am very happy for Colebourne and Lady Frederica," she said, the last of her heart tearing in two. She pushed it aside, ready to move on.

Haskett looked hopeful. "Then you wouldn't mind if I called upon you tomorrow?"

Samantha was at a crossroads. She could crawl under a rock and lick her wounds and refuse to come out—or she could forge ahead and make a life—with this good man. He happened to think quite a bit of her. The viscount was kind and would treat her well. And it helped that he did live far, far from the Duke of Colebourne.

She smiled at him. It was genuine. She might not love him but she doubted she would ever love anyone other than George. She could, however, build a life with him. Respect him. Learn to care for him.

"I was hoping you would say that, Lord Haskett. I look favorably upon your calls."

"You do?" he asked, his eyes widening.

"I do. I enjoy your company." Deciding to speed things along, she added, "I hoped when you said you'd like to call tomorrow that you meant you would be speaking with my brother."

Understanding dawned in Haskett's eyes. "You would look kindly upon my suit, Lady Samantha?"

"I would," she assured him.

His smile spread across his face, lighting his blue eyes, making him even more handsome. He placed a hand atop hers, the one that already rested on his.

"You have made me very happy, my lady."

She decided to tease him a bit. "Why, Lord Haskett?"

"Because you've agreed . . . oh, blast, I haven't asked you, have I?"

Samantha smiled. "No, you haven't."

"Then let's do this properly." He rose and placed her hand into the crook of his arm and led her through a set of French doors and out onto the balcony. It was close to midnight now and the June evening had turned cool.

Haskett took her hands in his. "Lady Samantha, I think you are the most beautiful woman in the world. You're intelligent and friendly and kind to everyone you meet. I have formed a great affection for you. Would you do me the honor of becoming my wife?"

Samantha hoped she wasn't making a mistake as she replied, "I'd be happy to wed you, Haskett."

CHAPTER TWO

St. George's Chapel, London—September 1808

"WHERE THE BLOODY hell *is* he?" roared the Duke of Colebourne as he paced restlessly in the small vestibule just off the chapel.

His friend, the Duke of Blackmore, shrugged. "You know Weston. He's always marched to his own time. He'll be here. Soon, I hope."

Would he?

Doubt flooded George, despite Jon's reassurance that Weston would show up. Where was his friend? They'd done everything together their entire lives, including their decision to wed together in a double ceremony this morning. The entire *ton* awaited them in the chapel.

Could West have changed his mind? No. It wasn't possible. He'd told George how utterly in love he was with Lady Juniper Radwell. They could barely keep their hands off one another in public—and George was certain in private they did as they pleased.

It was different with him and his fiancée. Lady Frederica Martin had only allowed him to kiss her twice, once before he proposed and once when he offered for her almost three months ago. Both kisses had been blissful, causing George to anticipate their couplings in the near future. Frederica was a beautiful young woman, a bit shy, but one who would make for a wonderful duchess. He'd followed his father's advice regarding seeking his duchess. The duke had told his son to always keep affairs of the heart separate from having a wife. George was to choose a woman of good family, one whose dowry would add to the family coffers, as well as add prestige to the Colebourne name. Frederica did both, bringing a princely sum of a dowry. Her father, Lord Mowbray, was the fifteenth earl of that name and had an impeccable reputation in Polite Society.

Still, he couldn't help but remember Samantha cautioning him when he revealed to her his choice of wife. West's sister was like a sister to George, as well. Her vehemence regarding the way he looked upon life with his future spouse had surprised him. The Pest had talked of sharing dreams and laughter with her husband, something he couldn't imagine his own parents—or many of society's couples—doing. Yet her passionate speech to him had given him pause over the last few months. What if Sam was right? Should he try to make friends with Frederica? She seemed as much of an enigma to him now as when he began pursuing her, a beautiful, unopened package that would forever remain a mystery.

He hoped at least Sam was happy in her own marriage. She'd wed the Viscount of Haskett two weeks ago and had delayed returning to his estate up north so she could attend the nuptials of her brother and George today.

Again, where was his closest friend?

The door opened and Reverend Chatterley entered the small room, concern on his face.

"Are we ready to start, Your Grace?" the clergyman asked.

"No. Do you see the Duke of Treadwell here?" he asked angrily. "We will start when he arrives."

"Are you certain His Grace is coming?" Chatterley asked meekly.

"Go," commanded George and the good reverend fled the room.

He regretted his rude behavior to the man but didn't wish to run after the clergyman and apologize. Not in his current state, which now had him alarmed and discombobulated.

Jon regarded him warily. He was to stand up with George and Weston at today's ceremony. George only wished their other good friends, Andrew and Sebastian, could be here. Both men had purchased commissions when the five of them graduated from Cambridge and they now fought against Bonaparte on the Continent. It almost seemed wrong, marrying with his friends missing out on the ceremony.

The door opened again. This time, it was the Duke of Treadwell, though West looked more bedraggled than George had ever seen him. He wore the same clothes as he had last night when they'd parted outside Viscount Kingsbury's home. The viscount, Lady Juniper's brother, had hosted a dinner for the two bachelors, along with several of their friends. They stayed up late, drinking and swapping tales of their younger days.

West looked as if he'd continue drinking the rest of the night. His hair was askew. His eyes bloodshot. His beard thick. He also smelled like a distillery. Besides the rumpled clothes, West wore a look of hopelessness, as if he were haunted by some great tragedy that he could never heal from.

"Good God, West! What happened to you?" George asked.

Since he looked on the verge of collapse, Jon took their friend's arm and guided him to a chair. West fell into it. He slumped, his hand going to his stubbled jaw, rubbing it, a sure sign of his distress. George took the seat next to him.

"Tell us," he urged softly.

"I can't," West ground out. "It's . . . so awful." He looked at George, pain filling his eyes, misery on his face. "I won't ruin your wedding day, George. You need to go out there and make your vows to your bride. I'm sorry." He shook his head. "I cannot stay. Not with the whole of Polite Society out there."

"I can make a brief announcement," Jon volunteered.

West nodded wearily, stroking his jaw again. "Yes. That will do.

Just say . . . say there will be only one wedding today. News of my broken engagement will get out soon enough."

George lay his hand on his friend's shoulder. "Is there anything I can do?"

"No. You've been my best friend all my life. Keep being my friend is all that I ask, despite whatever you hear."

"Will you tell me someday?"

"I'll have to. Else I might go mad," West admitted. "For now, go wed Lady Frederica and take her on the honeymoon. Once you return to Colebourne Hall, send word to me. I will be at Treadwell Manor." He stood and placed his hands on George's shoulders. "I wish you the best of everything, old friend. A happy marriage. A happy life."

With that, the Duke of Treadwell left.

Jon looked to him. "Are you all right, George? Do you need a few moments to collect yourself?"

He did—but he'd already kept his bride waiting far too long.

"No, let's go."

Reverend Chatterley lingered in the hall. It was obvious he'd seen West come and go and merely fell into step with George and Jon as they entered St. George's Chapel. A murmur swept through the crowd. He knew they were almost half an hour late starting the ceremony. He and the clergyman went to stand before the altar.

Jon stepped to the center of the aisle and announced to those in attendance, "Please accept our apologies at the delay. Only one wedding will take place today." He turned and returned to George's side as the crowd tittered.

George scanned the crowd and found Samantha, sitting with her new husband. Their gazes met, hers confused at not seeing her brother and learning West would not be speaking his vows today. He wished he could go and comfort her but it wouldn't do to draw further attention. Whatever had caused West to decide not to stand in front of the *ton* today and wed Lady Juniper would be scandalous enough. At least The Pest was already safely wed. If not, whatever scandal that broke might have affected her chances at making a good match.

The guests calmed down and the organist began playing. The doors at the rear of the chapel opened and he caught sight of his lovely bride. Frederica came down the aisle on her father's arm, her pale pink dress trimmed in rosettes, flowers artfully wound through her hair. She looked extremely nervous and he regretted making her wait so long. He hadn't thought to send word to her as he'd waited for West. That fact spoke volumes to him. He would need to be more respectful of his wife in the future. Put her before his friends. Though he would never love her, she should be afforded the courtesy a duchess should receive.

They reached him and her father kissed her cheek and stepped away. George moved to take her hands and found them ice cold, even through her gloves. Her lips trembled. In fact, her whole body did. He'd never seen someone so jumpy and anxious.

"It's all right," he whispered, trying to assure her.

Tears welled in her eyes. "No. It's not." She looked at Chatterley. "Give us a moment."

The clergyman looked startled. "I see." He took several steps back, allowing them some privacy. The entire chapel was silent, ears straining to hear what the bride had to say to her groom.

Facing him, Frederica whispered, "I cannot marry you today, Colebourne."

"Are you upset that Lady Juniper did not show up?" he asked gently. "I know you are close friends. If you wish to put off the ceremony, we can wed another day. It can be private. A quiet gathering, with just family and a few friends."

She shook her head. "No. You don't understand." She shuddered and his hands tightened about hers.

"I felt I owed it to you to tell you in person." She bit her lip.

His stomach roiled violently. "Tell me what, my lady?"

"I cannot marry you. Ever."

Her words stunned him.

"I am in love with Viscount Richmond. He's waiting for me." Frederica turned and looked to the back of the chapel.

George did the same and saw the viscount standing at the doors, a look of determination on his face. All the wedding guests in attendance also glanced back when the bride and groom did and now a thousand pairs of eyes returned their gaze to the couple.

His bride faced him again. "I could not marry you in good faith, George. Not when my heart belongs to another. I've come to say goodbye. Richmond and I are leaving for Gretna Green now."

Her words bewildered him. His fiancée was jilting him at the altar, in front of the entire *ton*. He'd always led a charmed life, everything going his way. Now, he was being publicly humiliated.

He would be a man, though. A gentleman. He bent and kissed Frederica's cheek.

"I wish you and Richmond much happiness, my lady."

A single tear cascaded down her cheek. "Oh, thank you," she said gratefully.

She squeezed his hands and then pulled hers away. With her head held high, Lady Frederica Martin marched back up the aisle. Not as the new Duchess of Colebourne but as a woman who went to the man she loved. The chapel's guests watched, collectively holding their breath.

Richmond's smile lit his face when she reached him. Together, they left the church.

All eyes whipped back to George.

"I see there will be *no* weddings at St. George's today," he quipped.

With that, the Duke of Colebourne moved down the same aisle, past all the invited guests, forcing himself to stroll at a steady pace and not run screaming from the building. Jon followed him and the two men reached the outside doors and pushed through them in time to see Richmond hand Lady Frederica into a carriage.

His friend accompanied him to the second waiting carriage, the one that was to have taken him and his new duchess to their wedding breakfast.

"Do you wish to be alone, George?" Jon asked.

He nodded and called out to the astonished driver, "Take me to Colebourne Hall."

"Send for me if you need me," Jon said, offering his hand, and the two men shook.

"Thank you."

With that, George climbed into the grand carriage bearing the ducal seal and collapsed against the velvet cushions.

CHAPTER THREE

Rockwell—Durham County—September 1811

SAMANTHA WONDERED HOW a wife could tempt her husband back into her bed.

It had been far too long since Haskett had come to her. She understood from the doctor that time had to pass after her miscarriage before she could resume marital relations. She'd lost the baby five months ago, though. Those months had been lonely ones. Samantha had hoped to receive comfort from her husband of three years.

Comfort didn't seem to be a word in Haskett's vocabulary.

She had known the viscount was shy when they'd wed. She'd actually liked that about him. Too many men of the *ton* were brash and acted entitled. Charles Johnson, Viscount Haskett, had seemed different. He'd been taken with her but very unassuming. He'd expressed surprise when she'd chosen him from all her many suitors.

Her reasons for selecting Haskett as a husband had seemed good at the time. Samantha had wanted to wed George, whom she'd been infatuated with. When she'd finally realized that dream would never come true, she'd turned to a man George's total opposite. Where George was outgoing and oozed charm, Haskett was introverted and a bit awkward in social situations. George ignored her. Haskett hung on her every word. George had been on his own most of his life and didn't understand the importance of family, while Haskett vocally valued it.

Haskett would one day be the Earl of Rockaway. His country seat was in the far northeast of England. Other than during the Season, Samantha wouldn't have to socialize with her brother's best friend since the Duke of Colebourne's main country residence was located in Devon, two miles from where she'd grown up at Treadwell Manor. She doubted she would ever return to Devon in her lifetime.

Unfortunately, Haskett had turned out to be a most unsuitable husband. He wasn't the companion she'd sought. Though they'd had plenty of wonderful conversations in London after they'd become engaged, that changed once they returned to Rockwell. She soon realized her husband was under the thumb of his domineering mother and didn't speak or act without her permission. The man who'd begun to blossom during his time with Samantha in London had returned to the man his mother wanted, one who was docile and did everything she told him to do. His father, the Earl of Rockaway, was apparently cut from the same cloth, having been wed for thirty years and utterly trained to do his wife's bidding without question. Lady Rockaway ruled the roost and acted as if she were the earl and not a countess.

Samantha had lost her mother when she was young and had dreamed that her mother-in-law would become like a mother to her. Lady Rockaway had proven to be unmaternal and openly jealous of Samantha. She'd come to the realization they would never have a close relationship—or any relationship at all.

The longer she had been at Rockwell, the more Haskett withdrew. He rarely spent time with her and only infrequently came to her rooms at night. It was almost a shock when she found herself with child because they'd had relations so seldom. She had longed for a child from the moment they'd wed, though. Losing the baby at four months along had been the worst day of her life. Though the doctor assured her she'd done nothing wrong, guilt still filled her.

She'd hoped the tragedy would bring her closer to Haskett. That they'd comfort one another. Instead, he'd retreated so far into himself, he probably had spoken to her no more than a handful of times since the miscarriage. It hurt her beyond measure, losing her baby—and then her husband.

Samantha had no one to turn to during this dark time. She'd quickly discovered not only did she have no support from the family she'd married into, but the servants and locals also looked at her with suspicion, merely because she wasn't born in the north. She was used to the warm ways of the West Country, where's she'd grown up. These aloof northerners would never accept her. Only Lucy, the maid she'd brought with her, had been a friendly face.

Once upon a time, she would have confided in Weston. Her brother had always been her closest friend. No longer. Not only had the distance come between them, but whatever had occurred to end his engagement to Juniper Radwell had changed Weston for the worst. The first Season she and Haskett had returned to London after their marriage, Weston—and George—had run wild. They were known as the Bad Dukes. Weston had received the nickname the Duke of Disrepute by Polite Society and did everything he could to live up to the sobriquet. Samantha had been shocked by both his and George's behavior as London's most notorious womanizers. It was so unlike who they'd been before each had experienced a broken engagement. Last Season, they had behaved even more outrageously, so much that she'd had nothing to do with either of them.

She had no idea how this Season had gone since she'd remained at home because of her increasing. When she'd lost the baby, she'd written to Weston. He had sent a terse reply. No more letters had followed. She supposed he was too busy hopping from one woman's bed to the next to bother writing to his brokenhearted sister.

Lucy came in and smiled. "Good morning, my lady. How are you today?"

"Fine, thank you," she told the maid perfunctorily.

Even Lucy had no idea of the depths of Samantha's despondency.

There were days when she wished she could run away. Weston had given her some money before her marriage, telling her even though Haskett would provide her with pin money, a women needed a little extra to spend however she liked. Samantha hadn't spent a farthing of it, keeping the money hidden in case she ever did need it. She fantasized about buying a naughty night rail that might tempt Haskett back into her bed but had no idea where to go for something of that nature. She couldn't ask the seamstress in the nearby village. Durham was the nearest large town but they rarely went there.

Lucy helped Samantha dress for the day. At home and in London, she'd always enjoyed breakfast in her room, sipping chocolate in bed as she read the latest gossip columns in the newspapers as she ate buttered toast points. That practice had been declared lazy by Lady Rockaway. Samantha was expected to dress and be downstairs for the morning meal with the rest of the family.

She made her way to the small dining room where the meal would be served. Lord Rockaway didn't bother to look up from his newspapers, which Samantha never had access to since her mother-in-law deemed them coarse and unsuitable for a lady. Lady Rockaway nodded brusquely. Missing from the table were her husband and Cousin Percy. Percy Johnson was considerably younger than Haskett and had come to live with the family when he was an infant after his parents were killed in an accident. Haskett acted as a dutiful older brother to Percy and had accompanied the young man to Cambridge last week, where Percy would be starting university soon. Haskett wanted to see his cousin settled in properly.

Samantha didn't like Percy in the least. Though he rarely addressed her, she caught him looking at her furtively, a lascivious look always on his face. His behavior bothered her enough that she tried never to be alone in a room with him.

A footman placed a plate in front of her. She ate the same approved breakfast every morning. Samantha despised that even her meal selection was controlled by her mother-in-law. Another footman brought her a cup of tea. Though she enjoyed two lumps of sugar in it, Lady Rockaway deemed that wasteful and only allowed one. Before her marriage, she drank chocolate for breakfast. Again, Lady Rockaway deemed that too decadent and refused to have it served in her household. Her mother-in-law had constantly lectured Samantha on the need for frugality, something that was cherished by northerners.

"What will you do today with my darling boy gone?" asked the countess.

Samantha curbed her tongue and refrained from saying she was composing a list of ways to seduce her husband into her bed.

"I thought I'd go for a ride this morning," she said. "Haskett will want a report regarding the tenants when he returns and I'd like to be the one to give it to him when he does."

A distasteful look crossed the countess' face. She had as little as possible to do with both their tenants and most of the household servants, feeling herself far above others in their station.

"After that," she continued, "I have a committee meeting at the church. The altar guild."

Her mother-in-law visibly shuddered. "I don't see why you go to those things."

"I believe it is important to become part of the community. To get to know the people. I am still new here and want to feel as if I belong."

In truth, the women at church hadn't accepted her in the least. She'd heard snippy remarks about how the earl barely tithed. How his family should be responsible for putting a new roof on the church. The only one of them who had extended the slightest bit of friendship was Mrs. Kith, the clergyman's wife. Samantha supposed the woman had to be charitable to all of the flock, even outsiders.

"See that you don't tarry long at this meeting," her mother-in-law ordered.

She couldn't understand why this woman felt the need to manage every aspect of her family's lives. What did it matter if Samantha was at the meeting one hour or two? At least it gave her something to do and an excuse to get out of this gloomy house. She had never visited, much less lived in, such a dark, dismal place and found it quite depressing.

When breakfast ended, she returned to her room and had Lucy help her change into her riding habit. Riding had become an escape for her. Though she had planned to ride daily with Haskett, he rarely accompanied her. She had no idea what her husband did with his time. He didn't seem interested in their tenants or managing the estate, despite what she'd just said. He was intelligent. She'd learned that from their conversations in London. Every now and then, she came across him with his nose in a book but when asked about what he was reading, he told her she wouldn't be interested. Finally, she'd stopped asking. She worried if he didn't get her with child soon that they would become total strangers.

A groom saddled her horse and helped her to mount. Samantha rode away from the house, relief filling her. Then she spied something coming up the lane toward the house and decided to ride in that direction, curious about any visitor. As she drew close, she saw it was a wagon. A rider rode next to it and broke away, headed toward her at a gallop. She pulled up, recognizing Percy.

Why on earth was he back at Rockwell?

He approached, slowing his horse as he reached her.

"Good morning, Samantha."

She didn't like him using her Christian name. He'd never done so before. Percy must be feeling brave outside the presence of his tyrannical aunt.

"Did you change your mind about university?" she asked, thinking him thickheaded but knowing he couldn't already have failed to meet expectations in such a short amount of time. "And where is Haskett?"

"We must talk about that." Percy frowned. "You must prepare

yourself."

"About you not going to Cambridge?" she asked, puzzled by his appearance back at Rockwell.

"Perhaps you should dismount," he suggested.

The thought of his hands secure against her waist brought distaste.

"No, tell me what you wish to before I go visit our tenants."

He remained silent a long moment and finally said, "It's about Charles."

"What about him?" she asked, now on guard. "I have already asked where he is and you've failed to tell me."

By now, the wagon had reached them. Samantha glanced at it and froze.

A pine box lay in its bed.

"No," she whispered. Her eyes whipped to Percy. "No," she repeated.

He shook his head sadly. "We were coming out of a public house. We'd stayed quite late because Charles was leaving the next morning to return to Rockwell. We both had overindulged in strong drink but that shouldn't have mattered."

He paused, sympathy in his eyes. She felt her throat tighten.

"We were accosted by three men a few blocks away." Anguish filled Percy's eyes. "We were almost back to my rooms when they appeared at the mouth of an alley, brandishing knives. They wanted our money. I handed over what I had immediately. Charles . . . he fumbled with his pockets. He was too inebriated. One of them got angry. Accused him of stalling. But he wasn't, Samantha. Charles was trying."

Percy swallowed, shaking his head sadly. "It didn't matter. The thief moved in and punched Charles. He fell to the ground. The man went through his pockets. Charles started protesting. Then . . . oh, God, it was awful. He . . . he *stabbed* Charles. Right there in front of me. I'll never forget the look on his face. He was confused. In pain.

The man yanked out the knife and thrust it into him again."

Samantha's fingers squeezed the reins tightly. Percy's words didn't seem real. Yet she saw how upset he was.

"They ran. I feel to my knees. I tried to cover his wounds. There was blood everywhere." He choked. "I'm so sorry, Samantha. I couldn't save him."

Without a word, she wheeled her horse and galloped away. The countryside went by at a dizzying speed as tears welled in her eyes. She rode for a few miles and finally brought the horse to a halt. She slid from its back and buried her face against its mane, sobs finally erupting.

Her husband had been murdered. Poor, decent Haskett, who never raised his voice or had a cruel thing to say about anyone. To be waylaid by strangers and then die so violently was unimaginable. She drew away from her horse and vomited, sickened by the idea. She wiped her mouth on her sleeve and wandered for a few minutes. She regretted not making more of an effort to help her husband open up. To make him realize he had great potential—if he quit letting his mother do all of his thinking for him.

Samantha returned to her horse, taking deep, even breaths. She hurt for the man who could have been so much more than he was and would mourn that they hadn't been closer. Yet at the same time, a small part of her knew she was finally free.

Chapter Four

London

GEORGE SLOWLY OPENED his eyes and cursed under his breath.

He'd fallen asleep.

He never stayed over with a lover. Never. It was one of his rules. Of course, he and West were all about breaking rules but, between the two of them, they had a certain code of honor to which they adhered to. They both agreed that it was never a good idea to stay overnight with a lover. Definitely Rule Number One.

"Darling," a sultry voice murmured next to him, stroking his bare chest.

No, this wouldn't do at all. He was the one who called his lovers *darling*. They called him Colebourne on rare occasions. Most of the time they merely called him Charm. He was so used to it by now that if a woman called him by his title, he knew it was one he hadn't bedded yet. Or she was over eighty and he had no intentions of bedding her.

That was another rule. Rule Number Two. The Bad Dukes took lovers between the ages of eighteen and eighty. Never younger. Never older. Of course, those on the low end had to be special cases. Neither Charm nor Disrepute would bed a virgin. If they were under a score, they had to already have been wed and proven to be terribly unhappy in their marriages. Usually, because they were wed to some old goat three times their age.

Rule Number Three is where he and West differed so it split into two sub-rules. West only slept with the same woman once. Once was all he wanted with a lover. George stuck with his three times and begone rule. Less than three and he felt unfulfilled, as if he let a woman down. He didn't want to leave any lover unsatisfied, much less himself. More than three couplings, though, and a woman—even married ones—became too possessive. They began to dig their claws into him. They started expecting things that he was incapable of providing. Thus, he stuck vigorously to his three times only rule.

Tonight with Lady Digby made three times. It was why she thought she could affectionately call him *darling*. She would think she was special and let other women believe it, as well. He wasn't having any of it.

That meant turning on the charm he was known for. He would need to leave her now. For good. Yet still make sure it occurred on good terms so when they saw one another at some *ton* event there would be no awkwardness. No unpleasantries.

Her nails raked across his chest lightly, causing his manhood to stir. Well, nothing in his rules said he couldn't make love to her again. He was known for multiple sessions a night with the women he seduced. As long as she understood when he left her bed this time, it was for good.

Capturing her wrist, he brought it to his mouth and kissed it. Thoroughly. Then he proceeded to kiss her senseless. He moved to every nook and cranny along her body, nipping and licking and kissing until he reached her core. Soon, his latest lover writhed on the bed, calling his nickname as she panted and moaned and wept with joy. He entered her and rode her until he felt drained and knew she was, too.

George slipped from the bed and began gathering his clothes as she lay there unmoving, her breath rapid and shallow. She watched him as he began slipping on the various layers of a gentleman. He didn't even know why he paid a valet since he undressed and dressed himself more than Briggs ever did. When he had on all but his cravat, he returned and sat on the bed. Lady Digby watched as he expertly knotted the cloth.

"This is it, isn't it, Charm?" she asked, a hint of sadness in her voice.

"It is, darling," he agreed. "But we've had such fun, haven't we?" He ran his index finger down the length of her nose, stopping at her lips. She bit his finger lightly before allowing him to trail it down her chin, her throat, and to her breast for a final caress.

"Am I the best you've had?" she asked wistfully.

George leaned down and softly kissed her. "If you believe you were, then you were, darling. The times we shared, I only thought of you and no others."

"I'm going to miss you, Charm. You've spoiled me for other men."

He cradled her cheek. "I merely listened to you, my lady. The next lover you take, you'll tell him what to do so that he pleases you."

"It was a good last time, wasn't it?" she asked hopefully.

Smiling, he nodded. "It most definitely was. Now, close your eyes, my sweet. Dream of happy things. Good night, Lady Digby. And goodbye."

With that, he rose and slipped from her room. As he descended the stairs, he heard a clock chime five. He reached the front entrance, where a footman dozed. The servant woke as George threw the lock, jumping to his feet.

"Goodnight, Your Grace. That is, good morning."

"Don't worry. I won't be back. No more late nights—or early mornings—where you must wait up to let me out."

The footman hesitated and then asked, "Is it true you only bed a woman thrice?"

He cocked his head. "Three nights, my good man." Waggling his brows, he added, "Sometimes, thrice in one of those nights, however."

Now, the servant looked at him in awe. "Goodness gracious, Your

Grace. That's bloody wonderful."

George winked at him. "I think so."

He opened the door and stepped out into the cool, late September morning and walked the two blocks to his carriage. Not his ducal one but a plain black vehicle. He never liked to disclose which beds he slept in and always had his night driver park a few blocks away in an anonymous coach. His day driver drove the one with the Colebourne crest.

His driver spotted him and sat up. "A rather long night, Your Grace," he commented. "We're usually home by now."

"Get me there as soon as you can," he instructed. "I am worn out and in need of sleep."

The coachman chuckled and George was barely inside the vehicle when the carriage took off. With the streets deserted, he was home quickly and went upstairs to his rooms. He discarded his clothing and fell into bed, a dreamless sleep enveloping him until the light hurt his eyes.

He shielded them before he opened them, squinting. Briggs was drawing back the curtains. The aroma of coffee hit him and he pushed himself to a sitting position.

"Good morning, Your Grace," his valet said, coming to the bedside and pouring George a cup of the fragrant brew, adding just the right amount of sugar and milk and stirring it before he handed the cup over.

Taking a sip, George slowly came awake. He continued drinking it as Briggs bustled about the room. After he'd finished the first cup, he set it down. Immediately, his valet prepared a second one and lifted the covering of the breakfast. George ate and drank more coffee as servants appeared with buckets of hot and cold water. Briggs supervised as they entered the dressing room and poured the buckets into the tub. When the last one left, George rose and padded naked to the bath.

He always took a bath when he rose. He didn't like the smell of last night's woman on him. As he bathed, Briggs would see that the maids stripped off his bedsheets and replaced them with fresh ones. Though he'd enjoyed last night with Lady Digby, he didn't need her lingering on his skin or sheets. That had become Rule Number Four. Both he and West religiously stuck to this rule. Rule Number Five was closely related. It said they were never to have a woman in their personal bed.

Of course, that rule was broken at house parties. The rule was made to include their own residences, both in London and any of their country estates. It was far easier to leave a woman's bed and return to his own. It might prove difficult to get a woman out of his bed and send her on her way. If a woman slept in a man's bed, she thought she belonged there. She would start whining about marriage. Both he and West knew matrimony wasn't for them. Therefore, their beds were considered sacrosanct. Unless at the given house party, when they made an exception to the rule. A house party meant you were a visitor somewhere so it wasn't truly your bed. And any woman you slept with would have to return to her guest room. George didn't make a habit of it, though. Even at a house party, he preferred going to the lady. Not the other way around.

George rose from his bath, taking the bath sheet Briggs handed him and thoroughly drying himself.

"What do I have today?" he asked, knowing the valet knew his schedule better than he did.

"You have a fencing match with the Duke of Treadwell at three, Your Grace. Then dinner at eight with your cousin. No plans after that—unless you've made some on your own and neglected to inform me."

"Very well. I suppose I should get dressed."

"Will you defeat His Grace this time?" Briggs asked.

"I doubt it," he said, knowing full well it was the truth.

George rarely beat West at anything. Though George had a natural grace and athleticism and could box, fence, ride, shoot, and dance better than all but a handful of men in Polite Society, his friend had become maniacal when it came to any kind of competition. After both men suffered broken engagements, West poured his anger into sports, especially boxing and fencing. He spent hours at both activities and had reached a level of skill so high that he rarely lost any match at either sport.

It didn't matter. George enjoyed pitting himself against West, testing himself, pushing himself. On the rare occasions he defeated his friend, West cursed like a sailor and then drank for days. Then he'd rally, putting himself through a grueling training regimen until he challenged George again. It was almost easier to try his hardest and still manage to lose than see West put himself through the process.

He reached the fencing academy, located by Gentleman Jack's gymnasium, where all good gentlemen of the era went to box, and entered. Going straight to the changing rooms, he found West already there putting on his fencing kit.

"Have you dumped Lady Digby yet?"

"Last night was our third encounter. You know I did. Have I ever broken one of our rules?"

"Good." West grinned. "Even rulebreakers have to stick to some rules in order to survive."

"Is that anything like there being honor among thieves?" George asked as he stripped off his coat and waistcoat and then untied his cravat and draped it on top of them. "I would advise you to steer clear of the aforementioned Lady Digby."

"Why? Did she become too clingy? I hate when that happens."

"She called me *darling*," he revealed.

West shuddered. "No Lady D for me then. I'm no one's darling. I'm made for disgrace."

They finished putting on their garb and went into the main gymnasium. Several pairs of gentlemen were sparring, while others were involved in lessons with fencing experts.

"If you ever get bored by bedding women of the *ton*, you could become a fencing master," George suggested.

West chuckled. "As if I could ever get bored."

But George saw a distant look in his friend's eyes that told him a different story. One he himself felt all too familiar with.

They went up against each other, Mr. Nixon refereeing their match. In the end, though it was close, Disrepute outdueled Charm. George didn't care. He enjoyed the physical activity and time spent with his closest friend. They changed in the dressing room and exited the fencing academy.

"Would you care to come home with me for a drink?"

West's question definitely told George something was on his friend's mind.

"Yes. I'll be right back."

He went to his day driver. "I'm going to Treadwell's. Pick me up there in an hour."

"Yes, Your Grace."

George returned and climbed into West's carriage. They were silent on the way home. It was a good silence, not an awkward one. A satisfying one that spoke of their long friendship, growing up on neighboring estates. Though they'd gone away to school together and added three others to their circle, Andrew and Sebastian were now off at war, fighting the menace of Bonaparte. At least Jon was still around and they saw him regularly.

They arrived at the Treadwell townhouse and went inside. Caldwell, the butler, greeted them.

"I am ravenous, Caldwell," West declared. "A full tea in the library for Colebourne and me."

"Of course, Your Grace."

He followed West to the library. His friend poured a hefty amount of brandy in snifters. They retreated to their favorite pair of wing chairs and sipped in silence until Mrs. Caldwell, the housekeeper, arrived with a footman rolling in the teacart. She poured out for them, knowing exactly how each took his tea since she'd been giving it to them for over two decades. Once she left, both men piled their plates high with sandwiches and tea cakes.

"What's on your mind?" George asked.

"I got a letter from Sam." West paused a moment.

They hadn't discussed Samantha in a good while now. George hadn't actually spoken to her since the last time he'd danced with her years ago. She'd questioned his choice of a wife and he'd resented her for it. Sam had been right. Frederica Martin hadn't been for him. He'd never told Sam that, though. The next time he'd seen her had been the next Season. By then, he and West had cut a swath through society, already creating the reputations they would live up to. He'd only seen Sam from a distance at a few social gatherings and had observed the disappointment in her eyes. The next Season had been the same. He and West were the Bad Dukes and George didn't bother approaching his old friend.

Sam hadn't come to London this past spring for the Season. She'd been increasing and remained in the north. West had told him she'd lost the child. George knew she would be devasted and yet he couldn't bring himself to write to her. Neither he nor West had mentioned her for several months now.

"How is she?" he asked, taking a bite of a delicious roast beef sandwich, which felt like sawdust in his mouth. He washed it down with half a cup of tea.

"Haskett is dead."

He stilled. "My God. What happened?"

"He was murdered. Assaulted on the streets of Cambridge late at night. He'd taken that churlish cousin of his to university and they'd been out late drinking. A trio of men robbed them. I don't know if

Haskett tried to fight back or what but the bottom line is he wound up dead."

George shook his head. "First her child. Then her husband. Poor Sam."

West frowned, staring into his cup. "Of course, he's buried by now. By the time the news reached me, the funeral would have been over and done."

"Is . . . is Sam coming back home?" he asked quietly.

"Home?" West asked. "Where is home? You and I live in London most of the year. Yes, we make a cursory visit to Devon to visit our country seats once a year or so but we don't live there. I doubt she'd even want to be around me. The last time I saw her, we spoke very little that Season. That was almost eighteen months ago. My sister is very disappointed in how I turned out. She made it quite clear she didn't approve of my behavior or lifestyle. She was embarrassed being related to the Duke of Disrepute."

West drained his teacup and set it aside. He raked a hand through his hair, misery plain on his face.

"What am I to do, George? You know what I have become. I'm no longer fit to take care of myself, much less Sam. I have no right to swoop in and order her about, telling her what to do. She was right to wash her hands of me. I have been a terrible brother to her. As it is, I am no brother to her at all now. A good brother would never have acted as I have. I let us drift apart. I never should have allowed a wedge this deep be driven between us."

He shook his head and blinked away tears that had formed in his eyes. "I love her—but it would be best if she had nothing to do with me ever again."

West stood and began pacing the room. "She's better off with her new family. I'm all she has as far as Wallaces go and she doesn't want me. Bloody hell, I wouldn't want me if I were my sister. I'd avoid having anything to do with me."

Unease filled George. He'd never liked the Earl and Countess of Rockaway though he knew very little of them. They seemed like very difficult people to him, neither sympathetic nor likeable.

"Do you think the Rockaways can comfort a grieving widow?"

"Who better? They worshipped the ground their son trod upon. Sam will be fine," West said. To George's ears, it sounded as if his comrade was trying to convince himself.

He placed his saucer on the table. "I've got to go. I've a dinner to attend. And a new conquest," he said lightly.

"Same here," West said dully, as if his heart wasn't in it. "I'll see you later."

"Goodbye."

As George went outside and climbed into his waiting carriage, he thought of how lonely he felt at this moment.

And how lonely Samantha must feel.

He'd write her. No, he wouldn't. He didn't know what to say. She was someone from his life before. One of the best parts of it. He wouldn't taint her and suck her into what he had become. She had a new family gathered about her, one who would surely support her and grieve with her. She would eventually marry again and hopefully have the children she would be so good with.

Samantha Wallace, no, Johnson now, was his past. George didn't wish to look back—or look forward to his empty future.

It was enough to get through every day, living a lie.

CHAPTER FIVE

Rockwell—September 1812

SAMANTHA OPENED HER eyes, resolve filling her. She tossed back the covers and went to stand at the window, looking out on the lawn as the sun moved above the horizon.

Today marked the anniversary of the death of her husband.

Today would be the day she would reclaim her own life.

The last year spent in mourning had dragged on as if it were a decade in length. She found it hard to grieve for a man she'd barely known after three years of marriage. One who had constantly disappointed her, wrapped around his overbearing mother's finger. Samantha had worn her mourning attire for the first six months to mark her husband's death and then switched to half-mourning, wearing grays and lavenders for the last six months. Despite the disapproving looks from her mother-in-law, she had kept to those colors.

Not today. She went to her wardrobe and chose a gown of deep hunter green, one of her favorites. Her clothes must be hopelessly out of date since it had been so long since she'd been in London. That would now change. She would write Weston after breakfast and tell him she was ready to return home. She hoped he would come for her himself but didn't count upon it. The few newspapers she got her hands on, thanks to Lucy digging them out from the garbage bin, told her that both the Duke of Disrepute and the Duke of Charm were still running unchecked through society, bedding a bevy of women and continuing to claim their places as the most loveable and outlandish rogues of Polite Society.

Still, she knew he would welcome her back. The bond between them was too strong to ever be permanently broken. Perhaps she could finally learn what had happened that day when he didn't show up for his wedding. She had tried to get the truth out of him but he'd told her it was unfit for her ears and she was to drop the matter. Since she and Haskett left for Rockwell two days later, Samantha hadn't been able to press Weston further. By the time she returned for the Season the following spring, her brother had already embraced his wicked nickname.

Not only would she return to Devon, but Samantha would partake in the Season next year. She had long ago given up on her childish dream to wed George, even after being widowed. Her brother's best friend also had been changed after being publicly humiliated by Lady Frederica when she jilted him at the altar. It seemed George and Weston continually competed to see which one could push the boundaries of society's rules. Knowing George would never settle down, she knew she must look elsewhere.

Her heart still longed for children, though. While she might also have put aside her notion to wed for love, she did believe she could find a good man who would act as both a friend and lover. A man who would be a good husband to her and a doting father to their children. Though Weston's friend, Jon, had always been kind to her, he also sowed his wild oats with Weston and George. The three of them seemed determined never to wed. Samantha wished Weston's other two friends, Andrew and Sebastian, weren't away at war. Both of them were honorable and loyal and would make for fine husbands. She prayed for their safety each night, hoping the war with Bonaparte would finally come to an end and the two men would return safely to England.

She had been courted by several eligible bachelors when she'd made her come-out years ago. She realized she was already four and twenty and considered old in Polite Society's eyes but surely there had to be a few good gentlemen who wouldn't mind wedding her. She determined to find one next Season and begin the family she longed for.

To do that, she must leave Rockwell. She would announce her decision today. Lord Rockaway and Percy wouldn't care. Lady Rockaway could gaze at her judgmentally all she liked. Samantha didn't care. She was tired of the cold north and this even colder family. She would go home and reclaim her life. If she had to walk out now and leave everything behind, she would.

Except for Lucy. Her maid remained loyal to her and she would never leave the girl in this horrid household. Together, the two of them would head south and begin a new chapter in their lives.

Lucy entered at that moment. "Good morning, Lady Samantha," she said with her usual good cheer. Glancing to the bed where Samantha had laid out the green gown, the maid smiled approvingly. "I see your official mourning period is over today. Good for you, my lady."

"Yes. I intend to return to Devon and will make that known today. Are you willing to come with me?"

Lucy's eyes misted with tears. "I have dreamed of it, my lady. I would have left long ago if not for you. I could never leave you behind."

Samantha embraced the girl. "Very well. Help me dress and I will break the news to my mother-in-law at breakfast."

"You know that old dragon will spew fire at you," the maid retorted. "She's a bad one. The servants are all frightened of her. I know to keep my mouth shut—but I think everything they say."

"I'm sorry it's been a hardship being at Rockwell," she apologized.

"Don't you worry, my lady. We'll get back to Devon and then on to London. You'll find a kind, handsome husband and we'll be set."

Lucy helped her from her night rail and into her layers of clothing. She sat at her dressing table while the maid arranged her hair.

"Keep it simple," she instructed. "Lady Rockaway frowns upon anything extravagant. I don't want her to see me and already harden her heart before I speak a word regarding my plans."

Lucy brushed the raven hair and wound it into a simple chignon. Samantha nodded her approval and stood.

"Shall I begin to pack?" the girl asked eagerly.

"Not yet. I will write to my brother today to inform him of my decision. Hopefully, we'll been gone from here within the month."

"Very well, my lady."

Samantha exited her bedchamber and descended the stairs. She entered the small dining room where they breakfasted each morning.

"We'll discuss it together after breakfast," her mother-in-law said to her nephew and then eyed Samantha as a footman seated her.

No one acknowledged her presence. Lord Rockaway's gaze was focused on his newspaper, as usual. Cousin Percy began cutting into his breakfast ham. Lady Rockaway sipped her tea. It didn't matter. Samantha liked being left with her own thoughts and began composing her letter to Weston in her head as she ate.

Once she'd finished eating, she tried to catch the countess' eye. It was as if her mother-in-law avoided her. She realized it was probably because of the color of gown she'd donned, which acknowledged Samantha no longer was in mourning for Haskett. Lady Rockaway had worn black from head to toe for the last twelve months as she grieved for her only child. Samantha hated how the countess always called Haskett *my darling boy*. He'd been a grown man of thirty when he died.

She glanced at Cousin Percy and wondered when he was returning to Cambridge, thinking he should already be gone by now. After Haskett's funeral last year, Percy had left for university once more and stayed a few weeks after the final term to catch up in his studies since he'd missed almost a month at the beginning of them. Still, he should be returning to Cambridge. That would make her last few weeks at Rockwell almost bearable.

"We will all go to the drawing room now," commanded Lady Rockaway as she rose.

Samantha decided that would be a better place to break her news. With footmen surrounding them, announcing her decision to leave Rockwell in front of so many servants might be looked upon in poor taste. The drawing room would give the family privacy in which to hear her plans.

The four retreated upstairs and her mother-in-law said to Samantha, "Sit here," pointing to a settee. "Percy, join her."

She did as asked and Percy sat next to her. Lord and Lady Rockaway took a seat opposite them.

"Today is the day we lost our beloved, darling boy," the countess began.

Immediately, Samantha thought about the monthly trips the family took to Haskett's grave. How Lady Rockaway made them stand there for a good half-hour or longer so they could be with the deceased and revel in their memories of him. She'd finally learned the thing to do was bow her head and close her eyes so she wouldn't have to make eye contact with anyone or see the grief ravaging Lady Rockaway's face at the loss of her beloved son. She wished she could mourn for Haskett more. She wished they could have experienced a good life together. Her heart told her it was time to move on, though.

"He was the best of men," Cousin Percy said solemnly.

"My boy was my heir. He was my flesh and blood. I miss him most dreadfully," Lord Rockaway added.

They all turned to her and she decided it was her turn to say something nice about her husband.

"I enjoyed my conversations with Haskett when we met in London. He was always kind and unassuming, unlike most gentlemen of the *ton*," she said with honesty. "I know how much his family will always miss him."

Lady Rockaway nodded her approval. "That being said, my darling boy would not wish us to grieve forever. He would want us to go on with our lives."

Samantha could hardly believe her ears. It might be much easier than she'd thought to tell them of her decision to return to Treadwell Manor.

The countess smiled fondly at Percy. "You were the younger brother Charles always wished for, my dear Percy. He took such good care of you from the moment you came to us as a baby."

"I worshipped Charles," Percy said, brushing away a tear. "I know that I am now the heir apparent to the earldom. While I hope it will be many years before I assume that responsibility from Uncle, I will always hold Charles in my heart and do my best to be the kind of earl he would have been. Thoughtful. Caring. Responsible."

"You'll do fine, my boy," the earl said. "Just think in everything you do, do it the way Charles would have done. My son, your cousin, can be your guiding light."

Samantha thought the conversation bordered on being excessive. Yes, Haskett had been a good man but not the saint these three portrayed and certainly not one who would have done an ideal job of running the estate.

"As for you," the countess said, turning to her daughter-in-law, "I know you will always honor my darling boy in your heart."

"I will certainly look upon my husband with fondness," she replied carefully, wondering how to speak out regarding her plans.

"The perfect way to do so—and keep you in the family—has been decided," the countess continued. "You will wed Percy."

"What?" she cried. "No, that's not a good idea at all."

Lady Rockaway's eyes narrowed. "It is *my* idea and therefore an excellent one."

Samantha glanced to her right and saw amusement in Percy's eyes. It told her he had known about this ambush.

"We wouldn't suit at all," she said. "We barely know one another. Percy is more than five years my junior. Frankly, I don't much like Cousin Percy," she admitted.

The countess looked at her disdainfully. "Nevertheless, you will wed. Percy is to finish university first. An education is important for a young man. It will give him time to sow his wild oats before he settles into marriage."

"You think I will remain here another three years and wait for him?" Samantha asked, her voice rising in hysteria. "No, my lady, I intend to return to my brother."

"You mean the brother who barely writes to you?" The countess clucked her tongue. "No, we are your family. Besides, you're the daughter of and the sister to a duke. We would not want to lose that family connection. You will remain here at Rockwell."

"I will not," she said firmly. "I am an adult. Of legal age. I will leave."

Lady Rockaway's face grew red in anger. "And I say you will remain here."

Samantha turned to Lord Rockaway. "Please, my lord. Say something. Tell me I will not be held prisoner here."

The earl frowned and turned his gaze away, remaining silent.

She looked back at his wife, who now wore a triumphant smile. Waving her hand around, she said, "You think this is a prison? Why, Rockwell is the finest houses in Durham County. You should appreciate living in such a place of beauty. After all, one day you will be its countess."

Shooting to her feet, Samantha said, "This discussion is over. I will have Lucy pack my things and we'll leave immediately." Softening her tone, she added, "I am sorry Haskett was murdered. I wish I could change that but I can't. You said we need to continue on with our lives. That is what I plan to do, my lady. I wish the best to all of you."

She crossed the drawing room and opened the door. Standing in the corridor were the butler and two footmen. She started to pass but the two footmen stepped forward, blocking her way. Panic filled her as she met the eyes of one of them.

They had been stationed here to intercept her. Lady Rockaway had known she would object to a marriage with Percy Johnson. Both men clasped her upper arms. Samantha tried to jerk away but they only tightened their grips. She began struggling.

"Let go of me!" she shouted.

"It would be best if you came along quietly, my lady," the butler said.

"I'm not going anywhere I don't want to," she told him.

Pity filled his eyes and he nodded to the footmen. They began dragging her down the hallway. Samantha screamed, over and over, her cries piercing the air. They passed startled servants as she fought to free herself.

They arrived at her bedchamber. The butler opened the door and the footmen hauled her inside. They tossed her onto the bed and hurried from the room. She ran to the door and reached it as she heard the lock turn. Trying it, she realized she was locked in.

"You can't keep me here forever," she shouted. "Let me out!"

She banged and kicked at the door for several minutes, continuing her tirade. "You can't hold me against my will, you bloody fools!"

No one came.

She slunk to the floor. The anger which had fueled her outburst now dissipated, leaving her exhausted. Collecting her thoughts, she rose and went to her desk, pulling out fresh parchment.

She would write to Weston. He would come for her. Her brother would end this farce. He was a duke. They couldn't refuse him.

Samantha poured her heart out to her brother, telling him how lonely and isolated she had been and how her in-laws now thought to hold her captive and force her to wed Haskett's cousin in a few years. She begged him to come for her. Sealing the letter, she left it on the desk and went to her bed. She curled up in a small ball, sobbing into her pillow so no one would hear her.

Someone shook her shoulder. Disoriented, she opened her eyes, figuring she must have fallen asleep.

Glancing up, she saw Lady Rockaway hovering over her like an avenging angel. She held something in her hands.

The letter . . .

"That's mine," Samantha said, leaping from the bed and grabbing for it as her mother-in-law stepped back and then ripped it into shreds.

"I read it," the countess said. "Treadwell will not be coming for you."

"You cannot hold me prisoner."

"I can do anything I want, you flighty, stupid girl. You weren't my choice for my darling boy. It's the only decision he ever made that went against my wishes. You do have the proper bloodlines, though. That's the only reason I'm keeping you. You will wed Percy when he finishes at university. You will give him children. Until then, you will remain in this room until you can act properly. I want you docile and agreeable."

"I'll never be that," Samantha swore.

Lady Rockaway slapped her and she stumbled, grabbing on to the bedpost.

"You will. If I have to beat you every day. If I have to starve you. I will make you into whom I want. The perfect daughter-in-law."

Stunned, Samantha watched the countess rush from the room and slam the door.

Chapter Six

Two years later . . .

SAMANTHA NERVOUSLY LICKED her lips as Lucy dressed her hair. She hadn't been allowed to see her maid since she'd been held captive in her room. Lucy pulled the brush through Samantha's long tresses, their eyes locked upon one another in the mirror. A burly footman stood at the door, guarding it. Once upon a time, she would have rushed him and tried to make her way through. She'd learned her lesson, though. Lady Rockaway had been adamant that she would turn Samantha into the perfect daughter-in-law. It had taken the better part of a year for Samantha to give up her rebellious ways.

The past year, she'd bided her time. The day would come when they would have to let her out of here. For the wedding. She quit her protests. Stopped fighting back. Pretended to be calm as the hate for these people grew in her heart. The beatings finally stopped. Lady Rockaway no longer had her starved. Samantha lost the haggard look that she'd seen reflected in the mirror. Her hair, which had begun to fall out, finally returned with its luster and sheen.

She also exercised all the time. They didn't allow her books. With nothing to pass the time, she'd decided to make herself strong. She ate everything they brought to her. Practiced lifting heavy items within the bedchamber. Paced the length of the room and back for hours at a time. When the day arrived and she was outside these four walls, she would make her move. She wouldn't tire or give in. She would push herself until she escaped—or dropped dead from exhaustion.

Lady Rockaway had stood next to her, dictating various letters for Samantha to write to Weston. She'd written him once a month during her marriage and continued to do so. The words she placed upon the page were stilted. She doubted the countess knew how to carry on a conventional conversation on the page. It didn't matter. Her brother had only answered two of them and, even then, his replies were brief. She wondered if he'd truly read the letters sent to him.

Hadn't he wondered about her? Part of Samantha's anger was directed toward him for not coming to rescue her. She knew it was ridiculous. Weston had no idea she'd been held against her will for so long, certainly not from the trite, dull letters she'd sent.

At least Lucy had been allowed in to arrange Samantha's hair for today's wedding. She'd insisted upon it, in part to see if her maid still worked at Rockwell. When Lucy came through the door earlier to help her dress for the wedding, Samantha could have wept. Except she didn't cry anymore. She doubted she ever could or would. Her insides were now as molten steel, ready to harden at any moment. Crying served no purpose.

Revenge did, however. She didn't know how she would exact it but she promised herself daily that these people would be made to pay for her years of suffering.

Lucy came from behind Samantha and fiddled with an errant curl. She leaned close to smooth and pin it, frowning as she concentrated.

Samantha whispered, "We escape today. Meet me at the stables."

To her credit, Lucy didn't acknowledge what had been said. She continued studying her mistress carefully until she moved away, a smile now on her face.

"There you go, my lady," Lucy said softly, her eyes welling with tears. "You look right lovely."

"Thank you, Lucy. You have turned me into a most beautiful bride."

Lucy asked, "Anything else, my lady?"

She stood and turned, seeing Lady Rockaway standing next to the footman who guarded her. Looking at the countess, she said, "I'd like Lucy to accompany me to the church. You never know if a button might come off or if a stray curl needs to be restrained by a pin."

"I don't see the need—"

"I do, Lady Rockaway. If I'm to wed again, I want everything to be perfect. I want to be perfect in every way."

Knowing how the countess insisted on total control in every situation, Samantha knew her request would be denied. She wanted it to be denied.

"Nothing will go wrong. The maid stays here."

"Aren't all of the servants coming to the wedding?" she asked, knowing she was pushing her mother-in-law. "Except for Cook and her staff. I know they've the wedding breakfast to prepare."

Lady Rockaway glared at her. "I said your maid remains behind. I will not be challenged on the matter."

Samantha took her cue. Lowering her eyes, she meekly said, "Yes, my lady. You're right. Lucy isn't needed."

Behaving in a subservient manner to this woman caused her to seethe inwardly but she had trained herself not to show her feelings to the world.

She raised her head, aiming to look contrite. Holding her head high, she mustered as much dignity as she could as she rose and crossed the room. She didn't stop at the threshold but pushed onward and found herself walking down the corridor. Seeing so much space around her almost made her grow dizzy. Fainting wasn't an option so she dug her nails into her palms, feeling the bite of them through her gloves. She took the stairs slowly and arrived at the bottom. The butler stood, watching her every step. He opened the door and she sailed through, sensing the others behind her.

A footman swung the carriage door open and she took his hand

and entered the vehicle. Lady Rockaway followed, then came the footman who had stood at her door for so long, preventing her from leaving or attacking anyone who brought her food or water to bathe in. She didn't know his name but his features would be forever burned into her memory.

No one spoke as the carriage rumbled along the lane and turned toward the village. She suppressed a sigh of relief. She had worried that with a second wedding not as many guests would have been invited and that Lady Rockaway might have had the ceremony held in the chapel at Rockwell. It was imperative that the marriage take place in the village.

One person she knew who hadn't been invited was her brother. She'd only been allowed to write regarding mundane matters in her letters to him, though the mention of Percy had been a constant thread over the last year. She supposed this was so Weston wouldn't be surprised when she wrote to tell him she'd married again. Not that he cared.

Gazing out the window, she watched the landscape roll by until they passed the cemetery. Then the church came into sight. The carriage stopped next door at the vicarage. Mrs. Kith stood outside, an encouraging smile on her lined face. Samantha prayed that the clergyman's kind wife would aid her escape. If she didn't?

Samantha couldn't begin to think about that.

The guard opened the door and jumped to the ground. He handed Lady Rockaway down first. Samantha swallowed, hoping all would go as she'd planned. The man had always handled her roughly before and she counted on him to do the same now. He seemed to enjoy the power he'd been given over her. She placed her hand in his and he jerked her down. She'd already tucked her boot into the deliberately loosened hem and, as she stepped, it tore exactly as she'd wanted it to do.

"Look what you've done," she cried angrily. "My hem is ruined!"

Her mother-in-law frowned deeply and Samantha curbed her tongue from reminding the countess that they should have brought Lucy along.

Instead, she looked to Mrs. Kith. "Oh, Mrs. Kith, you've always been so skilled with a needle. Might we go inside the vicarage and have you repair the damage? I do not want my groom to see me with a damaged dress."

She'd attended many an altar guild meeting where ladies sewed altar cloths and knew the good reverend's wife was talented with a needle and thread.

"Of course, my lady. Let's go inside." Mrs. Kith took her arm.

"Go with them," Lady Rockaway ordered. "Stand outside the door and bring her over the minute it's finished." To Mrs. Kith she added, "Hurry. I don't want to keep anyone waiting, least of all the groom."

"I can have it done in fifteen minutes," Mrs. Kith assured the countess.

"Make it ten," Lady Rockaway snapped and turned away to head toward the church.

The three went to the rectory and the footman remained outside. Relief poured through her.

The moment the door closed, she grabbed Mrs. Kith's arm. "I haven't been ill as they've led you to believe. I've been held hostage and am being forced to wed. Will you do your Christian duty, Mrs. Kith, and help me escape?"

The woman's eyes grew large and she nodded. "I've never liked them Rockaways, my lady. Not a one of that family. They're miserly and mean and should have put a new roof on the church years ago."

"My brother is a duke. I'll see that he gets you a new roof. Listen carefully."

As Samantha spoke, she untied the sash around her waist. She'd been allowed to sew her own wedding gown and had created an overskirt for it. The material at its waist had only been basted so she tore it off.

"You will sit in here and hem the garment as asked. I begged to use the chamber pot in private. I was nervous and my stomach was upset. You sent me into your bedchamber. I'll go out through the window."

"But . . . where will you go, my lady?"

"You can't tell them what you don't know, Mrs. Kith." She embraced the woman. "Thank you. You have saved my life."

Samantha handed the overskirt to the woman and hurried to the bedchamber. Locking the door, she hiked up her skirts and untied the reticule she'd fastened to her thigh. It would be easier to run without it slapping against her leg. Crossing to the open window, she climbed through it. She'd worn her boots, not the satin slippers that matched the gown. She'd made sure her skirts were long enough so that the boots wouldn't show.

She crept away from the house, cutting through the cemetery. Once past it, she entered the woods.

And ran.

All those months of strenuous exercise would now pay off. The boots were sturdy and much easier to move in. Samantha ran at a steady pace, knowing her life depended upon it. She wouldn't put it past Lady Rockaway to have her killed if she were caught fleeing. It would be made to look like an accident, of course, but dead was dead.

Samantha planned to live.

Rockwell was a good two miles from the village by the road. But cutting through the woods reduced that distance almost in half. She wasn't even winded by the time she reached the stables. She caught sight of Lucy standing in front and flung herself at the girl. They clung tightly to one another.

"I brought the money I have, my lady," Lucy shared.

"I have some my brother gave me," she revealed. "Now, we need a horse."

They entered the stables and ran into a young groom who was

exiting. His eyes widened at the sight of them.

"Peter," she greeted. "You've grown quite a bit taller since the last time I saw you," she said calmly, wondering why he was there and figuring at least one groom had been left behind to watch over the animals.

The boy had often saddled her horse when she'd ridden around the estate during the years of her marriage. He must have grown half a foot during her exile, though, and now must be seventeen or so.

"What do you need, my lady?" he asked eagerly, the look in his eyes telling Samantha he was on her side.

"A horse saddled. Not one that will be missed right away."

"On it," he said, sprinting away.

"Where are we going, my lady?" Lucy asked worriedly.

"They'll think we went to Durham. It's the closest town where we could catch the mail coach. Or beyond it to the east to Hartlepool if they think we've tried to sail away. Because of that, we'll ride northeast to Sunderland."

"That's almost twenty kilometers," Lucy fretted. "And the opposite way of where we need to go."

"I know. They'd never imagine we'd travel away from our intended destination. From there, we can take a mail coach to Lancaster and stay a day to rest. Then we'll continue on a mail coach to Exeter. It will be hard journey, Lucy. Possibly two weeks or so, even if we rest overnight once or twice. Are you still willing to come with me?"

"I would do anything for you, my lady. After I realized they weren't going to let you out, I tried to get word to your brother." Lucy burst into tears. "They . . . found out. I don't know how. But the poor footman I gave the letter to was whipped. Scourged so badly he couldn't work for a month."

The maid trembled violently and Samantha wrapped her arms around her. "It is all right, Lucy."

Tears streamed down Lucy's face. "And Lord Rockaway? He . . .

punished me himself."

Samantha stilled, her belly twisting into knots. "What did he do to you?"

Lucy angrily wiped away the tears with the backs of her hands. "I won't be telling you about that. It's not fit for your ears, my lady. But he told me if I tried to send for your brother—if I tried to leave—he would do to you what he did to me.

"Every day."

Grief and anger and hatred swelled within her. She hugged Lucy fiercely.

"Thank you, Lucy. I am sorry for what you suffered."

"It was nothing compared to you, my lady," the girl protested. I would have left long ago but I couldn't leave you behind." She took Samantha's hands in hers. "We'll do it together, my lady. We'll look out for one another."

Samantha gazed into Lucy's eyes. "We most certainly will."

Peter returned with a horse and led it outside. The two women followed.

Samantha opened her reticule and retrieved several bills. She handed them to him but Peter refused to accept the payment.

"No, my lady. You were always kind to me. The Rockaways are hard people. No one likes them. I won't say a word. I promise."

"Would you be willing to leave here if I could guarantee you employment?" she asked. "Whether you admit you helped us or not, they'll eventually find a horse is missing and you'll be blamed. Fired without references."

He brightened. "I'd be happy to leave."

She pressed the money into his hands. "Then take this. Hide it. Stay a week. Two would be better. If they do fire you, go to Durham. Use this to stay a night or two. Make sure no one is watching you and then take a mail coach to Exeter."

"Where's that?" he asked, curiosity and eagerness mingling on his face.

"In the southwest of England. A good two weeks or more away. Once you reach there, head northwest about thirty miles to Treadwell Manor. Walk. Hitch a ride. I don't care how you get there. My brother is a duke and it is his estate. I promise you will have a position waiting for you. You may choose whatever job you wish."

Peter nodded. "I'll keep silent as the grave, my lady. And I'll see you in a month or so. Good luck to you."

"Thank you."

The groom helped her into the saddle and then hoisted Lucy up behind her. Samantha looped her reticule around the saddle horn several times and then took the reins.

"I ain't never ridden a horse," the maid said, terror obvious in her voice.

She looked over her shoulder. "It's our only means of escape. It's all right to be afraid. Hold fast to me."

Lucy gripped her tightly and Samantha took off. Within a league, they reached the turning point in the road. East for Durham. North-east for Sunderland. Without slowing the horse, she rode in the opposite direction of Treadwell Manor, hoping the ruse would throw those who came after them off their trail.

As the miles passed, the air she breathed seemed sweeter. The countryside prettier. The sky bluer.

Freedom.

Chapter Seven

London

George leaped from the carriage and raced to West's door, banging on it and shouting.

Immediately, the door swung open and Caldwell said, "May I help you, Your Grace?"

Pushing past the butler, he entered and said, "Close the door."

Caldwell did as asked and awaited his instructions, as unflappable as ever.

"Lord Ivy is looking to issue a challenge to His Grace. It seems he had been intimate with his young stepmother and learned that His Grace recently spent a single night with her. The chit was foolish enough to tell Ivy she preferred Treadwell over him. Ivy's on a rampage and out for blood."

"What do you suggest, Your Grace?" Caldwell asked calmly.

"Lord Ivy's father has one foot in the grave already. The son will inherit soon and turn his attention to other matters, including women. He's always been fickle that way. If I can get Treadwell out of town and let Ivy cool off, I can prevent a disaster." He thought a moment. "Have the valet pack His Grace's trunk and see it delivered to my residence at once. We both were invited to a house party at the Duke and Duchess of Windham's in Devon."

"His Grace never responded to the invitation," pointed out the butler.

"Well, I declined it but Windham is not going to shut the door in the face of two of his closest friends," George pointed out. "Where's Treadwell now?"

"He is boxing this afternoon, Your Grace."

"I'll collect him from Gentleman Jack's. You see that trunk is packed and delivered. We'll leave as soon as we can collect it. And Caldwell, have a footman send a message to my townhouse, as well. My valet also needs to pack for me."

"Very good, Your Grace. I'll handle the matter at once. I will send word when I see in the papers that the gentleman in question has gained his new title."

"Good thinking, Caldwell. After the house party at Windowmere, we'll retreat to our own country homes in Devon until we hear from you. Thank you."

George left, knowing the butler would see to things in his efficient manner. He told his day driver to head to Gentleman Jack's establishment and entered the carriage. Lord Ivy had been a year behind them in school. He was a hothead and ignorant fool, a man who thought he was smarter than almost anyone in the room. Ivy would be an idiot—a dead idiot—if he challenged West to a duel. West was a fantastic shot and would aim to kill, merely because he'd despised Ivy as a boy and even more so as a man. That had probably led him to couple with Ivy's stepmother, who was barely out of the schoolroom.

He sat back and took several calming breaths. It would be good to see Andrew and Phoebe again. His friend had returned from war because of his brother's death and father's grave illness. The Duke of Windham had a heart attack when he'd learned of his eldest son's racing accident and death. Windham had lingered long enough for Andrew to make it back to London before he died, making plain Andrew Graham the new duke.

Of course, nothing seemed to run smoothly for him and his friends. Andrew's younger half-brother, a wastrel who spent lavishly, had shot Andrew and left him for dead. Fortunately, Phoebe had found the bleeding duke in the surf and taken him to her cottage by the sea, where she'd nursed him back to health. After being separated, the two had come together and wed three months ago. The house party was a way to help Phoebe get to know some of her husband's friends. George had actually wanted to attend but West had thrown a fit, growling about being buried in the country and bored to tears. In a show of solidarity, George had declined the invitation but their friend Jon, Duke of Blackmore, had accepted on behalf of himself and his sister, Elizabeth, who'd just made her come-out this past Season.

His day carriage pulled up at Gentleman Jack's and George quickly disembarked, wishing he'd thought to use the more inconspicuous night one. The vehicle started up again and turned the corner. Per his instructions, his driver would wait in the alley.

Turning to the footman, he said, "You know what to do. Find Treadwell's clothes and place them in the coach. Be quick about it."

"Yes, Your Grace." The servant quickly entered the building.

He walked over to West's carriage and greeted the driver.

"Good morning, Your Grace," the coachmen replied.

Before George could tell the man to go home, he spied a carriage approaching quickly. It stopped across the street. Lord Ivy leaped from it.

"Drive around London," he ordered the coachman. "Lord Ivy will be in pursuit. Don't stop anywhere. Don't go home for a good three hours or more. Lead him on a merry chase through the city. Understood?"

The driver nodded and flicked the reins, taking off as Lord Ivy dashed across the street, shouting, "Stop! I say halt!"

Ivy dashed toward George and demanded, "Where is he going?"

He arched his eyebrows and in a bored tone asked, "Am I Treadwell's keeper? I think not."

"You must tell me where he's headed."

"So you can challenge him to a duel over the honor of a woman who has none?"

Ivy grew red in the face. "You Bad Dukes are horrid."

With that, the viscount dashed across the street, shouting, "Follow Treadwell's carriage."

As the driver turned the coach around, Ivy climbed up next to the driver. "I see it! Hurry, man. Drive!"

George watched the vehicle race off. Treadwell's driver had a decent head start on them. He sighed and went inside in search of West. He followed his ears, hearing numerous cheers and seeing a large group of men gathered in a circle. Spying Gentleman Jack himself, he went to stand next to the proprietor.

"How long has Treadwell been at it?" he asked.

"Not long," the former boxer replied. "Two minutes or so."

He watched as West landed several punches and danced away from his opponent, a viscount who was a few inches shorter but with a heavily muscled chest.

"We need to leave quickly. A back way if you have one," he told Jack.

"Trouble with the ladies? Or wait, no. A gentleman of one of those ladies, I assume."

"You assume correctly," George said. "Lord Ivy, to be precise."

The gymnasium owner frowned. "He's a troublemaker, that one."

"He was even back in school. The fact he's never liked Treadwell only adds to the mess. He aims to challenge Treadwell to a duel."

Gentleman Jack sighed. "Do you want me to end the bout?"

"No. Treadwell can. He's only toying with his opponent."

George waited until the men circled one another and West faced George's direction. He caught his friend's eyes and tugged on his ear. It was their signal to leave. They'd used it in countless situations. Boring routs. Dull garden parties. Tedious conversations at White's.

West gave an imperceptible nod. Grim determination crossed his face. He moved in on his opponent with lightning speed, landing a serious of quick blows to the viscount's torso and then his head. Within a minute, the viscount lay unconscious on the floor and raucous cheers filled the gymnasium. West quickly darted through the thick crowd, reaching George.

"Follow Jack," he said and they fell into step behind the proprietor.

"You don't want me to stay behind and receive enthusiastic congratulations from my admirers?" West asked.

"You're already full of conceit. Come along."

They went to a part of the building George had never seen, down a long hallway. Gentleman Jack went to the last door on the right and unlocked it.

Pointing to a door directly across the room, he said, "Go through there. It leads to the alley."

"But I'm not even dressed," West protested, his upper torso bare and glistening with sweat.

In response, George tugged on his friend's arm, bringing West into the office as Jack relocked the door. George crossed the room and threw the lock on the outer door and opened it. His carriage waited in the narrow alley. The footman opened the vehicle's door as far as it could go and West climbed in. George followed and the vehicle quickly took off.

"I see my clothes are here." West crinkled his nose. "I assume you expect me to put them on."

"That's why they're sitting there."

West picked up the shirt and lifted it over his head. "Well, when are you going to tell me why I had to rush things? I'd planned to string the viscount along for a good ten minutes. You know I adore toying with my opponents."

"Lord Ivy wants to shoot you."

"Hmm." West slipped into his waistcoat and did a credible job of tying his cravat. "I suppose it's over his rather young stepmother?"

"It is. He was tupping the girl himself as he waits for his father to die. You know he's never liked you. Finding himself cuckolded—even though he, too, was doing the same to his own father—has him on a rampage. He plans to challenge you to a duel."

West shrugged. "Let him. The Duke of Disrepute would have two choices. Refuse Ivy's challenge and be truly disgraced. Or accept it and kill the fool. I'm leaning toward the latter."

"You'd have to go into exile," George proclaimed.

"For a while, I suppose. But dukes are generally forgiven anything and everything. I could go abroad."

"With the war going on? I think not, West. We'll follow my plan instead."

"What's that? Oh, I know. We're going to run. How truly shameful! Another horrible, despicable act to add to my legend."

George studied West a moment. "Do you ever get tired of living up to your nickname? Is there a time when you wish you could merely be Treadwell and not the Duke of Disrepute?"

West frowned. "What are you saying?"

He decided nothing but honesty would do in this instance. "I'm bloody tired of being the Duke of Charm. I'm tired of the empty life. The meaningless affairs. The fun and drink and laughter. Aren't you? We've been at it for years now."

West grew contemplative. Finally, he spoke. "Even if I were, it's too late for me, George. You are all charm and a duke. You've merely engaged in light affairs whereas I have done other despicable things. If you want to change—to try and be who you once were—I won't stop you."

"I can never be that man from before," he said grimly. "But I am tired of the one I have been for so long since then. I'm over the humiliation of being jilted in front of all Polite Society. That seems a lifetime ago. I'm ready to put aside all the emptiness inside me."

"Hmm. It sounds as if you long for a wife, my friend."

George thought a moment. "I think you're right. I want a family. I want a true home. I want one woman."

West shuddered. "You may do as you like but the thought of harnessing myself to one woman gives me hives." He paused. "Will you still be my friend? Even if I continue in my dissolute ways?"

"Of course. We've always been friends and brothers. I will never abandon you, West. Never."

"A wife would change things, George. You think she won't but she will."

"Not if I choose the right one."

For some reason, his thoughts turned to Sam. His old friend was a widow now. Though they hadn't spoken in years, he longed to talk this over with her. If she were willing to forgive him and they wed, George knew he could have a good life. Still, West was his best friend. One didn't just go up and marry a best friend's sister. That's even if Sam would consider his offer. They'd parted on poor terms and hadn't spoken for years. He had no idea if she would be interested in becoming his duchess.

"What's that odd look on your face?" West asked.

George decided he would share what was on his mind. "Don't laugh. This talk of wanting to settle down made me think of . . . Sam."

"Sam? *Sam?* Are you serious?"

"Well, you did say she's a widow. Do you think she's formed any connection with a gentleman since then? What's it been—a year?"

West thought. "More like two, I believe. Yes, two. I remember now."

"When is the last time you wrote to her?" George asked. "I know you haven't seen her since the Season before last. No, it's been longer than that."

West shrugged. "I'm not sure. I fear. I truly can't remember. I haven't been a very good brother."

"No, you haven't. You've been too busy being disgraceful."

"You haven't been any better yourself, Charm."

"No, I haven't," he admitted. "And I think I am finally ready to be."

They pulled up to his townhouse. "Stay in the carriage," he ordered. "I don't want anyone seeing you."

Going into his residence, his butler greeted him.

"His Grace's trunks have arrived, along with his valet. Briggs has your trunks packed as well, Your Grace. They are being placed in the carriage now."

"Good. I don't know when I'll be back. I'm off to the Duke of Windham's house party in Devon and will go to Colebourne Manor after that. If Lord Ivy shows up here, under no circumstances tell him where Treadwell or I have gone."

"Yes, Your Grace."

He spied a footman. "Run and tell the coachman carrying our valets that we're departing now."

"Yes, Your Grace." The footman took off.

George returned to his carriage and waited until the second one pulled around before telling his driver, "We're going to Devon."

He climbed inside and saw West had finished dressing.

As the vehicle pulled away, his friend said, "You've never said where we're going."

"We're off to Andrew and Phoebe's house party."

"Then I hope Phoebe has invited some very beautiful guests else I'll die of boredom."

George quipped, "That would be better than dying from Ivy's bullet."

CHAPTER EIGHT

SAMANTHA GAZED OUT the window of the crowded mail coach. For the last two weeks, she'd striven to always sit by the window so she could stare out at the countryside rolling by. With it being early October, the colorful leaves gave her plenty to look at. The weather was chilly at the beginning and end of each day but in-between she thought it lovely, especially the further south they pushed. She would not miss the frigid winters of Rockwell and her icy bedchamber, where Lady Rockaway never allowed a fire to be lit.

"Are we close?" Lucy asked, her tone weary.

Turning to her companion, she nodded and quietly said, "Exeter should be coming up in a few minutes from what I was told at our last stop."

Everything had gone as planned, which surprised her. They'd reached Sunderland and purchased two tickets for the mail coach all the way to Lancaster. In the two hours before it left, they'd gotten something to eat and Samantha had given away the horse they'd ridden to a young man close to Peter's age. She hadn't wanted to sell it and when she saw the lad walking, she'd stopped and spoken to him briefly. He had seemed as decent a person as she might find on such short notice and handed him the reins. Stunned, he'd watched her and Lucy walk away and then given a shout of joy for his good luck.

With their coach going a different route from those leaving Durham, Samantha prayed that no one from Rockwell would discover them. She didn't waste time wondering who might have been sent after them though she did hope the cruel man who'd guarded her would be fired without references. Negative thoughts had dominated every day for too long and she wanted to remain positive.

"What will we—"

She shook her head, frowning at her maid. Immediately, Lucy fell silent. Samantha had been careful the entire journey, not wanting to discuss where they were going with strangers surrounding them. She'd even warned Lucy about calling her *my lady* or *Lady Samantha*. She didn't want anyone who might be questioned later remembering her name and confirming she had traveled that way. Not that she would ever return. Once she reached Treadwell Manor, she would be safe. She never wanted to be under a man's thumb, or a woman's for that matter, for as long as she lived. No one would ever control her again. Tell her what to do or what she could eat or how to dress.

In exchange, she would have to give up the idea of bearing children. Though she still longed for a baby, that meant marriage. Samantha never wanted to be confined by that institution again. She'd toyed with the idea of taking a lover in order to have a child but it wouldn't be fair to the son or daughter she birthed. It didn't matter to her if Polite Society ostracized her but she would never want her child to suffer because of her sins.

Instead, she had decided she would take lovers. As many as she chose. There had to be more to the act of love than what Haskett and she had done or there wouldn't be so many in the *ton* finding new partners to couple with every Season. As a widow, it would be easier for her to take on a lover, as long as she was discreet. If she couldn't have children, at least she could discover satisfaction in the bedroom.

They rode for another half-hour and then she saw Exeter come into view. She and Lucy had already rested overnight at two of the stops along the route and she planned to do the same here before she hired a post chaise to take them the thirty miles home.

The mail coach rolled into town and stopped at the very heart. Passengers began to disembark. It amazed her how many people could be packed into these mail carriages. She and Lucy exited the vehicle and walked slowly away since they had no luggage to claim.

"We're almost home," her maid said dreamily. "It will be so nice to spend autumn and winter in southern England. Rockwell was so unpleasant."

"I came to hate the cold," Samantha agreed. "I know you must be hungry because I am, but I want to go to my dress shop and purchase us new things to wear. We've been in the same clothes for over two weeks. I never want to see this gown again."

She looked around to get her bearings. "It's this way," she indicated.

"What?" Lucy cried, grabbing Samantha's elbow. "We cannot do that. What if someone sees us? What if they catch up to us? I won't go back there," she said frantically. "I can't go back."

Samantha guided the girl several feet away to the mouth of an alley and pulled her inside it.

"We have done it, Lucy," she said firmly. "We have outsmarted them. Frankly, I am astonished it went as well as it did. But you have been with me every step of the way. We have looked over our shoulders even in our sleep. But look around! No one is here. No one has followed us."

The maid glanced about furtively. She swallowed hard and then calmed. "You are right, my lady. I don't mean to argue with you. I have trusted you every step of the way and you have brought us to our freedom."

Samantha wrapped an arm about Lucy's shoulders. "I have been on edge this entire time. But we have come this far. We are in a town I know well. People know me here. We are *safe*," she insisted.

Lucy's mouth trembled but she nodded in agreement. "We will do as you wish, my lady. I am sorry I questioned you."

"You were merely looking out for us. There is nothing shameful in that. After what we have endured, it was a natural reaction. But I believe if anyone is searching for us, they are far behind us. So please, let us go purchase something new for ourselves. We deserve it, don't you agree?"

The servant nodded.

"Come along. The dress shop isn't far from here."

They went six blocks east and entered the building. A sense of nostalgia filled her as she saw Mrs. Echols approach.

"Why, Lady Samantha, this is certainly a surprise," the proprietress said. "I heard of your marriage several years ago."

"It is good to see you, Mrs. Echols. This is my maid, Lucy. I was hoping that you might have something close to our sizes already in progress that could be finished by tomorrow morning."

"Hmm. Let me think. I'll check in the back." The dressmaker left them and returned a few minutes later with a few half-finished garments over her arms.

"What do you think of these?"

Samantha looked over the three gowns Mrs. Echols returned with. "I'll take the blue first. You can finish up the green for me, as well. I'll also need to place an order for several more gowns and undergarments." She turned to Lucy, indicating the last gown. "Do you like this one?"

"I do, my lady."

"Then Lucy will take that one and another two. I'm sure you'll need to measure us."

She used her no-nonsense voice and Mrs. Echols quickly agreed with her. The woman measured them both and then asked if Samantha wanted to look about the shop at various bolts of material. She did, choosing several fabrics for additional gowns. She would want most of her clothes made up in London by her usual modiste but she would need things to wear between now and next spring. Mrs. Echols was talented enough with a needle so Samantha didn't mind ordering a small wardrobe from her now, including a new riding habit. Riding had been the activity she missed the most. She planned to spend as much time as she could outdoors and atop a horse for the rest of her life.

"Lucy and I will return for our gowns tomorrow morning," she said. "When would you like me to return for a fitting on the others?"

"Give me a week, my lady. I will have as many ready as possible by then. Lucy's two gowns will be finished at that time, as well," the dressmaker said.

"Thank you, Mrs. Echols." Then softening her tone, she added, "I have come home. I lost my husband two years ago and have missed Devon very much."

Sympathy flickered in the dressmaker's eyes. "I am sorry to hear that you are a widow but I understand it's good to get home to family."

Samantha didn't know about that. She assumed Weston was carousing in London. They were the last of the Wallaces. Still, returning to Treadwell Manor was a dream finally come true.

"We'll see you in the morning."

She and Lucy left the shop. Dusk was almost upon them.

"Since we must spend the night in Exeter, we'll go to the inn I've eaten at several times while in town. We can book a room and share it. Then I'll hire a post chaise to take us the rest of the way in the morning."

"That sounds lovely, my lady."

They weren't far from the inn she was familiar with and Samantha determined they could walk there. By the time they reached it, the sun had set. She was glad they arrived when they did, not wanting to be out and about after dark. The innkeeper greeted her by name and she requested a room for the night.

"We have only one left, Lady Samantha," he apologized. "I'm

afraid it's rather small."

"That is quite all right. Lucy and I will share. Might we have supper brought to us and eat there instead of in the common room?"

"Of course. Let me see you upstairs now and then I'll let our cook know."

The innkeeper escorted them upstairs. The room was cramped but considering it was the only one available, she didn't remark on its size.

"I'll be back in a quarter-hour with something for you," he promised.

"I know it will be delicious. My brother and I always have enjoyed dining here when we were in Exeter."

The meal didn't disappoint. They dined on a hearty mutton stew and fresh vegetables. The bread and creamy butter spread upon it bested any she'd eaten while at Rockwell. The cook had even included fruit tarts for them.

"I can't believe I ate all of that," Lucy proclaimed. "It was ever so good."

Samantha was also full but in a very good way. Her mother-in-law had restricted what she ate. To be able to eat her fill was still a bit hard to believe. She would have to watch herself in the future and not overindulge, else she'd weigh a good stone more in no time.

The landlord himself came and cleared their dishes and she and Lucy drew back the bedclothes and helped one another strip down to their chemises. Each placed their clothes over the one chair in the room and they climbed into bed. A heavy, dreamless night of sleep allowed Samantha to awake refreshed the next morning. They dressed and went to the common room, where the barmaid brought them plates of country ham and eggs. She even asked for a cup of chocolate and when it came, she savored every sip.

"Please send my brother the bill," she told the innkeeper as they left the establishment and made their way back to Mrs. Echols' dress shop.

"I stayed up half the night but your dresses are finished, my lady," the dressmaker said.

After trying them on and seeing they fit, both Samantha and Lucy left their former gowns behind.

"Do with them as you wish," she told Mrs. Echols. "Use the material or throw it away. I will see you in a week."

"I look forward to it, my lady. I hope you'll be pleased with what I make up for you."

"Remember, the riding habit before anything else. I am eager to get back on a horse as soon as possible."

When they left the shop, they stopped at the milliner's next door. Samantha selected several pairs of gloves and a few hats and encouraged Lucy to do the same, placing the items on a bill to be sent to Weston.

A small part of her worried about blithely telling the various shopkeepers that her brother would pay for the goods she had purchased. She and Weston had been estranged for a good number of years and there was no guarantee that he would feel obligated to reimburse all these merchants. Though he had changed so much from the brother she knew and become thoroughly debauched, she still believed that, deep within him, his love for her had never died. Whatever had happened to him that altered him so radically, Samantha was determined to find out. In the meantime, she didn't think he would begrudge her for purchasing a few needed things. Weston had always been one to pay his bills in a timely fashion, unlike many gentlemen of the *ton*. She doubted that had changed. In fact, she was counting on it.

Wearing their new outfits, the two women walked three blocks to where they could hire a post chaise to take them directly to Treadwell Manor. It felt marvelous sporting a new gown after wearing her supposed wedding dress for half a month. The fact that the new gown was green, her favorite color, made it even more special.

When they reached the office, she inquired about the availability of a post chaise.

The clerk said, "We got one." He named the price and Samantha reached into her reticule. Her funds would be exhausted after paying for this but it wouldn't matter because she would finally be home.

She felt inside and her fingers touched nothing. Concerned, she opened it wider and dug around.

Empty.

"What's wrong, my lady?" Lucy asked, worry etched on her face.

She sighed. "Apparently, we were robbed last night. I was so full and content after our large meal that I fell into bed without securing the door latch."

"Oh, no!" Lucy cried.

"That's all right." She turned back to the clerk. "You'll have to present me with a bill. My brother, the Duke of Treadwell, will pay it."

"I can't do that," the clerk said, his mouth twitching nervously.

"Why not? It's done all the time."

When he shook his head, she demanded, "Let me speak with the owner at once."

"He ain't here and won't be back until the end of the week. And he's the bloke who said I had to get the money. No credit. He's been stung a few times lately." The clerk looked her up and down. "By people like you. Pretending to be gentry."

"I *am* a lady," Samantha said firmly. "The daughter of the previous Duke of Treadwell. Sister to the current duke."

"Well, we ain't seen that duke around here in a long time. He's one of them Bad Dukes, you know. The Duke of Disrepute. I wouldn't know him if he walked in here."

"How am I supposed to get to Treadwell Manor?" she demanded. "It's over thirty miles away."

He shrugged. "I don't know and don't care. I ain't losing my job over the likes of you. Now, be gone."

Stunned, the two women left the building. Lucy looked ready to burst into tears.

Samantha embraced the maid. "Come, now, Lucy. It's not that bad."

As she comforted the girl, she thought about tracking down the local magistrate to report the robbery but realized there was little the man could do. With no one to accuse of the crime of petty thievery, a magistrate would have no suspect to track down. Since magistrates were laymen who were not paid for their efforts, she decided it would prove to be a waste of time.

What concerned her more was getting to Treadwell Manor, which would be a daunting task. The few people they had come into contact with, such as the innkeeper or Mrs. Echols, would not possess a team of horses that could carry Lucy and her the thirty miles, much less make the return trip to Essex after resting the horses for a night.

Determination filled her, though. They hadn't come this far to give in to defeat.

"We will start to walk in the direction of home," she told Lucy. "Hopefully, we can find a ride along the way. Perhaps a farmer is driving his cart in the direction we are headed and will allow us to ride with him."

They started down the street. She linked her arm with Lucy's. The servant began to sniffle.

"We'll be fine. It's an adventure we've been on. This is merely the final piece of it."

They walked to the end of the main thoroughfare and turned north. After a few minutes, Samantha remembered that Andrew Graham's family estate was only a couple of miles outside the city. She didn't know if he'd returned from the war or not but she had visited Windowmere before with Weston. Surely, the staff would remember her. Even if the Duke of Windham or Andrew's aunt weren't in residence, hopefully the butler would see that she was provided transportation home.

When they reached the cutoff for Windowmere, she tugged on Lucy's arm.

"We're going to the Duke of Windham's estate. His son is friends with my brother. I know someone there will help us."

It took almost twenty minutes to go the length of the lane before they reached the imposing house. Samantha went and rapped on the door. She breathed a sigh of relief when she recognized the butler that answered the door.

"Mr. Pimmeline? I am Lady Samantha, sister to the Duke of Treadwell." She deliberately refrained from using her married name and title.

He brightened. "I thought it was you, my lady. We haven't seen the likes of you in some time. Please, come in."

She and Lucy entered the foyer. "I am in a bit of a troubling situation, Mr. Pimmeline. My maid and I are trying to reach Treadwell Manor and I was robbed in Exeter. Would it be possible for the duke—or if he isn't in residence—for Lady Helen to allow us to borrow his carriage so that we might reach home more quickly?"

"Lady Helen is visiting a childhood friend of hers but His Grace would be delighted to help you. He'll want to see you, of course. He's quite fond of your brother."

His words confused her. "What do you mean?"

Pimmeline said, "Well, His Grace went to school with your brother."

"*Andrew* is the duke?" she cried. "I had no idea he was even home from war, much less the duke."

"Why, yes, my lady. His Grace passed shortly after the marquess' death. Your brother's friend is the Duke of Windham."

Joy filled her. "Oh, that's splendid. I would love to see him."

Pimmeline turned to a footman. "Take Lady Samantha's maid to the kitchen so she may have some tea while I take Lady Samantha to His Grace."

She followed the butler up the stairs to the drawing room.

"Wait here, my lady. I'll see where His Grace is."

"Thank you, Mr. Pimmeline."

She wandered about the room, looking out the windows over the park.

"Samantha!"

Turning, she recognized Andrew, even though several years had passed since she'd last seen him. Accompanying him was a beautiful woman with caramel hair and eyes of sky blue.

"Hello, Andrew," Samantha greeted and smiled. "I hear you've become a duke."

He kissed her cheek and then said, "More than that. I also have a duchess. Lady Samantha, I'm honored to introduce you to my wife, Phoebe, the Duchess of Windham."

"You're a duke *and* married? How delightful!"

"It's a pleasure to meet you, Lady Samantha. I have met your brother."

"Oh, so you've met the Bad Dukes?"

The duchess laughed. "I have. I even invited them to our upcoming house party, which starts in a few days. We have a dozen guests that we know of who will be in attendance, including my sister and her husband. We'd be delighted to have you join us."

"That is very gracious of you to invite me, Your Grace," she said. "I'm afraid I've only the clothes on my back, though. It's a long story. I was widowed and my maid and I were on our way home when we were robbed in Exeter. I was hoping His Grace would help provide a way for us to reach Treadwell Manor."

"That's terrible," the duchess said. "But you must stay. We're of a similar size. You can borrow clothes from me. I have more than I ever thought I could wear. Besides, even though your brother never responded to our invitation, he might turn up."

"It sounds just like him to ignore sending a reply. Now that I have returned home, I hope I can make some headway with him and get to the bottom of why he's become the Duke of Disrepute."

"I'd like to know that myself," Andrew said. "It happened while I was away on the Continent and I can't get out of him or George why they've become such terrible rakes. I know, deep inside, they're still the good men I've always known."

The mention of George caused her heart to flutter but she dared not ask about him.

"What do you say, Samantha?" Andrew asked. "Will you stay and get to know my precious Phoebe? And now that your mourning period has passed, it would be a way to ease back into society."

Samantha didn't hesitate, ready to have some fun in her life. "I can't think of anything I'd like more."

CHAPTER NINE

"WE NEED TO see about getting you some more clothes," the Duchess of Windham said. "And I'm sure after your travels, you'd enjoy a nice, long bath."

Samantha almost melted at the thought of a hot bath. "Being submerged in a tub of hot water would be my fondest wish."

"Traveling does make one long for a good long soaking," the duchess said. "We'll get you clean and then look over my wardrobe and see which gowns suit you."

Andrew shook his head. "When talk turns to women's clothing, I know to politely excuse myself. It is good to see you again, Samantha. We can visit more later."

The duke took his leave and the duchess slipped her arm through Samantha's. "Let's go up to my bedchamber. You can stay there during your visit."

"I couldn't, Your Grace," she protested.

"Why not? The only time I use it is to dress. If you don't mind sharing it with me for a few minutes each day, there's no sense in you not having it."

She realized what the duchess' words meant. "So, you and Andrew are a love match?"

The duchess smiled. "Very much so. My nights are spent with my duke. Come along. I'll tell you all about how we met once you've had your bath. I'm sure your maid would like one as well. Where is she?"

"Mr. Pimmeline had her go to the kitchen for tea."

They left the drawing room and crossed paths with a familiar, matronly woman.

"Mrs. Hanks," the duchess said, "this is Lady Samantha. She will be staying with us through the house party. I'm giving her my bedchamber. Would you have hot water for a bath sent up for her? And her maid will also need a bath."

"Yes, Your Grace. I'll see to it at once." Mrs. Hanks smiled. "I do remember the time you and your brother visited Windowmere, my lady. It's very nice to see you again."

"Thank you, Mrs. Hanks. You made my last visit so pleasant."

"We'll make this one even better, my lady," the housekeeper promised. "I'll see to your bath now."

The duchess led Samantha to the bedchamber. It was extremely large and very light and airy.

"Are you certain you don't mind me staying here?" she asked.

"Not if you don't mind me coming in to change clothes. With the house party beginning in a few days, it would be silly to place you in a smaller room and let this one go to waste."

Soon, a parade of servants arrived with buckets of water and the duchess showed Samantha several vials of oil that could be added to the water. Once again, a luxury she'd been made to give up during the time she had resided under Lady Rockaway's roof. She opened and sniffed several, settling on one that smelled like orange blossoms. It was a scent she had always loved and reminded her of a happier time in her life.

Lucy entered the room. "I'm here to help with your bath, my lady."

"You're to have one, too," the duchess said. "Mrs. Hanks will take care of it for you."

"We'll be staying for a bit, Lucy," she told the girl. "The duke and duchess have invited me to attend the house party they are giving. It will start in a few days."

Lucy's eyes widened and then a smile broke out. "You need a little fun in your life, my lady. A house party is just the thing."

Once the bath had been prepared, Lucy helped Samantha undress and washed her hair and scrubbed her clean. The bath sheet Lucy wrapped around her was so soft. Nothing like the rough ones at Rockwell. She'd almost forgotten these small luxuries existed.

"Here, Lucy," the duchess said. "I've a dressing gown for Lady Samantha to put on and I've called for tea. We'll visit a while and then find a few gowns of mine for her to wear. I'll ring for you when your mistress is ready to dress."

"Yes, Your Grace," Lucy said, helping Samantha into the dressing gown and then bobbing a curtsy before leaving them.

"Come into the next room. I use it as a sitting room and write out my letters and menus there. Tea is waiting for us."

Samantha tightened the sash on the dressing gown and accompanied the duchess to the next room. It looked cozy and inviting, with comfortable chintz chairs and plenty of sunlight streaming in. The duchess poured out while Samantha made herself a plate. Her stomach rumbled noisily.

Her hostess chuckled. "I can hear you are hungry. Let me know if there's anything else you might like."

"This is more than adequate, Your Grace," she replied.

"Please, call me Phoebe. Andrew and I are holding this house party so I can get to know some of his friends better and make some of my own. I would be happy if I could call you my friend."

She looked at the duchess' shining blue eyes. "I would like that very much, Phoebe. I haven't had a friend in a very long time."

Phoebe reached and took her hand. "Other than my sister, I haven't either," she said quietly. "I am not glad that you were robbed but I am grateful that you turned to Andrew and agreed to stay with us." She squeezed Samantha's hand and released it.

"Tell me about how the two of you met. You promised you would."

"Andrew lost his older brother in an accident and sold his commission in order to come home and be with his father. The old duke didn't take to the news of his son's death well and he didn't last long. Andrew, not having been brought up to claim the title, decided to tour all of his properties and get to know his staff and tenants. He went to Moreland Hall in Cornwall. I was renting a cottage nearby."

"So, Cornwall is not your home?"

"No. I'd gone to Falmouth once as a child and enjoyed being close to the sea." A faraway look came into Phoebe's eyes. "I needed time to myself." She turned back to Samantha. "You see, I am also a widow."

"Oh, I am sorry. You went to Cornwall to mourn?"

"Yes. For my son."

Samantha wanted to jump in and ask a thousand questions but she saw Phoebe needed to say things in her own time and waited patiently.

"Borwick and my son, who was five, were killed in a carriage accident. My husband and I had a polite but distant relationship. My son was my life."

This time, it was Samantha who reached for Phoebe's hand to reassure her.

"I was with child. I lost the baby. Hearing the news of my husband's and son's deaths was just too much."

"I lost a child," Samantha revealed. "I was over four months along. It was the most devastating thing that had occurred to me."

Phoebe's eyes brimmed with tears. "We do have things in common."

"We do."

Her new friend reached for her teacup again and sipped thoughtfully. "You'll probably hear some of this story from the gossipmongers of the *ton*. Did you meet Francis Graham when you came to Windowmere?"

She frowned hearing the name, remembering Andrew's younger half-brother. "I did. While the marquess was charming and Andrew was so easy to be around, Francis was . . . unsettling."

"He tried to murder Andrew."

"What?"

Phoebe shook her head. "Francis had accumulated a plethora of debts. He wanted the title and funds that went with being the Duke of Windham. He shot Andrew."

"No!"

"I found him and took him back to my cottage. Nursed him to health."

Samantha smiled. "And that is where you fell in love. How romantic."

The duchess chuckled. "Especially when I thought he was a smuggler."

"Andrew, a smuggler? You're joking."

"It was Cornwall. Smuggling is prevalent along the coast where I was staying. And Andrew was dressed rather meanly. I thought he'd quarreled with a fellow criminal and that smuggler had tried to eliminate him."

"Surely, he cleared up your misconception."

Now, Phoebe laughed heartily. "No, he didn't. I think he rather enjoyed the fact that I thought him to be so disreputable. Even so, I did fall in love with him. Due to circumstances beyond our control, we were separated without saying goodbye. The next time I saw Andrew was this past April at the first ball of the Season. All of a sudden, my smuggler was a very proper peer—and I wasn't the middle class widow he'd thought I was. The Duke of Windham met the Dowager Countess of Borwick that night."

"I am so intrigued. This is fascinating."

"Polite Society had nicknamed Andrew the Duke of Renown because he'd been thought dead. When Andrew's body wasn't discovered, Francis murdered a man and identified the body as that of his half-brother in order to claim the title without having to wait years to have Andrew officially declared dead. Because of this, the *ton* thought Andrew dead—and then he came back to life, so to speak."

She laughed. "Oh, I wish I could have been in London to see this played out. Did Andrew sweep you off your feet and declare his undying love?"

Phoebe grinned. "I made him work for it. I told him he must court me. He chased off every suitor of mine and insisted we wed. We did so in June and, after a brief honeymoon, we came to Windowmere and have remained here these past few months. That's why we are having the house party."

"I am happy for you," she said. "And for Andrew. He was always a good friend to Weston. He's the Duke of Disrepute, in case you have him mixed up with George, the Duke of Charm."

"The Bad Dukes? They're always together. Often with Blackmore," Phoebe added. "Jon and his sister, Elizabeth, will be attending the house party. She made her come-out this year. From what I gather, Blackmore has calmed down quite a bit. At least until his sister finds a husband." She paused. "Would you like more tea?"

"Yes, please."

Samantha added two lumps of sugar and a healthy dose of cream, feeling decadent as she did so.

"You know my story now," her hostess said. "Is there anything you wish to share with me?"

She thought a moment, wondering how much she should reveal.

"I married after my first Season," she began cautiously. "I had wanted to wed a man I respected. One whom I could converse with. I thought Haskett was a good match. Once we returned to his family's estate in Durham, however, he changed. He could barely act without looking to his mother for approval. Her husband was the same way.

The Countess of Rockaway ruled her household with an iron fist. The men seemed inconsequential."

"How disappointing for you," Phoebe said, sympathy in her azure eyes.

"It got worse. Haskett rarely spoke to me during the day, much less visited me at night. The fact I found myself with child was almost a miracle." She paused. "Then I lost the baby and my husband had nothing to do with me after that."

She stared out the window as she continued to speak, not sure she could meet Phoebe's eyes.

"Then Haskett was murdered by thieves when he went to help establish his cousin at university."

Phoebe's quick intake of breath was the only noise she made.

"I spent a year in mourning," Samantha continued, "wanting to be respectful to my husband's family. At the end of that time, I told them I was returning to Devon and my brother."

Her nails dug into her palms as she remembered that long-ago day with bitterness.

"Lady Rockaway informed me that I would be staying in their family. I was to wed my husband's much younger cousin, Percy, once he completed university. When I told my mother-in-law that we wouldn't suit, I was carried kicking and screaming to my bedchamber.

"Where I remained for the next two years."

Phoebe shot to her feet. "Oh, no. No. Samantha."

Her new friend pulled Samantha to her feet and wrapped her in a tight embrace as Phoebe wept. Phoebe's arms felt good about her. It was nice to finally share what she'd suffered. She wouldn't give Phoebe any of the details of how harsh that existence had been but at least Phoebe knew the bare bones of the story.

Phoebe pulled back. "I cannot begin to tell you how sorry I am. That is criminal what they did to you."

"I think so, too. I suppose they could have placed me in an asylum.

That would have been much worse. I escaped—with Lucy—on what was to be my wedding day to Percy. We fled and took an unusual route, not a direct one. I didn't know if anyone would give chase."

Her new friend hugged her again. "You are safe here, Samantha. You may stay as long as you like. And when Weston does come, you must tell him this so he can make the servants at Treadwell Manor aware."

"I don't think they would try to take me back. I am a lost cause."

"Do the earl and countess come to London for the Season?"

She nodded. "They do for part of it. Usually, at the beginning. My romance with Haskett occurred after they left. We even wed in London without his parents present. Lady Rockaway told me I would not have been the choice for her son."

"Yet she wanted you to wed her nephew, the new heir?"

"I was the daughter of a duke and sister to another. She thought my pedigree would benefit the family."

"I am glad you got away from such evil people. What you did was so brave. I am proud to call you my friend."

"Don't tell Andrew any of this just yet," Samantha said. "Can you do that?"

Phoebe thought a moment. "If it's what you wish. I think, eventually, he should know."

"I understand. I just need a little time to get used to my freedom. Once the house party begins, I'll tell Weston—and Andrew—what happened. *If* Weston bothers to show up."

"Your brother should have stopped this," Phoebe said, her mouth tightening. "He was too busy being a dissolute rake." She huffed. "I'm sorry. I know he's Andrew's friend and your brother but—"

"I know. I'm disappointed what he's become ever since he didn't wed Juniper Radwell. I'm hoping I'll finally learn what happened between them and why he is as he is now." She looked to Phoebe. "Don't blame him. Lady Rockaway had me write letters to Weston each month. She dictated what they should say. He had no idea my life was a living nightmare. Give him a chance, Phoebe. For most of his life, Weston was a wonderful brother and my best friend. I'm hoping we can regain our closeness during this house party."

Phoebe stood. "Then you'll need to be properly attired. Let's go peruse my wardrobe."

Samantha followed her new friend into the next room. She had said the right words but she didn't know if she had forgiven Weston yet.

Or if she ever could.

CHAPTER TEN

GEORGE ROSE AN hour before noon. They'd arrived in Exeter late last evening. He thought it best to stay in town and not show up on Andrew's doorstep at eleven o'clock at night, especially when he'd declined their invitation and Weston hadn't bothered replying at all.

As usual, his friend stayed up most of the night, drinking and carousing, a wench on his lap. George had left them at three in the morning and gone to bed. Weston had spent every day of their journey from London sleeping like the dead in the carriage and then repeating the same behavior every night. Since they were so close to Windowmere, George decided to sleep in and ate and dressed at a leisurely pace. When noon arrived, though, he went to his friend's chamber where Wilson, West's valet, paced nervously in the corridor.

"I'll wake His Grace. Fetch hot, black coffee and something for him to eat, Wilson."

"Yes, Your Grace. Oh, uh . . . His Grace's . . . guest is still inside."

"I'll take care of her, as well. Move, Wilson."

The valet took off, looking relieved to have something constructive to do. Not bothering to knock, George opened the door and went straight to the window. He pulled back the drapes and opened the window, allowing sunlight to stream into the room and across the bed. West groaned and threw an arm over his eyes. The woman stirred.

He picked up her gown and chemise and went to the bed. Shaking the woman's shoulder, he said, "Your presence is no longer required by His Grace."

She blinked sleepily and then her eyes widened. A hand snaked out from the bedclothes and she snatched her clothes.

"Turn around," she ordered.

Though it was nothing he hadn't seen, George did as she requested, saying, "Be quick about it."

He heard the rustle of her clothing and then she padded barefoot across the room, collecting her stockings and shoes before leaving. He turned around and said, "It's time to get up."

"Why?" mumbled West, his arm still draped across his eyes.

"Because I said so. Wilson is fetching you fresh coffee." He reached for a pillow and smacked Weston hard.

"Ow! Sod off."

"No. Sit up."

West pushed himself up and opened sleepy eyes. "What time is it?"

"Time to wash, shave, and dress. I won't have you going to see Andrew and Phoebe looking as you do."

A loud sigh sounded. "Do we really have to go, George? We're close enough to Colebourne Hall and Treadwell Manor. We can easily bypass Windowmere and be home by the end of the day."

"No," he said firmly. "Andrew wants Phoebe to get to know his friends better. That means getting to know *us* better. He's been through the bowels of Hell with that blasted half-brother of his trying to murder him, not to mention his years at war. Andrew has always supported us. The truth be told, he's the best of the five of us, though Sebastian runs a close second. It's time we show Andrew that we value his friendship. Besides, I let you sleep until the noon hour."

Weston made a garbled noise and vomited all over himself and the bed. The stench turned George's stomach.

"I'll see that water is brought for a bath," he said curtly.

As he left, Wilson arrived with a tray bearing a pot of coffee and rolls. George told the valet he expected Treadwell's hair trimmed, his beard shaved, and his friend should be impeccably dressed. He then moved past the valet and asked the innkeeper's wife to see that bathwater be heated and sent to Treadwell's room. Returning to his own, he sat on the bed and looked out the window.

Both his life and Weston's had gone out of control when they'd both suffered broken engagements. George felt as if he had hit rock-bottom and he wanted a way out of it. He was tired of playing the charming, gallant, ne'er-do-well. It was all an act. Though he had been known to be charming back in the day, he was ready to move on from his wastrel ways. It didn't seem as if Weston were ready to do the same, though, but it didn't matter. He would stand by his friend even as he tried to make sense of his own life. He'd take time during the house party to reflect upon the changes he wished to make.

And then he'd write to Samantha.

Better yet, he'd go see her. She had always been a good friend to him. Even if she had moved on and found someone else after Haskett's death, the advice she would dispense to him would be immeasurably better than any he could receive from anyone else.

Yet a part of him hoped that she hadn't found someone new. That no other man was in her life. That she would be willing to take a chance.

On him.

After two hours, he returned and found Weston looking chipper. "Are you ready to leave? You look it."

"I feel splendid, George. Let's go to Windowmere," Weston said enthusiastically.

He wondered if laced in the enthusiasm was a healthy dose of sarcasm.

They accompanied their valets and luggage to the waiting carriages and George told his driver he would signal when they approached the turnoff to Windowmere. When they neared it, he rapped his cane on the roof of the carriage and the vehicle slowed and turned down the lane. They pulled up in front of the beautiful house and the butler came out to greet them.

"Your Graces. What a pleasant surprise."

"I am sure it is, Pimmeline. Do you think Mrs. Hanks can find each of us a room? I know the house party starts in a few days and we're somewhat early for it."

"Windowmere is large enough to accommodate even unexpected guests, Your Grace. Especially two old, dear friends of His Grace."

Footmen appeared, along with the housekeeper, who said, "It's ever so nice to see you, Your Graces."

"We are delighted to be here, Mrs. Hanks," George replied. "Sorry if we showed up a bit before all of the other guests."

"The duke and duchess will be happy you have arrived," she said with warmth. "Would you like to go to your rooms first and freshen up a bit?"

"No," Weston said, speaking for the first time. "We want to surprise them. Where are they?"

"In the drawing room, Your Grace," the butler replied. "But please let me at least announce you."

"Very well," Weston said. "Come along then."

George fell into step with West and Pimmeline raced ahead, admitting them to the foyer and then hurrying again to reach the staircase before they did. West, devil that he was, moved quickly, causing the butler to almost run up the stairs and down the corridor in order to reach the drawing room first. West grinned at George, who managed to keep up with them.

Pimmeline threw the door open. "Their Graces, the Dukes of Treadwell and Colebourne," he gasped, panting.

George and Weston entered the room.

SAMANTHA HAD ENJOYED the most extraordinary day. It was extraordinary merely because it was ordinary. A day that, years ago, she would have taken for granted. After her experience at Rockwell at the hands of Lady Rockaway, though, she would remember to cherish the mundane and even celebrate it.

She had risen and taken breakfast with Phoebe and Andrew. The conversation was lighthearted and she learned of the activities being planned for the house party and who some of the guests would be. She was happy to at least know one guest, having met Jon, who was now Duke of Blackmore, years ago. He would attend with his younger sister. Samantha had never met Elizabeth and looked forward to doing so.

She'd been given her choice of the type of eggs she wished to eat and selected the meat which would accompany them. She chose the flavored jam for her toast points. And she indulged in two cups of her precious chocolate, though she reminded herself not to overeat. Just because food was readily available now didn't mean she needed to eat everything in sight.

After breakfast, Phoebe had called for the carriage and they had gone into Exeter to visit Mrs. Echols. Samantha's second dress was ready and the other two for Lucy had been finished. They had tried on the gowns and Mrs. Echols made a slight adjustment to one before they were allowed to take them from the shop.

Phoebe insisted they go look at more hats. Usually, it wouldn't have taken much persuasion because Samantha adored hats. Once again, though, doubts surfaced regarding payment of the growing bills. When she voiced them to Phoebe, her new friend brushed off the concerns, assuring Samantha that Andrew would step in and see that Weston would make the payments. If for any reason he did not do so promptly, Phoebe promised that Andrew would see to the bills in a timely fashion. Because of Phoebe's reassurances, Samantha went ahead and purchased several hats and additional gloves, as well.

The rest of the day had been spent getting to know more about her new friend. She and Phoebe walked in the Windowmere gardens. They took luncheon with Andrew. They went down to the stables afterward and visited the horses. Phoebe's seamstress was already making minor alterations to several gowns Samantha would wear, including a riding habit. The seamstress promised the riding habit would be ready to wear by tomorrow morning and so the two women looked over several mounts, deciding which one might best suit Samantha. She'd shared how much she enjoyed being on horseback and Phoebe insisted they would ride every day while Samantha was at Windowmere.

Now, they had come in for tea and awaited the teacart to be rolled into the drawing room. Andrew had just joined them.

He kissed his wife's cheek and asked, "How was your day, my love?"

She saw the love shining in Andrew's eyes and how it was reflected in Phoebe's. She pushed aside the wistfulness that rose within her. While she was delighted that Andrew had found a wonderful woman to love, Samantha knew that love wasn't meant for her.

"We had a marvelous day," Phoebe replied. "I am so glad that Samantha is staying with us."

Suddenly, Mr. Pimmeline rushed in, his calm demeanor gone.

"Their Graces—the Dukes of Treadwell and Colebourne," he sputtered.

The words had barely been uttered when Weston and George rounded the corner. Her heart skipped a beat at the sight of them.

Especially George.

Since she'd last seen him, he had only grown more handsome. More self-assured. His tawny mane of hair was thick and worn a little too long. His vivid, green eyes met hers and she saw the surprise register. His jaw dropped.

Quickly, she cut her eyes to Weston, who looked a little tired but just as handsome.

"Sam!" her brother cried and rushed toward her, pulling her to her feet and enveloping her in a bear hug. "What on earth are you doing at Windowmere?"

"I could ask the same of you since you never bothered to respond to Phoebe's invitation," she quipped.

Weston pulled away and stared at her and then burst out in laughter. He kissed her brow. "There's a story here, I'll daresay. I'll take you and Phoebe berating me all you wish. I'm just so happy to see you."

He released her and turned to Andrew and Phoebe, whom George had gone to greet. As Weston moved away, George stepped to her.

"Hello, Sam," he said, his voice low, his eyes twinkling. "It's good to see you."

George embraced her. While her brother's hug had felt familiar, tugging at her heart, George's brought a sense of security.

Which was absurd.

He was one of the Bad Dukes. He flitted from lover to lover. It would do her well to remember that. She innately understood this man still had the potential to hurt her heart. She was never going to let anyone hurt her again.

Least of all the man she had once loved.

Releasing her, he said, "If I had known you were at Windowmere, I would have come sooner. Why are you here and not at Rockwell? Or Treadwell Manor?"

"Shall we sit?" Phoebe asked. "The teacart has arrived."

"You'll sit with me," Weston said, returning to Samantha's side and capturing her hand. He tugged her to a settee. "Catch me up, Sam. What in blazes brought you to Devon?"

Her gaze met Phoebe's as her hostess handed her the first cup of tea poured. Having something in her hands helped to calm her.

"You know I lost Haskett a couple of years ago," she said, pausing to take a sip of tea. "I found nothing of interest to hold me in the north any longer."

"Not even . . ." Weston's voice trailed off and his brow furrowed in thought. "What was his name? Perry? No, Percy. Percy Johnson. That's it."

Her belly tightened at the mention of the groom she'd fled from. "What do you mean?" she asked sharply.

Her brother shrugged. "It seemed from your last letter or two that you were somewhat interested in him."

She arched an eyebrow. "Oh, so you did receive my letters. Funny. I wondered about that because you never seemed to reply to them. Unless those were lost in transit."

Weston looked sheepish. "I have never been much of a letter writer. That's more left to women. But seriously, I thought you might have a *tendre* for the fellow. He was a cousin of Haskett's, isn't that right?"

"Yes. He is now heir apparent to the Earl of Rockaway. And no, the only feelings I possess for Cousin Percy are ones of loathing," she said evenly.

Weston looked taken aback. "I see."

Samantha took the plate Phoebe handed her, again glad for the momentary distraction as she reined in her rage and then said, "I decided it was time to return home. To Treadwell Manor. I hope that won't inconvenience you, Weston."

He chuckled. "Not in the least. I'm rarely there. But I will return with you after the house party. I'd like to spend some time with you, Sam. It's been too long since we were together."

"That would be lovely," she said and focused on her plate of food, too many emotions swirling within her. She was touched her brother wanted to spend time with her and still angry at him for not coming to her rescue. She also wanted to tamp down the sudden feelings stirred up at seeing George.

Silence filled the room until George said, "I hope you'll accept our sincere apologies, Phoebe, for arriving early. Especially when you weren't expecting us at all."

The duchess smiled graciously. "I had a feeling you might turn up and already had planned to set aside rooms for you in case you did show up at any point."

"I'm very glad you've both come," Andrew added. "I didn't see much of you in London this Season."

"Because you were enthralled with Phoebe," Weston said. "She took up all your time."

"I'll admit I worked hard at wooing her," Andrew said. He entwined his fingers with hers. "And I'm happy to report that it was worth it. I adore being a husband and love my wife very much."

He brought their joined hands up and kissed her knuckles. Phoebe rewarded him with a sweet smile.

"If you were on your way to Treadwell Manor, how did you wind up here?" George asked.

Samantha smiled. "As Lucy and I left Exeter, I decided to stop in and call upon Andrew on our way home. I was delighted to find that he'd wed and have already found a fast friend in Phoebe."

"I told Samantha about our upcoming house party and insisted she stay through it. Happily, she accepted the invitation," the duchess added. "I've given her my bedchamber so she has plenty of room."

The rest of teatime passed pleasantly. Andrew spoke about some of the improvements he was making at Windowmere and various other estates which he had inherited. Phoebe asked about what was new in London and Weston and George regaled them with tales of what had happened during the Season after the Windhams had departed town.

Finally, the teapot was emptied and Andrew said he needed to speak with his estate manager. Phoebe rang for Mrs. Hanks and had the housekeeper take the new arrivals to their rooms. She reminded the two dukes that they were in the country and kept country hours, meaning they would dine at seven. Weston had rolled his eyes and muttered something which Samantha was glad no one could understand.

She left the drawing room and decided to stroll in the gardens. It was good Weston had showed up, despite his ill manners in not notifying Phoebe he would attend. She planned to spend as much time with him as she could, hoping they could ease back into their familiar relationship.

George was another matter. She still felt an unmistakable pull toward him, even stronger than in the past. Before, she had been a very young woman smitten with her brother's incredibly charming friend. She was older now. A bit wiser. And she understood that desire simmered under the surface. Desire for George.

The question was—would she act upon it?

Chapter Eleven

GEORGE LOOKED OUT the window of his room across the yard, standing ramrod straight, his hands clutched behind his back.

Samantha was here. At Windowmere.

It was the last place he would have imagined her to be. He'd almost fainted at the sight of her, which would have been utterly ridiculous. She was a woman. A friend. Someone he hadn't seen in ages and hadn't spoken to in years.

Yet thoughts of her had plagued him repeatedly in the last week. She even haunted his dreams. At the moment he'd decided to make a new life for himself—hopefully with her—she'd turned up.

George considered it to be Fate. One didn't question it. One merely took advantage of it.

Samantha's beauty had only grown since the last time he'd seen her. He'd tried not to notice her at *ton* events she'd attended, especially because she ignored him so readily. He'd been hurt by that but understood why she no longer bothered with him or West. Still, every now and then, he'd stolen glimpses of her while she was engaged in conversation with others. He'd liked too much of what he saw and turned away, knowing she was a married woman.

She wasn't any longer.

Could he press his suit with her? Would she look upon him as more than an old friend? More importantly, could he convince her he was ready to change?

He caught sight of her at that moment. She crossed the lawn and entered the gardens.

Immediately, he said to Briggs, who was unpacking for him, "I'm going for a stroll. I've been cooped up far too long inside a carriage. I need to stretch my legs."

"Very good, Your Grace. I'll finish here and press your clothes for dinner this evening."

"All right."

George left the bedchamber assigned to him and made his way to the staircase. He reached the foyer and didn't want to waste time going all the way around the house. Instead, he turned toward the kitchens, cutting through them as scullery maids tittered. Let them say whatever they wanted. He didn't care for anyone's opinion now but Sam's.

Reaching the gardens, he entered and continued on the path, hurrying along, hoping to catch up. He saw Sam ahead, sitting on a bench. Her face was turned up to the sun, a dreamy expression upon it. He slipped past her and seated himself on the bench, drinking her in, inhaling the subtle scent of orange blossoms that came from her skin.

She must have sensed his presence. Her eyes opened and she turned her head in his direction. She'd always had remarkable eyes, a mixture of blue and green which made them aquamarine, the same as West had. The eyes stood out in a face that was heart-shaped, framed by her raven hair. He didn't think he'd ever seen a more beautiful woman.

"Hello, Sam."

Her brow knitted together. "I'd rather you call me Samantha. Sam was a tomboy who followed you and Weston around like a senseless puppy."

Her words took him aback. "I never thought you senseless. As for following us around, I rather liked having you nearby. You always hung on my every word. It made me feel important."

She looked at him disdainfully. "You're a duke now. Not that boy I worshipped. You have all the ladies of *ton* fawning over you, Charm."

"Don't call me that," he said testily.

"Why not? That's how the newspapers refer to you. I also heard most everyone speak to you that way the last time I attended social events in London."

He shook his head. "Charm is a persona that I adopted to get me through a difficult time."

Her features softened. "Does it still sting?"

George thought she finally seemed like the Sam of old. "Not really," he replied. "It did for a good while. I'd led a perfectly happy, carefree life until that moment when my fiancée threw me over for another man in front of Polite Society. That moment changed me. I wanted people to see it wasn't me who'd come up short. I did my best to charm everyone in society, from elderly matrons to young women making their come-outs."

She gave him a wry smile. "It seems you have done more than charm them, George. From what I gather, you have been intimate with a good deal of them. I'm sure that restored your reputation among the men at White's and if you please the ladies you couple with, they most certainly pass that along to their friends and acquaintances."

It seemed impossible they were having this conversation, talking about his multitude of lovers.

"I'll admit I have used my charm and looks." He took her hand and heard her quick intake of breath. "I'm tired of being the Duke of Charm, though. I merely want to be plain George."

She tugged on her hand but he refused to release it.

"You will never be plain, George. You're most handsome and a duke. Separately, those are impressive but, together, it makes for a devastating combination."

"Do you think so?"

She frowned. "Why does it matter what I think?"

"Because we were once friends, Sam. I'd like us to be friends again."

And more.

"Samantha," she prompted.

"Samantha," he agreed.

"I didn't think men and women could be friends," she said, gently pulling on her hand again.

"I'm not returning it just yet," he announced. "So you might as well stop trying to take it from me."

She looked taken aback—and then she laughed. He'd forgotten the sound of her laughter. How deep and rich it was for a woman. Tingles rippled through him.

"Are you willing to become my friend again, Samantha Wallace?" he asked, calling her by her maiden name.

She shrugged. "I don't see why not. You seem as close as ever to Weston. I suppose if I'm going to be around him, it's inevitable that we'll see one another from time to time, Charm."

"Please. Don't call me that."

She studied him a moment. "You truly mean that. You don't want the nickname."

"No, I don't. I told Weston on our journey here and I'll say the same to you. I'm tired of the empty existence I've led for so many years. Days that blend into nights. Weeks that become months and then years. I'm ready for a change. I've spent too long being lonely. Living a lie."

"Hmm. Does this mean you plan to act differently? Stop bedding any woman who catches your fancy?"

"Yes. I'm ready to settle down and act like a duke and a proper gentleman."

Sam laughed a bit harshly. "You might think you do, George, but will society let you? You've garnered quite the reputation over the past few years. They won't let you shed it freely, you know. Especially if you remain friends with my brother. I doubt he's ready to quit playing the lothario."

"You're right. West mentioned the same thing. He asked if we would still be friends. I told him we would always be friends."

She shrugged. "Then it will be guilt by association, I'm afraid. A leopard cannot change his spots. You trying to become a different man while still entangled with the Duke of Disrepute will result in failure."

"Not if I prove I am a changed man."

Her brows knitted together. "And however will you do that?"

"By being loyal and faithful to one woman."

He brought her hand up to his lips and kissed her fingers. She flushed an enticing shade of pink and jerked her hand away.

Rising, she said, "You are disgusting. All of this talk of wanting to be a different man. Is this how the Duke of Charm finagles his way into a woman's bed—through sweet lies?"

George stood and clasped her shoulders. "I'm not lying to you, Sam."

"Samantha," she ground out.

"Samantha," he said softly. "From the moment I thought of altering my direction and becoming the man I should have been all along, I began thinking of you. You have been in my thoughts for a week now. You were there all along and I was too ignorant to see it. And then destiny put you in my path."

His fingers tightened. "I don't want to charm every woman out there, Samantha. I only want to impress you."

She stared at him in confusion. He took the opportunity to press his mouth to hers.

Samantha had always enjoyed sparring verbally with George. They'd done so since childhood and even though they hadn't spoken since the night he announced his engagement to Frederica Martin, they had picked up as if no time had passed. The trouble was that his very nearness caused her pulse to pound wildly. Then he began talking about wanting to change who he was.

And then his lips pressed against hers.

She didn't know what to do. If she responded, she would encourage him. It was no certainty that he had changed. He might merely view her as another conquest. The George she'd known years ago would never stoop to something so low but the Duke of Charm most likely would.

Was he telling the truth?

Samantha decided it didn't matter. If he wanted to attempt to seduce her, it was up to her to decide how far it should go. She was the master of her life. She could permit a few stolen kisses. An illicit touch or two. Even if she allowed him to come to her bed, it would be her decision. Not his. She'd already determined she was going to live her life as she wished. Take lovers. Who better to invite into her bed than the Duke of Charm, the man who was said to give the most rapturous pleasure to every lover he seduced?

His hands slipped from her shoulders and cradled her cheeks, his thumbs softly stroking them. Samantha's hands went to his chest, her palms flattening against the hard wall of muscle. Even through his layers of clothing, she felt the heat of his body and smelled the sandalwood soap he was so fond of using.

His lips had brushed tenderly against hers and now he began kissing her with purpose. Her heart sped up as he did, his lips firm as he pressed them against hers. Already, he kissed better than Haskett ever had. Her husband's kiss was perfunctory and had never created any response from her. George's kiss already had her heart racing and her knees growing weak.

Then his tongue ran along her bottom lip, startling her. It caused her belly to tighten. No, lower than that. His tongue swept back and forth, lulling her until her breath came quickly and she clutched his waistcoat. It moved higher and teased the seam of her lips. She opened to him, unsure of what he would do but terribly interested to find out.

What he did shocked her. Surprised her. And caused her body to heat.

He slipped his tongue *inside* her mouth.

Haskett had never done something so outrageous. Or delicious.

George certainly knew what he was doing because her entire body began tingling. She heard a low moan and realized she had made the noise. His tongue mated with hers, calling it out to play, and she responded as he did, duplicating his every move. His arms came about her, enveloping her, bringing her flush against him. That wonderful heat from his body warmed her. Then burned her. Then scalded her.

Samantha answered every kiss, even as he deepened them. He tilted her head back in order to have better access. They breathed in each other's air as they continued to kiss. It was maddening. It was incredible. It was like nothing she had ever experienced.

This is what she'd wanted to learn about. If Haskett hadn't kissed her properly, what else had he been lacking in? Whatever it was, George could certainly teach her. She would learn as much as she could from him and then move on to other men.

Because she couldn't care for George. She refused to be vulnerable again. She would never be at anyone's mercy. She would live her life to the fullest.

His mouth left hers and trailed hot kisses along her jaw. Her head fell back, allowing him better access. His lips went lower, nipping and kissing her neck, licking where her pulse pounded out of control. Her breasts felt heavy. Her core throbbed steadily.

"Sam," he murmured against her throat.

She should correct him but didn't want him to stop. Sam no longer existed. She would never be that innocent, carefree girl again. But Samantha could navigate her way through the waters of society and know every pleasure to be had.

George's mouth moved up again and settled against hers. They seemed to be a perfect match, two halves becoming whole as they kissed. His teeth softly sank into her lower lip and she whimpered, a hot flash of desire running through her. The pounding between her legs ached something fierce. She knew he was the answer to it.

Samantha also knew that she needed to stop. Leave him wanting more. She certainly did. And if she did, he must, as well. Making him wait would be part of her exercising control. She would decide when. With whom. And how.

Turning her head, she broke the kiss, her breath coming quickly. His hand moved to her head and pushed it against his chest. His other hand stroked her back.

"Oh, Sam. Samantha," he whispered.

She longed to stay exactly as they were but knew that was what he wanted. Because of it, she pushed away and looked up at him.

His green eyes were darker than she'd ever seen them. She supposed that was from desire. His breathing, too, had been affected by their kisses.

"I will see you at dinner, George," she said calmly, turning away.

He caught her wrist. "And later?" He brought it up to his lips and kissed the underside of her wrist tenderly.

"Possibly."

With that, she eased her wrist from his hold and walked away.

CHAPTER TWELVE

GEORGE REMAINED ON the bench in the garden, totally overwhelmed by his encounter with Sam.

No.

Samantha . . .

She was every inch a Samantha now. Definitely not the small child who'd toddled about in their wake. Certainly not the long, leggy tomboy who'd gone fishing and hunting and riding with them.

The Samantha he'd just kissed was a woman in every sense of the word. One whose beauty had matured, making her absolutely breathtaking.

She was also a woman who didn't suffer fools. There'd been a sharp tone to her voice when she'd admonished him. She hadn't believed him when he said he wanted to change. It offended him that she actually thought he tried to ply her with sweet words to entice her into his bed. Of course, he did want her there. But things had to be different between them. Right. As of right now, he knew that wasn't the case. She should be wary of him, though. Any woman of the *ton* should. He had slept with a multitude of them over the last several years.

All he wanted now was one woman. His Sam—who had blossomed into a bewitching creature called Samantha.

What most surprised him was she hadn't a clue how to kiss. How could she have been married for as long as she had been and not known how to kiss? Surely, Haskett had been better to her. George's conversations, though, with other gentlemen at his various clubs led him to believe that most men didn't care to pleasure their own wives. They saved that sort of thing for their mistresses or lovers. Viscount Haskett must have been one of those men. George ached for Samantha, being shackled to such a cold husband.

He smiled. It also let him know that she had much to learn regarding the art of love. And he would be the perfect instructor. Her kiss already set him afire. She'd been a quick student, mimicking various things he did. Everything about her, from the scent of orange blossoms to the curves of her breasts and hips to the way her kiss sparked his desire led him to believe they were well suited.

George rose from the bench and leisurely made his way back to the house. He went around to the front door this time, knowing dinner preparations would be in full swing in the kitchen and not wanting to cause any problems. Upstairs in his room, Briggs dressed him for dinner. Restless, he headed to the drawing room and found Andrew sitting there alone.

"Ah, George. Come in. I was indulging in a brandy. Care for one?"

"I'll get it myself," he said, pouring two fingers into a snifter and then taking a seat in a wing chair nearby.

"Phoebe is delighted you came," Andrew said. "And anything that delights my duchess makes me happy."

"I can see that for myself. From the way you look at one another to the way you touch, it's obvious the two of you are a love match." He paused. "I want that for myself."

His friend looked at him in surprise. "Wait. The Duke of Charm is telling me—"

"There is no more Duke of Charm, Andrew. I'm abandoning all claim to the nickname I never wanted."

"What are saying, old friend?"

"That I've grown tired of making love to several different women in a week. That I long for one woman to share my bed and my life. I look at you and Phoebe and see that love is something that does exist. I never saw it with my parents. I've never experienced it myself. But I recognize it between you and your duchess." He lowered his voice. "And I'm desperate for it. With Samantha."

Andrew eyed him with interest. "So, that's how it is."

"Yes. The perfect woman was always standing right in front of me for years. I suppose because she's three years younger, I never saw her as a potential mate."

"What led to this?" Andrew questioned. "It seems rather sudden."

George thought a moment. "Were you ever lonely while away at war?"

"All the time," Andrew admitted. "I had to keep a professional distance between me and the men I commanded. It was hard enough writing condolence letters to the families of soldiers I lost. I couldn't befriend any of them. As for the officers, some were too cavalier for my taste. I took my position seriously. I held the lives of a good number of men in my hand. I had to protect them the best I knew how without growing close to them. It was isolating. It was a lonely existence."

He nodded. "I feel I've been at war for a long time myself. Oh, don't get me wrong. I didn't suffer anything near what you and your soldiers did. But I felt at war against myself. Against Polite Society. Against rules that bound me. So I broke every rule, both written and unwritten. I covered my embarrassment at being jilted by becoming the most charming rogue the *ton* has ever seen. Anyone looking at me from the outside would have thought I was carefree and happy, with no responsibilities and no worries.

"Instead, I was bloody miserable, Andrew. I played a role on a stage of my own making for far too long. I finally realized it was within my power—my power alone—to end the farce. To make something of myself. To be the duke and man my father would have wanted me to be. I'm only glad to see he didn't live to see how I've mucked up my life."

"You'll be thirty next year. All of us will. I find as we hit certain milestones in our lives that we become more reflective. For me, I had to learn and grow and change a great deal when my brother and father died. I was never meant to be the Duke of Windham. I've had so much to learn about my new role and all of the responsibilities that come with it." Andrew smiled. "But the most important thing is that Phoebe will always be by my side. If I make a mistake, she tells me things will be all right and cheers me on. When I do something well, she rewards me with the most beautiful smile. In everything I do, I strive to be the best man I can possibly be—because of her."

"That's how I want to live the rest of my life," George agreed. "If it can be with Samantha, I will be the richer for it."

"When will you speak to her?"

"I already have. At least, a little bit. I found her strolling in the gardens and told her of my admiration for her."

Andrew shook his head. "Let me guess. She didn't believe a word that came from your mouth."

He chuckled. "I believe she mentioned something about leopards not being able to change their spots. Yes, she questioned if I was sincere. She practically told me I couldn't change because society had pigeonholed me as a rake and a rogue and wouldn't accept me being anything else. I talked to Weston about this."

"About his sister? Or changing your tune?"

"Both, actually. I don't think he believed me about Samantha. We discussed it on the journey here. West worried that I would pull away from him. Not be his friend anymore. I assured him that would never be the case. Our fathers were the closest of friends from boyhood. West and I have been the same from the cradle, growing up on neighboring estates." He paused. "But I can see where my close association with the Duke of Disrepute might cause the *ton* to doubt my sincerity."

He stood and began pacing. "I did tell Samantha society would know I've changed if I showed myself to be faithful to one woman. Her."

Andrew chuckled. "I can see how your words might have taken her aback." He frowned. "I'm not saying you shouldn't pursue her, George, but I advise discretion and moving slowly. I'm not betraying any confidences here because I don't know Samantha's entire story—though I think Phoebe's gotten it out of her. All I know is Samantha and her maid showed up here two days ago with only the clothes on their backs. They'd come from Rockwell with no luggage. None at all. That triggered my suspicions immediately. And then Samantha said that they'd been robbed when they reached Exeter. She came here hoping my father would help her, not knowing he'd passed and I was the new duke. She seemed fragile and yet very determined. I think she ran away, George. The question is why."

His friend's words startled him. Why would Samantha have had to leave without any of her possessions? What would make her flee a place she had lived for years, with people she would consider family?

"Just be sensitive, George. Don't push her too fast. And for God's sake, don't go kissing her. Kissing can muck up everything."

He gave Andrew a sheepish grin. "Too late on that account."

SAMANTHA HAD LUCY help dress her for dinner early. She hoped to seek out Weston for a few minutes before they dined so they might have a private conversation. Something told her that her brother would do his best to avoid being alone with her despite his seeming eagerness to spend time with her. She did not want to postpone their difficult conversation.

Leaving her room, she went to the main floor and searched for Mr.

Pimmeline. A footman directed her to him.

"Mr. Pimmeline, do you happen to know where my brother is?" she asked.

"His Grace is in the library, my lady. Or he was as of five minutes ago. I brought him a new bottle of brandy."

"Hopefully, he hasn't drunk the entire thing already," she said. "Thank you."

She made her way to the library and slipped inside. Weston sat sprawled in a chair, his eyes closed, a snifter of brandy in his hands. With no one around and his guard down, he looked younger. More vulnerable. She'd always thought of him as her strong, capable, older sibling. He seemed far from that now.

Slipping into a chair next to him, she said softly, "I hope I'm not disturbing you."

His eyes opened. For a brief moment, Samantha saw a weariness in them. Then he seemed to rally and cynicism replaced it.

Giving her a rakish smile, he said, "I always have time for my favorite sister." He brought the brandy to his mouth and downed what was left.

"Considering I'm your only sister, I have to wonder about that statement." She took a deep breath. "Weston, why did you abandon me?"

"What? I don't know what you mean." He reached for the bottle and poured himself three fingers.

"You do know exactly what I'm speaking of. Put that drink down," she commanded.

He did as asked and settled back into the chair, eyeing her warily.

"I want to understand what happened to you. To us."

He shrugged. "You wed. I didn't. You moved to the north with your husband. I remained in London, a bachelor sowing his wild oats. You're a woman, which means you came out of the womb writing letters. I'm a man and can't be bothered to write them."

She shook her head. "You have a ready answer for everything. Not ones I'm pleased with, though."

He studied her a moment. "Accept my apology, Sam. I know I've been a terrible brother. I'm not a very good person and haven't been for quite some time. I thought you'd washed your hands of me after wedding Haskett. You never gave me the cut direct but you ignored me at *ton* events. I did try and write a time or two but I have little to say." He ran a hand through his dark hair. "How do you tell the little sister who worshipped you that you've become a scoundrel of the worst kind?"

"I suppose you dip the quill into the ink and move it across the page," she snapped.

Weston frowned. He took her hand. "What's wrong? Where is all of this anger coming from? Yes, I didn't write to you much. I'm sorry I lost contact with you. But you had a husband, Sam. A new life. A new family. I was the idle, worthless brother you'd left behind. I know you're ashamed of me and what I've become."

"You never checked on me," she accused. "I was miserable in my marriage. Lady Rockaway ruined every day I spent at Rockwell. Haskett was under her thumb and wouldn't take a step without her. The sweet, sincere, awkward gentleman I thought I'd married became a stranger once we returned to the north. His mother was unhappy he'd wed me and bullied me to no end."

Samantha jerked her hand from his. "Then I lost my baby. You don't know how devastating that was. All my hopes and dreams were pinned to that child. I wanted to turn to my husband for comfort but he rarely visited me in my bedchamber before that occurred. He barely spoke to me after it happened and never touched me again."

She stood and began pacing the room, rage coursing through her.

Weston came to his feet and hurried to her as she gripped the mantel and stared into the fire.

"I was so lonely. So alone. No one consoled me. No one cared if I lived or died. I was in a strange house in a strange place and no one cared a whit about me. I wanted my big brother to come rescue me. To take me away and bring me home, where I would be safe."

"What do mean—safe?" he asked.

She refused to answer, her hands tightening until her knuckles grew stark white.

"Why didn't you just leave after Haskett's death? I would have welcomed you."

"Because I . . ." Her voice trailed off.

She was too embarrassed to tell him. Speaking the words aloud would make her that weak, helpless creature again. She would never be that person again.

Weston placed his hand on her shoulder and she jerked away.

Staring into his aquamarine eyes, she said, "You let me down. You disappointed me. You abandoned me." Her eyes narrowed. "I don't know if I will ever forgive you."

"Sam." He pulled her into his arms and stroked her hair. She closed her eyes, determined to remain resolute.

When he released her, she stepped back, crossing her arms protectively in front of her.

"Maybe you need George as much as he needs you."

"What do you mean by that?" she asked sharply.

Weston shrugged. "I don't know what happened but the entire carriage ride here he went on and on about how he despised his life and wanted to change it. That he was ready to settle down and how much he wanted a family. And a wife." He shook his head. "He talked about *you*, Sam. I think he'd already made up his mind to leave Windowmere after the house party and go directly to Rockwell to see you."

His words stunned her. Maybe George had been telling the truth.

"At least George was thinking about me," she said. "You never did."

"You're right. I was a selfish bastard who forgot about you once you left London. You were someone else's responsibility. Not mine. And I relished that. I was tired of being decent and honorable and always doing the right thing. So, I stopped doing it. You weren't around to see my fall. When you returned the next Season, it had already occurred."

Weston sighed. "I've dug myself deep into a pit, Sam. An abyss of my own making. I didn't want to drag you into it with me. I thought with you gone, I could do whatever I wanted."

She touched his arm. "Why, Weston? What happened between you and Lady Juniper? What could be so awful that it would make you hate yourself and everyone around you?"

He shook his head. "No. You'll not get that out of me. Thank God she's dead and gone and I never have to see her again," he said, his voice laced with vehemence. "I am what I am now, Sam. I won't have a change of heart. Not like George. He might be able to save himself. *You* might be the one to help him. I'm just a blackguard of the worst kind. I have no heart or soul left."

Weston placed his hand over hers. "I do love you. I always will." He leaned to kiss her cheek. "But I never should have come to Windowmere. Say my goodbyes to everyone."

Her brother gave her a sad smile as he pulled away and left the room.

Chapter Thirteen

GEORGE SAW THE door open. Samantha and Phoebe entered the drawing room. He thought of what Andrew had said. That Sam was fragile. Vulnerable. He wondered if she would share with him what her life had been like at Rockwell or if it was something she wished to put behind her, as he did his dissolute ways.

As the two women came closer, he could see Sam was upset. She looked remarkably restrained—except for chewing on her bottom lip. Anytime she had been worried or upset as a young girl, she'd done the same thing. She worried it now, a thoughtful look on her face, and then she caught herself and smoothed out her features.

Looking at Andrew, she said, "I'm embarrassed to do so but I must inform you that Weston has left Windowmere. He ask that I give his excuses and tell everyone goodbye for him."

Andrew and Phoebe exchanged a glance and his friend said, "I am sorry to hear that. I was hoping for Phoebe to get to know Weston better over the next week. I'm sure you, too, are disappointed after having been apart for so long."

"Where did he say he was going?" George asked sharply.

Sam met his gaze. "Does it matter?" she asked, her eyes revealing the hurt her brother had put there.

"Actually, it does. We left London in a bit of a pickle. West should not return there. At least for now," he added, seeing the concern on both Andrew's and Phoebe's faces.

But Sam's face was a mask. George knew she cared deeply for her brother and wondered why she showed no emotion at his departure.

"You aren't his keeper, George," she said angrily. "If my brother wants to leave and return to London, that is his business. If you really care, though, ask your valet. Servants know everything. I'm sure your valet and Weston's speak all the time."

He looked to Andrew. "Might I summon Briggs? I feel an urgency to know about West's destination."

Andrew rang for their butler and when Pimmeline arrived, he said, "Please summon His Grace's valet to the drawing room at once."

"Which one, Your Grace? Briggs or Wilson?"

"Is Wilson still here?" George asked.

"Why, yes, Your Grace."

"Then please have both valets come," Andrew suggested. "And ask Cook to hold dinner for now."

They made small talk until the two servants arrived, both looking a bit uncertain as to why they'd been called to the drawing room by the Duke of Windham.

Andrew nodded and so George took the lead.

"Did either of you know Treadwell left Windowmere?"

"No, Your Grace," Wilson said. "His Grace wouldn't leave without me." The valet looked uncertain, though.

George looked to Sam. "When did he leave?"

"We said goodbye a little over half an hour ago," she said.

"Check his bedchamber, Wilson. Briggs, go to the stables and see if Treadwell left on horseback or borrowed a carriage."

Both valets nodded and left the room.

This wasn't good. George didn't like West up and leaving and not knowing where he went. If he journeyed to Treadwell Manor, that was one thing. He was merely being rude to the Windhams and would owe them an apology. If he thought to venture back to London, however, trouble could be waiting for him. George didn't want to have to follow his friend all the way there just to drag him away again.

Especially when he needed the time to convince Sam that he wanted her future to be their future.

"We might as well go into dinner while they track Weston down," Andrew suggested. He took Phoebe's arm and led her from the drawing room.

George offered his to Sam. She took it and he sensed a spark as they touched though she looked straight ahead and didn't speak as they made their way to the dining room.

They were finishing their soup when Pimmeline bent and whispered something to Andrew, who nodded. Moments later, both valets entered the room.

"What have you found out?" Andrew asked them.

Wilson spoke first. "His Grace wasn't in his rooms but his purse was missing. I searched everywhere and couldn't find it."

"His Grace took a horse from the stables," Briggs confirmed. "He told the groom he was going into Exeter for the evening."

George relaxed. West may have told Sam he was leaving but it sounded as if his friend merely went into Exeter for his usual drinking and wenching.

"Thank you. That will be all," Andrew said, dismissing the valets.

Once they'd left, George said, "I'm sure he's only gone into town for his amusement. He'll be up all night. If you'd like, I'll go into Exeter tomorrow and find him and bring him back."

"I don't think so," Sam said. "He seemed adamant that he was leaving."

He turned to her. "West's temperament can be mercurial at times. May I ask if you quarreled? That usually sends him away quickly. He doesn't like any kind of confrontation."

"We did have words," Sam admitted. "But I believe he was leaving Windowmere for good and not returning for the house party. He specifically asked for me to tell Andrew and Phoebe goodbye. He said he never should have come."

West hadn't wanted to come in the first place. George had practically kidnapped him from London and dragged him halfway across England to Devon.

"Even if that's the case, he's stopped in Exeter for the evening," he told the others. "West will no doubt be up late tonight. I'll ride into town in the morning and see if I can help straighten things out."

They continued the meal as worry ate away at him. He couldn't let his closest friend return to London and face Lord Ivy in a duel, yet he didn't know if he could drag West back to Windowmere. Perhaps the best thing to do would be to see him safely to Treadwell Manor. That meant time away from Sam, though. He'd wanted to spend the upcoming week with her. Getting to know her again. Or getting to know the woman that she'd become. If he had to search for West and then take him north to Treadwell Manor and back, he would lose a good two days. By then, the Windhams' guests would have arrived and some other gentleman may have caught her attention.

Damn Weston Wallace.

As the meal came to a close, Andrew said, "If you don't mind, I think Phoebe and I will retire for the evening. With so many guests arriving tomorrow, we have a full day ahead of us."

George could tell by the gleam in his friend's eyes and the blush staining Phoebe's cheeks that retiring did not mean sleeping.

"I am also still a bit weary from my long journey south," Sam added. "I think I will do the same."

George only wished he could engage Sam in whatever activities Andrew and Phoebe had planned.

"Then I will say goodnight to you all, as well," he said.

They left the dining room and went to their rooms. George remembered that Phoebe had given hers over to Sam and he made note of which room she entered before he returned to his own down the corridor. Briggs awaited and helped him out of his coat and waistcoat.

George untied his cravat and slipped it from his neck, handing it to the valet before pulling his shirt over his head. He reached for the dressing gown stretched across the bed and shrugged into it before sitting and allowing Briggs to remove his boots.

"Thank you," he said, dismissing the valet. "I'll see you in the morning."

"Do you need me or Wilson to go with you into Exeter, Your Grace?"

"No. That won't be necessary."

"Goodnight then, Your Grace."

After Briggs left, George restlessly paced the bedchamber. He wasn't the least bit sleepy. He thought of the time he'd waste chasing after West and seeing him to his country estate and how Sam would be at Windowmere enjoying the company of other men. He needed to stake his claim before he left for Exeter in the morning. Belting his banyan, he left his room and headed for hers.

It was a terrible idea. She could already be asleep. She had said she was tired. Still, he rapped softly on her door, hoping she would answer. He waited. No response. Raising his hand one more time to knock, it startled him when she opened the door.

She wore a blue silk dressing gown. Its rich color brought out the blue in her eyes, subduing the green in them. Her hair was in a single braid that fell over her shoulder. He longed to loosen it and see her dark hair spilled about her.

Sam frowned. "What do you need, George?"

I need you.

"I know this is unorthodox but may I come in? I wish to speak to you."

Wariness filled her eyes. "Why?"

"I have things I must say."

She bit her lip and a frisson of desire poured through him.

"Can it wait until tomorrow?" she asked.

"I plan to leave early for Exeter in order to hunt down West." He paused. "I'd rather tell you what's on my mind tonight. It's important."

"Very well." She stepped back and admitted him, closing the door behind her and remaining in place.

George had a dozen things he wanted to say to her and yet he didn't know where to begin. Should he tell her how beautiful she was? Or how he'd missed their bantering after she'd wed Haskett? Should he open his heart and let his feelings pour out, telling her what an ignorant fool he'd been to ignore what was in front of him all of those years?

Before he could decide how to start, Sam took two steps toward him. He inhaled the subtle scent of orange blossoms with her near. Her breasts brushed his chest as she leaned into him and wound her arms about his neck, pulling his lips down to meet hers.

Words could wait.

His arms came around her snuggly. He would release her only if she changed her mind. That didn't seem likely, though, as she kissed him. Her lips were soft against his, pillows of temptation. George let Sam take the lead, sensing that it would be important to her.

The onslaught of kisses had his head reeling. This was a woman with but a single purpose.

To tempt a man into her bed.

She was a widow. A willing widow. The George he'd become after his broken engagement wouldn't have had a second thought as to bedding her. The George he wished to be wondered at her behavior. These two parts of him warred as their kisses heated up. Sam's tongue emerged and teased his mouth to open. It was as if the role of rogue he'd played for so many years had now been reversed. She was the seducer. He was the seduced.

He gave in and opened to her, clinching her more tightly to him, deciding he should be in charge. Their tongues battled with one another, each fighting for dominance, both knowing they would win in the end. Her fingers played with his hair, tugging on it, threading through it, even as her kisses enflamed him. George hadn't felt like this. Ever. His hundreds of coupling had been a game. A pleasant way to pass the time and get through another long night.

Tonight was different. He was different.

He relaxed his hold on her and clasped her waist, walking her a few steps back until she met the door.

"Oh!"

Her eyes opened, those magnificent aquamarine eyes, and she stared up at him. Her mouth was already swollen from their kisses. She looked every inch the temptress. His fingers slid down, along the curve of her hips and back up several times. She watched him with those large eyes. He skimmed her body a final time and reached for her fingers, entwining them with his. He raised their joined hands until they were at her shoulders and pressed them against the door. His body also pressed against hers, pinning her to it.

Her eyes widened and her breath came more rapidly. He could see her pulse leaping in her throat. His mouth went to it, licking it as it beat. Sam moaned. He nipped at her and she started, pushing against him slightly. He soothed the love bite with his tongue and repeated the motions along the long, slender column of her neck. She moaned low in her throat and tried to move her hands to touch him but he held them in place.

"I'm going to take your mouth and make it mine," he said, his voice low and husky.

He did as promised, kissing her deeply. He could feel her breasts swell against his chest and wanted to taste them. Her dressing gown already gaped in front, giving him a glimpse of the round globes beneath it. He kissed his way down her throat. Down the valley between her breasts. Until his teeth came to the tie that belted the gown. It took a moment, but he loosened it and then used his teeth to pull it off. The dressing gown opened all the way.

Sam's breathing was quick and shallow, her chest heaving. Using his teeth again, he lowered the night rail so that one breast was exposed. The nipple stood taut, begging for his attention. He licked and sucked the breast as she writhed against him. When his teeth grazed the nipple, she jumped. It seemed as if no man had ever done this to her. He cursed the years she'd wasted with Haskett and promised himself he would make it up to her as he continued to lave and suck, delighted to hear the sweet noises she made.

He turned his attention to her other breast and spent an equal amount of time on it, enjoying her moans of pleasure.

"Do you like this?" he asked softly.

"Yes."

"Do you want more?"

Sam nodded.

"Tell me. Tell me you want more."

"I want more," she managed to say, her voice breaking on the last word.

"You want it from me. George."

"Yes," she said breathily. "From you. From George."

"And no one else."

"No."

"Good."

His kissed his way back to her mouth and thoroughly devoured it as she moved against him. If her husband hadn't suckled her breasts, he surely hadn't done other, more pleasurable things. George pushed their hands up the door until they were over her head. He moved them close together and untangled their fingers, quickly capturing her wrists in one hand and holding them there. That left a hand he could use to do with as he wished.

"What are you doing?" she asked, a catch in her voice.

"It seems I have a free hand," he whispered and caressed her cheek with his fingers as he kissed her.

She squirmed a little but he had a good grasp on her wrists. His hand slid down to her jaw and along her neck before dropping to knead her breasts. Sam's eyes closed, a dreamy expression on her face. He moved to her nipple and rolled it between the pads of his thumb and forefinger, once again loving the sounds she made.

He let his hand drift down to stroke her belly, hearing the sharp intake of breath. He moved lower and cupped her. She struggled now to free herself but he had her right where he wanted her. Parting the dressing gown from her lower body until he had access to her night rail, he allowed his fingers to bunch the material, bringing it higher and higher until he touched a bare leg, which felt as smooth as silk. His fingers danced along her inner thigh and he sensed her stiffening.

"What are you doing?" she demanded as they moved toward her core.

"Is it throbbing? Pounding so fiercely you can scarcely think? Is it crying out for my touch?"

Sam looked baffled. He doubted she'd ever experienced the sensations she had now. It gave him no small satisfaction to be the first to do this with her.

And definitely the last.

No man would ever touch her like this. George would make sure of that.

His fingers glided up her thigh and touched the hidden place between her curls.

"George," she said, a warning in her voice.

"You said you wanted more," he reminded her.

"I . . . I wasn't sure what I wanted more of," she said hesitatingly.

He grinned at her. "Oh, you'll want this, Samantha Wallace. I guarantee you will."

Chapter Fourteen

Samantha had absolutely no idea where this was going. George was eliciting feelings within her and doing things to her body that she never would have imagined possible. Once again, she felt cheated with all the wasted years she'd spent with Haskett, who'd barely kissed her and never had caused her body to burn as it did now.

George had imprisoned her hands high above her head, easily capturing her wrists in one of his large hands. It left her feeling exposed, her breasts jutting out. George had pushed aside her dressing gown and night rail and feasted upon each breast, causing her to squirm and twist as he teased her with teeth and tongue. His movements had not only caused her heart to pound loudly, the blood rushing in her ears, but at the apex of her legs and fierce drumming had begun.

She suspected it was desire for him, manifesting itself physically, something she'd never experienced before. She knew he was the only one who could quell this rising need within her.

When she'd decided to take lovers to pleasure her, she had no idea what it would involve. The Duke of Charm, though, was an expert in love play, as he now demonstrated. Samantha found herself greedy to take even more from him.

What more involved was a mystery—even though she had certainly coupled with Haskett. What George did went far beyond anything she had experienced in her marriage bed.

His fingers now danced along her nether curls. She felt her face flame. She never touched there, other than to run a quick washcloth over those parts. Haskett had pushed his cock into her there. This was different, though. Where her husband had indifferently—almost clumsily—slipped his manhood inside her, George seemed as if he were going to do much more than that. The thought intrigued her and yet terrified her at the same time.

"Open your eyes, Samantha," George commanded.

She hadn't realized they were shut.

"Why?" she asked as she did as he instructed.

"Because I want to see the light come into your eyes when I touch you."

She swallowed. What was she supposed to say that?

One finger glided along the seam of her sex. Samantha shivered.

"You like that?"

She nodded.

"Say it."

"I like it," she repeated shakily.

She'd liked everything he'd done so far. The way he'd kissed her. The way he'd fondled her breasts. Even the movement of his fingers sliding up and down her curves had brought immense pleasure.

"You're wet for me," he said.

"I . . . I don't know what that means," she sputtered.

"It means you like what I've done to your body. What I'm doing now." His eyes gleamed. "What I will do to you."

She shivered. "What will you do?"

"What would you like me to do?" he asked, his finger moving back and forth lazily.

She whimpered and he pushed it inside her. Now, she was truly surprised. She bit her lip.

His clasp on her hands hadn't wavered. He moved his mouth to hers and kissed her as his finger began caressing her. She shuddered.

George broke the kiss and softly bit into her bottom lip, then soothed it by stroking his tongue over it. His finger moved in and out and then another joined it. She mewled like a kitten and squirmed under him restlessly. He kissed her again, more deeply, and the throbbing raged out of control. She fought for a breath, overwhelmed. He broke the kiss.

"I'm going to watch you now. Carefully."

He pressed his thumb against something within her and she gasped.

"Oh, my!"

"That's good, isn't it?" he asked as the pad of his thumb ran in a slow, small circle.

Samantha's hips rose as she tried to press against it. His fingers continued working some kind of spell on her. She found herself growing hot. Hotter. Even hotter, as if someone had bound her in front of a furnace.

"You are so beautiful," he murmured, staring deeply into her eyes. "More than beautiful. Your eyes are alive with passion. Your cheeks flushed with desire."

Something began to build within her. "George," she said uncertainly.

"I know, love. It's coming. And when it does, you'll let it wash over you. Wring out every bit of pleasure you can."

His caresses increased as his eyes searched hers. She thought she might explode.

"Stop," she begged.

"Do you really want me to?"

"No," she whispered.

It was as if she ran from something unknown, up a hill, out of breath, only to find herself atop a cliff. The pressure mounted. She flung herself into the abyss as a wave of warmth and pleasure rocked her. She cried his name as she bucked against him, the wave bringing her higher and higher and then gently falling away. Samantha felt spent. If George hadn't been holding her up, she would have fallen to the ground like a rag doll.

His fingers left her. He brought them to his mouth and licked them. She watched, fascinated.

"You taste like honey and sunshine," he told her.

He released her wrists and lowered her arms as he swept her up and carried her across the room and gently placed her on the bed. He untied the sash on his dressing gown and tossed it aside.

His muscled torso was bare except for the golden hair that lightly covered it. She longed to reach out and touch it. She'd never seen Haskett naked. He'd always insisted he perform his marital duties in the dark. She doubted her husband's physique had looked anything like George's did. He was a golden god, perfection brought to life.

Samantha watched him loosen his trousers and strip them away. His manhood stood at attention. It was so large.

"If you think to put that inside me, you're going to have trouble," she said aloud then winced that she'd done so.

He chuckled. "You're already wet for me, love. I would know if we were in trouble. We aren't."

He came to the bed and slipped a hand under her neck, raising her and pulling on the sleeve of her dressing gown, then tugging on the other side to remove it. He clasped her waist and lifted her from the bed as if she weighted nothing and captured the hem of her night rail, bringing it up and over her head.

She stood naked in front of him. Her first thought was to cover herself and she fought to keep from doing that. She was a woman of the world now. She intended to have many lovers and so she stood there unmoving, proud of her full breasts and narrow waist.

He whistled low. "You are Aphrodite come to life. I've never seen a more perfect woman."

She winced at his words, knowing he'd seen enough naked women to fill half of London.

He pulled her into his arms, one going about her waist and the other cupping her nape. He kissed her, softly, gently, with a sense of wonder. Her palms flattened against the hard wall of his muscled chest and began sliding up and down him, reveling in the feel of something so different from her. They brushed against his nipples, the flat discs rising slightly. She'd enjoyed when he played with hers and wondered if he would feel likewise.

Carefully, she brushed her fingertips back and forth across them. He sucked in a quick breath. So he did like it. She turned her hand and lightly raked her thumbnail over each. A low curse erupted from him, causing her to smile. His mouth came down hard on hers, possessive and greedy. He kissed her until she clung to him, afraid to let go.

Then he placed her on the bed again and climbed beside her.

"May I make love to you, Samantha?"

She liked that he asked her permission. That he thought it important not to merely take what he wanted.

"Yes. Do you have a French letter?"

He cursed again. "In my bedchamber. I never go anywhere without one."

She winced, again reminded of all the beautiful women that he'd bedded over the years, while she had only been with one man before tonight.

He cupped her cheek. "It doesn't matter. I can withdraw."

"Good. I don't want to make a child."

Even if she madly wanted a little boy with George's mischievous smile or a girl with his golden curls.

He lifted her braid and began working on it, separating the strands until they were free and running his fingers through them.

"It's like silk," he said, awe in his voice. "Fine silk."

He buried his face in her hair, his body coming over hers as he nuzzled it. Then he lifted his face and gazed at her.

"I'm going to love every inch of you, Samantha."

Again, she had no idea what he meant.

Until he did so.

By the time he hovered over her, she believed he had touched every bit of her body. His fingers again stroked her inside, causing excitement and need to build within her. He withdrew them and quickly they were replaced by his manhood. George pushed it inside her.

"You are so tight. So wet. So very perfect," he murmured.

She had doubted he would fit but he seemed to do so as he slipped almost all the way out of her and then thrust into her again. She cried out.

"Did I hurt you?"

"No. You make me feel . . . incredible."

"Good."

George began moving within her and Samantha rose to meet each thrust. Her fingers clawed into his back as he kissed her and their dance of love began. After long minutes, it reached a fever pitch. She was on the precipice again, ready to tumble over. He pulled completely out and then replaced his cock with his fingers, bringing her to ecstasy again as something warm brushed against her belly. She looked down and saw he'd spilled his seed there.

He kissed her mouth lightly and then the tip of her nose before retreating from the bed. He returned with a cloth and wiped all evidence of him from her belly and slipped the cloth into his banyan. Sitting on the bed, he stroked her hair, brushing it back from her face. He bent and kissed her sweetly.

"We'll talk when I return tomorrow. With or without West," he said.

She watched him slip into his trousers and banyan again and then he left the room.

He had said he wanted to talk to her. That it was important. Samantha hadn't wanted to hear what he wished to say to her because she was afraid. If her brother was right, George really did want to change. He obviously had feelings for her and had allowed his body to speak tonight instead of revealing what was in his heart. But if he truly did want to step away from being the Duke of Charm and start a family, she was not the woman for him. As much as she'd enjoyed the past few hours with him, he would want marriage. She'd sworn to herself never to wed again. Never to be controlled by a man—or a woman—as she had been with Lady Rockaway.

Instead, she would use the lessons George had taught her tonight and put them to good use.

With anyone but the Duke of Colebourne.

Chapter Fifteen

George returned to his bedchamber, moved by his experience with Sam. He had made love to many women, where he controlled every kiss. Every touch. He held his emotions in check and kept his distance, never yielding power to his bedmate.

With Sam, he made love *with* her. They'd been equal partners, despite her lack of experience. Every movement, every motion, every touch and sigh had been because they both wanted it. Needed it. And because of that, he hadn't wanted to take or stay in control. He had done what came naturally. Their dance of love had been both give and take, each of them generous with the other one. It had made for something unlike he'd ever known when coupling with a woman.

If he'd had any doubts about pledging himself to a single woman for the remainder of his life, making love with Sam had dispelled them. Their encounter had been the most incredible sexual adventure of his life. He knew with time, Sam would grow as a lover and partner. There would be no limits as to what they might do together.

His only regret was that he hadn't told her that he loved her. He'd kept from murmuring the words he'd never spoken to anyone. Not to his former fiancée, whom he'd barely known. Certainly not to the hundreds of women he'd bedded over the years. He wasn't sure if Sam would have believed him, though, which was why it was the only thing he'd held back from her. Surely she knew, though, that after they'd come together in such a way that there was no other woman for him.

He fell into bed, craving a few hours of sleep before he went to search for West. He awoke happy. George couldn't recall the last time he'd experienced that elusive emotion. Boredom. Indifference. Anger. They'd all be constant companions of his over the years but, today, he opened his eyes and instantly felt his spirits light and discovered a smile on his face. Sam was responsible for this. He wished he could go to where she lay sleeping and awaken her with a kiss before making glorious love to her all day.

That was impossible since he needed to locate West. Instead, he rose and penned a brief note to Sam before ringing for Briggs. After his valet dressed him, he took the folded page and pushed it under Sam's door, knowing it was still far too early for her to be up and about. Going downstairs, he ran into Andrew.

"What are you doing up so early?" George asked.

His friend chuckled. "How long has it been since you were in the country? I'm up by this time every morning when we're at Windowmere. There are a dozen things to do every day, starting with making love to my lovely wife, who's already breakfasted and is preparing for our guests' arrival."

"You do love her," he said.

"Of course. I adore Phoebe. I worship her. I burn for her. She is my everything," Andrew said. "Yes, it begins and ends in love but there is so much else in-between."

"I'm off to Exeter to find our Prodigal Son," he said, beginning to understand Andrew's feelings for his wife after his hours with Sam last night. "It may take all day. Once I find West, either I'll convince him to return with me to Windowmere or I'll escort him to Treadwell Manor. If it's the latter, I probably won't return until tomorrow so please give my apologies to Phoebe and the other guests."

"And to Lady Samantha?" Andrew asked.

"I spoke with her last night and left her a note this morning. What you can do for me is make sure none of your male guests go sniffing about her."

Andrew laughed. "That might prove difficult. Samantha has matured into quite a beauty. The gangly tomboy of days of yore is no more."

"Well, do your best, Andrew, because I plan to make her my wife."

His friend studied him. "Does she know this?"

"She should have a good idea after last night," George quipped.

"Don't tell me what's been going on under my roof. What I don't know I can't talk about." Andrew grinned and placed his hand on George's shoulder. "I am happy for you, though. Samantha is a wonderful woman. It's time you came to your senses and settled down."

"Hopefully, I'll see you later today or by tomorrow, at the latest," George said and left the house.

He found his coachman in the stables and had him ready the carriage to travel the few miles to Exeter. Soon, they were on the road and arrived quickly at the edge of the city. George had his choice of several inns to visit or houses of ill repute. West could be sleeping at either. George would start with the inns since West wasn't fond of brothels. He could be a bit of snob, finding a good many of them—especially those outside of London—to have women he believed to be inferior. West would rather tup a buxom serving wench at an inn before a tart working in a whorehouse.

After visiting two inns and finding West at neither, he went to a third. As he exited his carriage, he saw a man with brown hair and a wiry frame leading a horse from the stables next door. He thought he recognized the horse and called out to the man.

"Can I help you, my lord?"

"Yes. Might this be one of the Duke of Windham's mounts?" he asked.

"Why, it is. I am about to return it."

George frowned. "Why? Won't the Duke of Treadwell come and claim it?"

"Ah, you know not only the horse but His Grace," the man said jovially. "The duke gave me a princely sum to look after the horse when he arrived last night. Asked me to return it to Windowmere today."

"Did His Grace stay at this inn last night?" George inquired, pointing to the structure to his right.

The man shrugged. "I don't right know, my lord. I just took the horse and agreed to return it this morning. It was too late to ride it back last night."

"Very well. Thank you."

He made his way to the inn's door and ventured inside, immediately being greeted by the proprietor.

"Good day. I am the Duke of Colebourne and I am looking for the Duke of Treadwell. I know his horse stayed here in your stables last night. Did His Grace take a room?"

The innkeeper's bewildered look gave George pause. "No, Your Grace. No duke has not come in here for some time now."

Thinking quickly, he said, "He might not have referred to himself as a duke. He would have had a good deal to drink, though, and claimed any pretty wench nearby."

"No, Your Grace. No one matching that description came in last night. It was very quiet. A family of five. Two gentlemen traveling from London. Another man who is headed to Cornwall to look into a mine he recently purchased. Those are our only guests. A few townspeople came in for a pint or two of ale but they all live nearby."

"I must have missed His Grace," George said. "I apologize for taking up your time."

He visited the last inn and the two houses of ill repute. No one matching West's description had visited any of those establishments last night. He checked with a man who rented horses and carriages. West hadn't done either.

Where could he have gone? Had he found a ride to Treadwell Manor? At this point, George had exhausted all leads in Exeter. Worried now, he returned to his carriage and told the driver to make for Treadwell Manor. He sat back against the plush cushions, wondering why West hadn't stayed in Exeter overnight before setting out for Treadwell Manor. If he even went there. Surely, he wouldn't be so foolish as to go back to London.

Of course, Sam said they did have cross words last night. West had already been unhappy at being dragged to Devon. It shouldn't surprise him if his friend up and went to London, despite Lord Ivy lying in wait for him there. George would go to Treadwell Manor first and if West wasn't to be found there, it would mean a return to London. Irritation built within him at the thought of having to journey all the way back to the city. Especially since he wanted to spend time with Sam.

He arrived at West's country estate and descended from his carriage. The butler and two footmen met him.

"Is His Grace in residence?" he asked.

"No, Your Grace," the butler told him. "We haven't seen him for some time."

Frustration filled George. The fool *had* gone back to London. He'd either get himself killed or kill Ivy in a duel and have to flee England. George dreaded the long trip ahead of him, cursing silently, but knowing he needed to find West.

"Thank you," he told the butler. "Would you send word to the Duke of Windham that I have returned to London? Tell him I hope to find Treadwell there."

"Of course, Your Grace. Are you planning to stay the night before traveling to London?"

Knowing his horses needed resting, he nodded. "If it's not an inconvenience."

"Of course not, Your Grace."

George went inside and was shown to a chamber. He requested hot water be sent up. As he waited for it, his thoughts swirled.

He loved West with all his heart. The man had been both friend and brother to him for almost three decades. Still, West was a grown man. And George was weary. Tired of the false life he'd led for so many years, filled with emptiness and no meaning. He had been given a gift by finding Sam at Windowmere. He could either chase West back to London and lose the opportunity of courting Sam—or he could return to Windowmere and let West do as he pleased, which he would do whether George showed up or not.

Though it saddened him to let down his friend, he made the decision that he hoped might change the course of his life.

He would return to the house party tomorrow and offer for the woman he loved.

SAMANTHA WAS ALREADY awake when she heard a noise. She sat up in the dark bedchamber and listened, wondering if George was back at her door. She pushed aside the bedclothes and tiptoed to the door, stepping on something. Bending, she retrieved a folded piece of parchment and took it to the window. She pulled back the curtains, which allowed enough light to fall against the page. Her name was scrawled across it. She recognized George's handwriting and opened it.

Samantha –

I'm off to find the errant West and am sorry so much of my day will be spent searching for him—when I'd rather be with you.

Last night was very special to me. I hope it was to you, as well. I told you I was ready to change and I will. I need you by my side to help me do so, though. I've made a mess of my life. You are the one woman who can straighten me out and make me laugh, all at the same time.

I'll return as soon as I can, either with West in tow or having delivered him to Treadwell Manor. I look forward to seeing you again and speaking to you about things that were left unsaid for too many years.

Yours,
George

When she'd made her come-out, she would have given anything for George to have paid attention to her. Even now, a small thrill rippled through her, knowing he harbored feelings for her. She hardened herself to them, though. George was her past. He knew her when she was a completely different person, naïve and untouched by the ugly realities of life. While last night had been eye-opening and had taught her much about the act of love, she couldn't pledge herself to him. What he required of her was far more than she would be willing to give.

Guilt filled her. He wanted to change and said he needed her help in this mission. She would tell him she would support him in whatever he tried to do. It wouldn't be as his wife, though. How ironic that all she'd wanted to be was married to George for so many years. Now that he wanted the same, she had moved on. Her experiences at Rockwell had changed her. She was not the idealistic young woman he'd once known. If he knew who she'd really become, George wouldn't want her at all.

Telling him no would be the hardest thing she would ever do.

Samantha sat in the chair, pondering her future, until Lucy arrived and helped her to dress. She brought a breakfast tray with her.

"Her Grace has already breakfasted. She is preparing for their guests. She thought you'd like to eat in your chamber but she wishes for you to help greet the arrivals."

"Thank you, Lucy. Go ahead and pick out something for me to

wear this morning while I eat."

Once she'd eaten and dressed, Samantha went downstairs and found Phoebe.

"Oh, I am so glad you're here," her friend exclaimed, handing her a sheet. "Look over this menu for tonight's dinner and tell me if you can think of anything to add. I need to get it to Cook."

She glanced over. "It looks quite thorough. Remember, I've seen all the menus for the upcoming week."

Phoebe sighed. "I know. I just want everything to go well. This is the first time we are entertaining as a married couple. I want every detail to be perfect."

She hugged Phoebe. "Everyone will enjoy being at Windowmere. They'll see how happy you've made Andrew."

"He's made me equally happy." Phoebe paused. "I think of how cold and distant Borwick was and how different my life is now."

Pimmeline appeared. "Your Grace, the first carriage has been spotted coming up the lane."

The two women went out to greet the guests, joined by Andrew.

"It looks as if it's Jon and Elizabeth," he said as the vehicle pulled up. "It's too bad George and Weston aren't here." He paused. "I received word from Treadwell Manor earlier. George is headed to London to seek Weston since he wasn't to be found in Exeter."

Samantha nodded but didn't say anything. It angered her that disappointment filled her. She didn't want to lead George on. Perhaps it was best he wouldn't be at the house party, after all. She could pursue becoming the new person she so desperately wanted to be, cutting ties with everything in her past.

Jon bounded out and grinned at them before offering his hand to his sister. Samantha had always liked Jon. He was friendly and loyal and he'd always teased her as if she were a sister to him.

He came toward them, leading Elizabeth.

"We are delighted to be here," he said, greeting Andrew and

Phoebe and adding, "and especially seeing Sam here. This is my sister, Elizabeth. She made her come-out this past Season."

Elizabeth had her brother's dark hair and dark blue eyes. While Jon was just over six feet, she was almost a foot shorter.

"I am happy to be introduced to you, Lady Elizabeth," Samantha said. "I knew your brother when I was younger. I am Lady Samantha." She introduced herself this way after hearing Jon call her Sam. She needed to leave all notions of Sam, the tomboy, behind and become Samantha, the intriguing widow. She especially didn't want to be known a Viscountess Haskett and would forsake that form of address, at least during the house party. That would change, though, next Season when she went to London.

"He mentioned you over the years, Lady Samantha. It's so nice to make your acquaintance." She smiled at Andrew and Phoebe. "Thank you, Your Graces, for inviting Jon and me to your house party."

"We couldn't have a party without you," Phoebe assured the young woman. "Won't you come in?"

As the rest of the houseguests showed up, she found herself drawn to several. Viscount and Viscountess Burton, who were Phoebe's sister and brother-in-law, had brought Basil, their new baby of almost eight months. The viscountess was full of life and excited to share everything her new son was up to. Samantha also liked Lady Boyston, a war widow who had no children, and Lady Henrietta, a friend of Elizabeth's who was slightly plump but rather pretty, with blond curls and large, blue eyes.

Of the men who'd been invited, she found three of them appealing, assessing their potential as future lovers. All were attractive and had eyed her with interest when they'd been introduced. Viscount Roach seemed close to thirty, with a solid build and kind, brown eyes. The Earl of Baywell was slightly older than the viscount and had served in the army with Andrew. Baywell had a lithe frame and quick wit. Baron Stilton was an old classmate of Andrew's, with a short, stocky build and lively, mischievous eyes.

Samantha decided she would at least kiss all three of them and see if it led to anything beyond a kiss.

Chapter Sixteen

All the guests had arrived by luncheon and Phoebe had them gather outside, where tables had been set up for them to dine *al fresco*. Though early October and slightly cool, there wasn't much of a breeze and their hostess deemed it a perfect way to begin their time together. Samantha sat at a table with Lady Henrietta, Baywell, and Stilton. The men kept the conversation lively, trying to entertain the two women. She found herself drawn to both of them and had to warn herself not to be too easily impressed. It had been years since she'd been in the company of gentlemen who actually spoke to her pleasantly and vied for her attention. It wouldn't do to appear too desperate.

Once luncheon finished, several of the guests retreated to their rooms to rest until teatime since their journeys had been long ones. Some of the women mentioned writing letters and some of the men convinced Andrew to take them on a tour of Windowmere. Samantha found herself with the earl.

"Are you off to rest or write letters?" he asked.

"No. I arrived a few days ago and have no need of rest. Actually, I'm a bit restless."

"So am I. It's being cooped up in a carriage for several days. Would you care to stretch your legs and walk the gardens with me?"

She thought of the last time she'd been in the gardens. George had kissed her quite thoroughly. At least she didn't need to worry about seeing him again anytime soon since he traipsed after Weston, whom she was beginning to believe might be a lost cause.

"I would enjoy that, Lord Baywell."

He offered her his arm and she showed him the direction to head.

"You mentioned you enjoyed riding," he said. "We will have to do some while we are here."

"Are you trying to worm your way into my heart, my lord?" she teased. "Talk of horses will endear you to me."

A smile lit his face. "Then I hope it works."

He placed his hand over hers. She wished neither of them wore gloves. She would like to see what it would be like to feel his touch against her skin. Her cheeks heated, thinking of the many ways George had touched her.

Did she really want other men doing to her what he had done?

They strolled across the lawn and turned to go to the rear of the house, reaching the gardens and entering them.

"Are you fond of plants and flowers, Lady Samantha?"

"I like looking at them but I know very little about them," she admitted. "I have only recently returned to southern England. I lived in the north for several years after my marriage." She thought it best to let the earl know a small part of her history. "My husband passed away and after my mourning period, I decided I wanted to be around family and friends again."

"My condolences," Baywell said.

"It was over three years ago," she added. "It's in my past now. I am determined to look toward the future."

"A wise decision."

They strolled slowly, with Baywell pointing out several of the various flowers.

"I love the asters best," he said as they passed a grouping of them. "So tall and proud. And beautiful shades of purples."

"What are those?" Samantha asked, pointing to their left. "They are such rich colors. Those reds and oranges would make for beautiful shades for a gown."

"Ah, those are dahlias." He stopped and picked one for her. "See all the layers of petals?"

Baywell tucked it into her hair, just above her ear. The brush of his lower palm against her cheek didn't cause any sort of tingles, which disappointed her.

"There. That looks lovely," he said and took her arm again, his hand possessively claiming her own.

Still, no kinds of feeling overcame her. Maybe it took time for that to build.

Then why had it seemed instantaneous with George?

They walked on some minutes, with the earl pointing out physalis, from the nightshade family.

"You certainly know your flowers," she told him.

"I used to follow our gardener around when I was young. He would set me to digging in the dirt, which is exactly what a little boy longs to do. I helped him plant shrubbery and flowers. He taught me the difference in annuals and perennials. I still take an interest in my gardens."

"Where is your country estate?"

"Wiltshire. Only a few counties away, so the growing season is similar to here in Devon. Autumn produces some of the best blooms, in my opinion."

"I think I will need to learn more about flowers," she said.

A gleam came into his eyes. "I'd be more than happy to teach you, my lady."

They continued on and found a bench.

"Would you care to sit?" he asked.

"That would be lovely."

The bench was just large enough for two—if Baywell rested his arm against the back of it. Samantha found herself snug against him as she looked at the flowers opposite them.

"What are those? They are the most amazing colors. Reds. Blues. Purples."

"You won't see colors like that very often. They're anemones. I like to think them the royalty of an autumn garden because of how vibrant their shades are."

"I wonder if we have these at Treadwell Manor," she mused.

"If you have a gardener worth his salt, you will," he said, laughing.

She looked at him and thought how handsome he was, more so when he laughed. He stopped and their gazes locked on one another. Neither looked away.

"I'd like to kiss you, Lady Samantha," he said huskily. "That is, if you have no other commitment to anyone."

"I don't," she assured him. "And I would very much like to kiss you."

She didn't know if she should have admitted that. But he seemed very nice and smelled wonderful and had been pleasant to talk with.

His fingers grasped her chin, holding it as he studied her. Then he tilted it up slightly as his head drew close. His lips met hers. They were firm and pressed against hers.

What was she to do? Haskett had never kissed her open-mouthed. She hadn't known that was a choice before George kissed her that way. Would Baywell wish to do the same?

Samantha tried to relax, deciding to let the earl lead the way. He continued to kiss her the same way, stirring no desire in her whatsoever. Disappointment filled her. He was so handsome and witty. She had wanted him to be a good kisser. Perhaps if she opened slightly, he would be better. She relaxed her jaw and allowed her lips to part slightly.

She sensed the change in him. He released her chin, his hand cupping her cheek for a moment before slipping to grasp her nape. His tongue played along the seam of her lips, urging them to open more, which she did. Soon, it slipped into her mouth.

This was better. She could tell he was skilled and had done this many times. She liked it. She liked kissing him. She liked him.

But he wasn't George.

That giddiness which had built within her when she kissed George was missing. Though Baywell made some of the same sounds as George had, she found she didn't wish to make any at all. She enjoyed what he was doing and still somehow kept her distance, as if she observed from several feet away.

With George, his kiss had been all-consuming, devouring her, causing her to be mindless, greedy for his touch.

Baywell pulled away, his eyes heavy-lidded as he stared into hers, his thumb stroking her nape.

"I hope we can be friends," Samantha said, wanting to gently let Baywell know that she wasn't interested in more from him.

The corners of his mouth turned up. "I hope we can be much more."

GEORGE TAMPED DOWN his impatience as the carriage turned and made its way up the lane toward Windowmere.

He needed to see Sam. Desperately. Even being apart from her for a day had been too much. Need for her overwhelmed him. He wanted to stroke her hair of silk. Kiss her rosebud mouth. Caress every curve of her luscious body. His every thought was consumed by her. He knew it had to be love because he'd never felt this way before. He'd always remained detached from each encounter with a woman, pleasuring them but keeping himself apart. With Sam, he wanted to crawl inside her. Ridiculous? Absolutely.

It still made him smile.

He wanted to know everything about her. Not just her body but who she was now. He knew the girl of long ago because he'd spent so much time in her presence, along with West. That last year before her come-out, though, he'd begun to pull away. It was almost as if he'd subconsciously realized his interest in her and had thought it wrong. Sam had been as much a sister to him as she had been to West. The feelings that he'd started developing for her had upset him. He'd dealt with them by avoiding being around her.

That was what had led him to courting Frederica Martin. She was what he thought a duchess should be. Beautiful. In control of her emotions. Polite. Distant. He'd known Lady Frederica would never make demands of him. He could wed her and continue to do as he pleased. She would be happy being a duchess, one of the few in the kingdom. They would have children. Entertain. Live separate lives, for the most part.

He hadn't thought about marrying at such an early age but West had been mad for Juniper Radwell, head over heels, with heart palpitations every time he saw her. Both he and West lost their fathers near the same time and they were aware of the massive responsibilities that awaited them by achieving their dukedoms at such a young age. West had suggested they look for brides, to be more settled into their roles. With his best friend deciding to wed and being so passionately in love, George had simply followed suit. They'd even planned to marry in a double ceremony at St. George's Chapel.

All these years later, he remembered how Sam chided him for choosing Lady Frederica as his wife, telling him she was utterly wrong for him. Sam had passionately declared she wanted a husband who would be her friend and equal, as well as her lover. The thought had seemed incredibly odd to George at the time. Now, he absolutely understood what she meant. He wanted to build a life with Sam. He wanted to share all the small things that happened during a day. He wanted to hold their children on his lap and read to them and put them to bed—then retire with her to their bedchamber and make more babies.

He saw now that Sam had been far more mature than either he or West, even though she was younger than they were by three years. He understood that she'd not been happy in her marriage. It didn't matter. He would be the husband she wanted. They would share everything.

If he could get back to Windowmere.

He'd left Treadwell Manor early, realizing as he did that he'd asked the butler to send word to Windowmere that he was traveling to London. That meant his hosts and Sam wouldn't be expecting him. A small part of him worried that of the gentlemen invited to the house party, several of them would already be flirting with her.

What if she wanted them instead of him?

No, that couldn't be right. They had been intimate only two nights ago. Sam wasn't the kind of woman who would hop from bed to bed without a second thought.

As the Duke of Charm had done.

George shook his head. When he thought of Charm, it was as if that man were someone totally separate from him. Why had he wasted years being something he wasn't? He told himself he did so because Sam hadn't been free. He could only be grateful that Haskett had died. Or been murdered. West told him something about it but, even then, his friend had known little. George had assumed that was because all his news came from Sam and she must be grieving immensely for her dead husband. Now that it seemed she didn't, it gave him hope that she was amenable to them coming together and marrying. Haskett had been gone long enough so that wouldn't raise any questions. True, some might think they wed fast but he'd known Sam all her life. And besides, who cared what the *ton* thought? If they were happy, that was all that mattered.

George planned to make his wife immensely happy.

The carriage slowed and then came to a stop in front of the house. He threw open the door and saw Pimmeline waiting. Phoebe came out and joined the butler, a sunny smile on her face.

"George! You came back!" she cried, looking radiant.

He kissed her cheek. "I did. It seems I left my valet and trunk behind," he teased. "And I owed my host and hostess my presence at their party because I certainly want to get to know the Duchess of Windham better." He paused. "I also hope to play my cards right and leave Windowmere with a fiancée."

"George," Phoebe said, a blush rising on her cheeks. "You don't say. Come in. Let's go to my sitting room."

He didn't wish to sit but he didn't want to disappoint Phoebe. She'd already been very good to him and she was a wonderful wife to Andrew.

They settled in and she asked, "You didn't find Weston?"

He explained his search in Exeter and trip to Treadwell Manor, where the servants hadn't heard from their master in a good long while.

"I thought to chase after him and return to London—but I had better things to do here."

"You are truly interested in Samantha?"

"I am. I spoke to Andrew about it."

"He shared some of your conversation with me," she confided. "I think you would make for a marvelous couple." She frowned. "I'd go slowly, though, George. Don't assume anything. Don't rush Samantha."

"That will be hard," he admitted. "I feel we've already wasted so much time the last few years. She was right before my eyes and I didn't recognize that. I raced back here, only to be detained by a coach that had broken a wheel. I wound up taking the stranded family into Exeter and then backtracking here. I hope I didn't miss too much."

"We had a lovely luncheon outdoors and most people are resting after their long journeys."

"And Sam?"

Phoebe hesitated and then said, "She went for a stroll in the gardens with Lord Baywell. He served with Andrew."

He pushed to his feet. "I've met him. He's bright. Handsome. Exactly the kind of man I wanted to stay away from Sam. I'll find them."

She rose and placed a hand on his arm. "Calm down. You haven't been listening to me so I'll speak more plainly. I'm warning you not to come on too strong, George. Samantha looks very much in control but she has had much happen to her and needs time to recover from it."

"I can't help it," he said. "I love her. I want to marry her."

Phoebe patted his arm, trying to soothe him. "All the more reason to calm down and approach her with care."

He took a deep breath. "All right. I won't dash out the door and run through gardens calling her name. I certainly won't slam my fist into Baywell's pretty face and break his nose."

She laughed. "Good. I knew I could count on you."

"I won't stand aside placidly, though, Phoebe."

"I'm not asking you to. Just . . . be careful. Now, go find her and tell them it's almost time for tea. That will be your excuse to retrieve them."

George excused himself and went toward the gardens, recalling his kiss with Sam there. No, Samantha. He needed to start calling her that in his head so he wouldn't make the mistake aloud. She was a lady. A widow. She'd matured from the carefree girl she'd been all those years ago.

He wound his way down the path, his eyes eagerly seeking her. Then he spotted her, seated on a bench with Baywell.

They were kissing.

His heart dropped to his feet even as his blood boiled. The woman he loved—and had made love to—was kissing another man. A very eligible one. Wealthy. Confident. A war hero.

What if Sam wanted Baywell instead of him?

He forced himself to remain rooted to the spot. He didn't want to spy on them but he certainly wasn't going to turn around and leave.

The earl broke the kiss and they stared at one another. Their lips were moving but he wasn't close enough to hear their conversation. Then he saw Baywell smile. That was what put his feet in motion. George tried to walk and not run and kept murmuring to himself not to smash his fist into the earl's face.

As he reached them, he heard Sam say, "I don't think so, my lord, though I do like you."

The earl chuckled. "Then I hope you'll partner with me in charades tonight. I think we would make for a team hard to beat."

"I'd be happy to do so."

"Good afternoon," George said and the couple looked up.

"Colebourne," Baywell said brusquely, a frown on his face as he stood.

"Hello, George," Sam said, also rising and looking surprised to see him, a blush staining her cheeks. "Andrew told me you'd left for London and wouldn't be returning to Windowmere."

"I changed my mind. May I join you?"

Chapter Seventeen

Samantha knew George's very charming smile hid his rage. When he became angry as a boy, he would ball his fists and place them behind his back to keep others from knowing how upset he was. His hands were out of sight now, thrust behind him, his features placid.

"I don't think—"

"I'd love to have your company." She interrupted Baywell and placed a hand on his forearm, feeling the muscles tight beneath her fingers. "Do you know Colebourne, my lord? He and my brother have been the closest of friends since birth. Our families' estates lie next to one another. George has always been like a big brother to me."

She felt the tension flee the earl, which pleased her, but George's smile faltered slightly.

"I know of the duke. And your brother," Baywell said succinctly and Samantha saw the earl didn't care for George—or rather, George's reputation.

"George, this is the Earl of Baywell. He and Andrew served on the Continent together. We've been enjoying a stroll through Phoebe's gardens. The earl is quite the gardener and has pointed out many varieties of flowers to me."

Samantha released her hold on the earl. "George and I saw some of the gardens the other day. Lord Baywell and I were about to walk through the rest. I'm sure he wouldn't mind you joining us."

She looked up at Baywell and smiled sweetly.

The nobleman looked torn. She knew he didn't want George tagging along with them yet he didn't want to leave her with the Duke of Charm. Glancing to George, she saw he understood the situation perfectly. His hands returned to his sides.

"Actually, it may be wise to head back to the house. I saw Phoebe before I came out to take a bit of air. She reminded me not to be late for tea. Why don't we all return to the house? I would hate to upset our charming hostess, knowing how much effort has gone into the house party."

George stepped to her and offered his arm. Samantha took it, not wishing to seem churlish.

"I know Phoebe has planned a wonderful tea," she said to both men. "I tried some of Cook's apricot tarts with Devonshire cream the other day and they were delightful. I know they will be served this afternoon."

Baywell moved beside her and offered his arm, as well. She placed her hand on it and said, "My, I am so fortunate to have two handsome men escorting me to tea."

The trio started back along the path. No one said a word the entire time though she could tell George was about to burst out in laughter. She wanted to flash him a warning look but knew that was the last thing she should do. When they were children and one of them on the verge of laughter, the other would fall apart in helpless giggles. She feared she would do the same if she looked in his direction now.

"I must go change my gown," she told them when they arrived at the house. "I will see you shortly."

Samantha left them in one another's company, wondering if they would sniff each other out as dogs might and become friendly—or wind up in a scrape. She hoped it was the former. It wouldn't do to begin a fight on the first day of the house party.

Lucy awaited her and already had out a gown for tea. She allowed the maid to undress and redress her, thankful that Phoebe had allowed Samantha to borrow some of her gowns. She would also need to go into Exeter in a few days to claim the other ones Mrs. Echols worked on.

"What would you care to wear for dinner this evening, my lady? The midnight blue is very nice. So is the emerald green."

"It doesn't matter. Whichever I don't wear tonight, I can wear tomorrow evening."

"I heard His Grace came back without your brother. I hope everything is all right."

She shook her head dismissively. "Weston will do as he chooses. If he's gone back to London, that means Treadwell Manor will be a more pleasant place when we go home."

"I'll press the blue for tonight then," Lucy said.

"Thank you."

Samantha went to the drawing room and saw a good dozen people already there, George among them. He came to her.

"I'm sorry I didn't find West. I am not sorry that I interrupted your tryst with Lord Baywell."

"Oh, bother," she said, making no effort to hide her annoyance. "It wasn't a tryst, George. I was merely showing the earl through the gardens."

One eyebrow arched. "It's hard to see flowers when your eyes are closed and your lips are engaged with his."

"You were spying on us?" she huffed as she felt her cheeks burn.

"No. I was merely stretching my legs after riding from Treadwell Manor to Windowmere and came upon you. At least I was gentleman enough to let you finish before I engaged you in conversation." He paused. "I thought you lady enough not to go kissing anyone while I was gone. Then again, you didn't think I was coming back. I suppose that excuses your actions in your mind."

"We will speak of this later," she hissed and turned away, moving to stand with Lady Elizabeth and Jon.

George followed and joined their circle, greeting his old friend as Samantha quietly fumed.

"Hello, Jon. I haven't seen you in a while." George smiled at Elizabeth. "And I don't believe I've been introduced to your lovely sister."

"That's because Jon wouldn't allow it," Elizabeth said, allowing George to take her hand and kiss it as Jon's eyes narrowed. "He said I wasn't to speak to either you or the Duke of Disrepute." Then her eyes widened. "Oh, I am sorry, Lady Samantha. Forgive me."

Samantha said, "I didn't speak to either of them when I went to London for the Season. They were much too disreputable for my tastes. George claims he's ready to change, however. You might want to give him a chance. I think the Duke of Charm is quite harmless."

She thought Elizabeth would be perfectly suited for George and used this opportunity to nudge them together.

Jon wasn't having any of it, though. "I love you as a brother, George, but you are to stay away from Elizabeth," he ordered.

"That will prove hard to do at a house party," Elizabeth said, smiling at her brother's friend. "I will trust my new friend, Lady Samantha, when she says you have been defanged."

"I think it's admirable that your brother has protected you, Lady Elizabeth," George said. "I hate to inform you, but he has proven to be quite the rake himself. It seems he, also, has turned over a new leaf."

"Only until my sister has wed," Jon declared. "Then I am back to my old ways. I'm trying my best to appear reputable so she can find a suitable husband." He paused. "I have a reason to behave for now. Why are you wishing to change? You don't answer to any woman. Nothing ties you down."

George smiled enigmatically. "Oh, I have found a special woman. She has already tamed me. I'm a mere pussycat now and not the roaring lion I once was."

Elizabeth's eyes lit with interest. "And who might this lady be,

Your Grace?"

"You're not getting it out of me yet," he said, laughing. "She's playing hard to get at this point. I am in the position of doing the pursuing for once." He grinned. "Don't worry. She may think she's run safely away from me—but I plan to catch her and never let go."

Samantha winced inside at George's description. At least he hadn't come out and named her to his friend. If he wasn't telling Jon, he was certainly acting as a gentleman. Still, she needed to get him alone at some point and gently inform him that they didn't have a future together.

"I've been told that dinner awaits us," Andrew said to the group. "Please, come join me and my duchess."

Jon offered Samantha his arm. "Let me escort you, my lady." He raised his eyebrows. "And you may take Elizabeth in, George. I better see you on your best behavior around her for the next week. That would prove to me that you are different."

Samantha found herself seated next to Viscount Roach and he greeted her warmly.

"I already hear Baywell has claimed you as his charades partner this evening."

"The earl tells me he is quite a decent player," she replied. "I agreed to partner with him because I do enjoy winning."

She spent the meal talking with Roach, who sat on her left, and Viscount Burton, who had been placed to her right. He, too, seemed as much enthralled with his infant son as his wife was and entertained Samantha with stories of things Basil had done. Seeing the viscount's pride in his only child made her wistful, knowing she would never have any of her own. Perhaps she could serve as a sort of aunt to Andrew and Phoebe when they had children since she doubted Weston would ever settle down with one woman. It saddened her because she thought if he stopped running about as a cad that he would make for a wonderful father.

After dinner, the men remained in the dining room to smoke their cheroots and drink a glass of port as the women retired to the drawing room. She found herself taking a turn around the room with Lady Boyston, who had made a good first impression on her.

"How do you know the duke and duchess?" Samantha asked.

"His Grace was my husband's commanding officer."

"Is it painful to speak of your husband?"

"No. I adjusted to him being gone a long time ago. We meet at an assembly room dance when he was in the neighborhood training soldiers. It was love at first sight." Lady Boyston's smile grew wistful. "We only had a few weeks together as husband and wife before he left for the Continent. He died in action a few months after that."

Samantha took Lady Boyston's hand. "I'm so dreadfully sorry."

"I am, too. He never came home on leave. We never saw each other again. He wrote wonderful letters to me, though. He enjoyed life in the army and thought the world of His Grace."

"Have you thought of marrying again?" Samantha asked carefully.

"I suppose I will at some point. I very much would like to have children. I was with child when the news came. I had just written a letter informing him he was to be a father. He died before he could have received it." Lady Boyston paused. "I gave birth too early. My baby was too small. Too fragile to survive."

Samantha squeezed Lady Boyston's hand. "Then you suffered two losses."

"Yes." She raised her chin. "Hopefully, I will have the opportunity to wed again. I know that is why His Grace issued an invitation to me. There are several bachelors here. I hear you, too, are a widow."

"Yes. My husband died a few years ago." She didn't mention he was murdered, nor did she wish to discuss her miscarriage.

The door opened and the men poured into the room.

"Have any of the gentlemen caught your eye?" Lady Boyston asked.

"No, but it's early," she replied. "I did walk in the gardens with Lord Baywell. He is quite knowledgeable regarding flowers and is also quick-witted."

The earl came toward them, George closely behind him.

"I hear that Lady Henrietta is going to sing and play for us and then we'll play charades," Baywell told the women.

"You should play, as well, Samantha," George urged. "No one has your skill when it comes to the pianoforte."

The pit of her belly felt cold and hard. "I haven't played since before my marriage," she said bluntly.

"Why?" George asked, puzzled.

She could tell him that Lady Rockaway wouldn't allow her to play because she thought music to be a waste of time. Or she could tell him it was hard to practice when locked away in a small bedchamber for two years.

Instead, she shrugged and said, "I lost interest."

A deep frown crossed George's face. Before he could speak, Phoebe claimed the room's attention, announcing that Lady Henrietta would entertain them for the next half-hour. Samantha and Lady Boyston took a nearby seat, while Baywell and George came and stood behind them.

As the young woman's fingers danced across the keys and her voice rang out across the room, Samantha felt the warm pressure of George's fingers on her shoulder. He squeezed it and they were gone.

She almost wept.

Chapter Eighteen

George couldn't fathom why Samantha had stopped playing. She had been the most talented pianist of any woman of his acquaintance and had played with such joy and abandon.

Something dreadful had occurred at Rockwell. Her years there hadn't just been lonely. Whatever it was had changed her fundamentally. The Sam he knew would never have given up music. It was a part of her. She'd loved playing for others, even dueting with those who played the pianoforte, as well as singing. He remembered coming in from playing outdoors with West and hearing her at practice. He would go and stand out of sight and listen to her, amazed at how one so young could bring such feeling to the notes.

He longed to touch her again but after the one brief squeeze of comfort, he kept his hands at his side. He knew Baywell was watching his every move. George couldn't decide if Sam was interested in the earl, but Baywell was certainly aware of her.

Lady Henrietta completed her set and those gathered applauded with enthusiasm. She had been quite good. He saw her blush as a few gentlemen praised her and then she returned to sit next to Elizabeth.

Andrew claimed everyone's attention and said, "Those who wish to play word games, including charades, should remain in the drawing room. Tables have been set up in the library for anyone wanting to play bridge."

Baywell immediately leaned over to Sam and said, "Don't forget,

Lady Samantha. We are to be partners at charades."

"I remember, my lord."

George looked to Lady Boyston. "Would you do me the honor of partnering with me?"

"Yes, Your Grace. Are you competitive?"

He laughed. "Very much so. I intend for us to beat Samantha and Baywell and every other pair who participates."

"Good," his new partner said, giving him a warm smile. "I'm afraid I've always been happier as a winner rather than a loser."

"Sounds like you're issuing us a challenge, Your Grace," Baywell said.

Shrugging, George said, "Lady Boyston and I are both clever and cutthroat. Make of it what you will."

Both women chuckled at his bold statement and stood as some guests left for the library. Those who remained gathered for the first round of charades. Phoebe went over the rules for anyone unfamiliar and said she would act as an impartial judge, providing each pair with a word or short phrase. She would also time the participants as far as writing their clues. A point would be awarded to the pair who correctly guessed the answer and another to the couple who provided the clues. If no one guessed the phrase, no points would be awarded in that round. The team with the most points would win a prize.

The duchess indicated slips of paper that had been folded and placed in a large silver bowl. George told Lady Boyston to draw for them. She brought back their phrase and they huddled as she showed him.

"Difficult—but not impossible," he determined. "Now, to divide it into portions and write our rhyme."

Pairs moved to different areas of the drawing room and a few couples retreated to the hallway so no one would overhear them as they talked over whether to separate their assigned phrase into syllables or portions. George and Lady Boyston quickly hatched a plan and began working quietly on their rhyme, which described their phrase both verbally and enigmatically.

Once they'd completed their clue, he asked, "Would you like to describe the first part?"

"No, I'd rather be involved with the latter. Shall we practice?"

"Two minutes until we begin," called out Phoebe.

"We'd better be quick," he said.

They were able to practice twice before the duchess called everyone back into a group and asked for volunteers.

"Lady Boyston and I would be happy to go first," he proclaimed, taking her hand and escorting her to the front of their audience.

They took turns reciting their portions of the rhyme they had composed. Jon called out for them to repeat it and they did so. Then the guessing began. It took several minutes before Viscount Burton called out, "A dripping June sets all in tune!"

"You are correct," George said. "An excellent job in deciphering our clues, Lord Burton."

The viscount grinned. "It was my wife who figured it out. I merely blurted out the answer with enthusiasm."

"Who's next?" asked Phoebe.

They played several rounds until Samantha and Baywell rose and went to the front. They were the last pair to present their rhyme. Rather, Baywell did while Sam stood nearby with an encouraging smile. It irked George that the earl performed the entire rhyme that they'd created, leaving her out.

Regardless, he quickly knew the answer and rose.

"Beauty is in the eye of the beholder," he calmly said, his gaze locked upon Sam.

She nodded. "His Grace is correct."

"I believe with that point, His Grace and Lady Boyston are our winners," declared Phoebe.

"What is their prize?" asked Lady Henrietta. "Some sweet?"

"No," the duchess said, retrieving the sterling silver bowl they'd drawn from. "The bowl is the prize."

George escorted Lady Boyston to the front and Phoebe handed over the bowl, which he gave to his partner.

"Lady Boyston deserves this far more than I. She is much better at creating rhymes. I'm sure she already has the perfect place for it."

"You are too generous, Your Grace." Her eyes glowed. "But I do have a wonderful spot for this. My roses will look lovely in this bowl."

Everyone laughed and applauded their win as they returned to their seats.

Samantha was the first to speak. "I congratulate you on your win, Lady Boyston. And you, George, for so graciously giving your teammate the prize."

He thanked her, avoiding glancing at Baywell, whose sour expression made him look as if someone had pinched him.

"I suppose it's time to turn in for the night," Lady Boyston said. "Are you heading to your room, my lady?"

"Yes, I'll go with you."

Everyone in the drawing room began embarking toward their guest rooms. George found Briggs awaiting him.

"Have a good day with all the grand company, Your Grace?"

"Yes. I won at charades."

"I wouldn't expect anything less. You're very witty, Your Grace," the valet said, taking off his master's Hessians.

George let himself be stripped of his finery and dressed for bed. He dismissed Briggs and went to stare out the window at the moon shining in the darkness. More than anything, he wanted to be with Sam now. He needed to find out what had happened to her in the years of her marriage and widowhood. She seemed so different now.

Yet he still wanted her.

He lay down but found he couldn't sleep. Country hours didn't suit him. No, that was the old George speaking. He just needed to get used to rising early and being in bed before midnight instead of arriving home before dawn broke the next day. If only Sam were here, he'd be happy to come to bed and stay there day and night.

Restless, he tossed back the bedclothes and stood. Perhaps a brandy would soothe him. With none in his room, he would have to go elsewhere to find a decanter. He fumbled about and found his banyan, slipping into it and tying the belt. He pushed his feet into his slippers and quietly left the room, moving down the dimly lit hallway and down a flight of stairs. He knew where the bottles were in the drawing room and so decided to go there. One quick drink and he'd go back to bed.

Opening the heavy door, he immediately heard music coming from far across the room. George closed the door and saw a figure sitting at the pianoforte.

It was Sam.

SAMANTHA ACCOMPANIED LADY Boyston from the drawing room. Lady Elizabeth fell into step with them and they discussed taking a ride after breakfast tomorrow morning. Though she hadn't been riding in ages, she had borrowed one of Phoebe's habits and was eager to get back on a horse. They decided to meet for breakfast at nine, already dressed in their riding clothes, and proceed to the stables after their morning meal.

She went to Phoebe's bedchamber and saw Lucy dozing in a chair. The maid awoke with a start.

"I'm sorry, my lady." She jumped to her feet and began fussing over Samantha, removing her evening gown and remaining layers and helping her mistress into her night rail and dressing gown.

"Let me unpin your hair," the maid said.

Samantha sat at the dressing table and closed her eyes as Lucy took down her hair and brushed it.

"Shall I braid it?"

"No. I may later. Go to bed, Lucy," she urged. "I will see you in the morning. I'll be riding immediately after breakfast so I'll dress in my habit."

"Very good, my lady. I will see you tomorrow morning."

After the servant left, Samantha continued sitting at the dressing table, pulling the brush through her long hair. She studied herself in the mirror. The woman staring back looked a bit tired. She needed to get some rest but knew sleep would evade her because she had too much on her mind.

More than anything, she itched to go back downstairs and play the pianoforte. As Lady Henrietta played and sang tonight, Samantha realized how much she had missed music in her life. Even during her long exile, she hadn't sung to pass the time, knowing how displeased Lady Rockaway would have been if she'd heard singing. Now, all she wanted to do was sing and dance and play and make merry. It was as if she'd been in a cocoon all those years at Rockwell and now she emerged as a butterfly, wanting to spread her wings and fly to the sun.

With George.

No, she couldn't have George. She'd already made love with him once and he was acting as if she were just another possession. He would want to marry her and tell her what to do and keep her from being the person she was meant to be. She would have to speak to him tomorrow and let him know nothing further could happen between them.

Even though her thoughts had been consumed with him. With his kiss. The way his hands skimmed her body. The electricity that existed between them. The way he'd awakened desire in her for the first time.

Samantha rose and took the candle in hand. Everyone would be in their beds by now. No one would be in the drawing room. She could go and play with no one any the wiser.

She padded down the carpeted hallway in her bare feet, silence surrounding her. The doors to the drawing room were closed. She pushed one open and closed it behind her, crossing the room with only the light from her single candle lighting the way. She placed it atop the pianoforte and sat on the bench. How familiar it felt to be sitting in a place she had loved for so long. Playing had allowed her to escape to other worlds. It had brought her such joy.

She vowed from this day forward, she would play every day.

Gently, she raised the cover, exposing the ivory keys. Her fingers caressed them lovingly. She thought about what to play first and then began.

Minutes later, frustration bubbled over. She'd struck wrong notes repeatedly, her lack of practice obvious. She started up several times and finally stopped, blowing out an angry breath. Before, tears would have come. No longer. The wells where they came from had dried up long ago.

"I *will* do this," she muttered, raising her hands again.

"You can do anything you want," a familiar voice said.

Samantha froze. She looked up and saw a silhouetted figure nearby.

"Hello, George," she said calmly, though her heart raced at the sight of him. "I didn't think anyone would be here at this time of night. If I had thought someone would come in, I never would have bothered to try playing."

She closed the cover. He came and sat on the bench next to her. His familiar scent and the heat radiating from his body enveloped her.

"Remember when I used to sit and turn the pages for you when you played?" he asked.

The thought brought an ache within her. "That was a long time ago. As you can tell, I'm sorely out of practice. I thought I wanted to play but it appears I've lost it. It was a mistake to think I could pick it up again."

"You may not have practiced for many years but I think it would easily come back to you. Don't give up on it."

His arm slid around her waist and she wanted to let her head fall to his shoulder. She refrained from doing so. She couldn't encourage him.

Instead, she stood and moved away from him, breaking the contact between them.

"No. Music was a part of my life long ago. It might take years to regain whatever talent I had. I have better things to do with my time."

Good God. She sounded like Lady Rockaway. The thought made her want to vomit.

George came and stood in front of her. He gently took her chin in his fingers and raised it so their gazes met.

"You played better than anyone I knew, Samantha. Your playing brought joy to others. It was obvious it also made you happy. Don't give up. You might not want to practice with so many in attendance at Windowmere, but you can keep playing once you leave here."

"I may," she said begrudgingly, not wanting Lady Rockaway to keep haunting her—or keep her from playing.

His hand cradled her cheek. "That's better. You're not someone to give up when you want something." He paused. "Neither am I."

His head bent and she knew any minute now their lips would touch. Though she craved it, she wouldn't allow it. She turned her head and they grazed her cheek. She stepped away.

"George, I can't do this with you."

"Do what?" he asked. "What's wrong, Samantha? You know you can tell me. I'm one of your oldest friends. I know I wasn't much of one the past few years but that's behind us now. I want to be your friend. I want you to confide in me what's made you change so. I—"

She turned away, immediately regretting that she lost his touch by doing so. "I *have* changed. That's what you don't understand. I finally grew up and saw what the world was like. I'm not that idealistic young girl you knew, George. There's a darkness inside me now."

"I don't believe that," he said. "Not for one minute."

His hands fastened on her waist and he jerked her to him. Her breath caught.

"I don't know if your husband ignored you or mistreated you or what. That part of your life is over now. He's gone. You're no longer with his people. You are with those who love you." He gazed into her eyes and she saw sincerity shining in his. "I love you, Samantha. When my feelings for you grew years ago, I shoved you away. That was a dreadful mistake. It pushed you into Haskett's arms and saddled me with Frederica for a short while.

"That's over now. They're gone. We're here. Yes, we both are different people but what I feel for you, I've never felt for anyone else. Let me love you, Samantha. Let me be with you. Let me learn who you are and who you want to be."

She stared up at him wordlessly. With a heavy heart, she said, "No. I cannot hurt you, George. I don't feel the same as you do. You are looking for a wife. I never wish to be one again. If you were still the Duke of Charm, I would happily engage in a quick affair with you and, afterward, we could both move on. You are different, though. It's because of that—"

His mouth seized hers, silencing her.

Chapter Nineteen

George didn't accept that Sam had no feelings for him, much less that she didn't want to ever wed again. He didn't have the words to charm her into admitting so. Instead, he would show her not only how much he loved her but her response would reveal to her that she did care about him. She might not love him yet but he knew that she could. His heart told him that they were soulmates, destined to be together in this life and the one beyond.

She opened her mouth to protest and he took the opportunity given him, sliding his tongue inside her mouth and stroking hers. His hands tightened on her waist, making sure she wasn't going anywhere. He shouldn't have worried. Her hands immediately went to his chest, caressing it. One slipped inside his banyan, finding bare flesh. He shivered at her touch.

George scooped Sam up and moved to the nearest chair without breaking their kiss. He settled her in his lap, her hands sliding around his neck, her fingers pushing into his hair. Satisfied she wasn't going anywhere, he gentled the kiss and broke it. Before she could speak, he began kissing her softly, not wanting to rush things. He kissed her for some minutes with only his lips, his fingers stroking her cheek and running through her unbound hair. He moved up her nose to her brow, kissing it and then her eyelids before sliding along her cheek to her jaw. Pressing soft kisses along it, he inhaled the scent of orange blossoms wafting from her skin as it heated.

His lips trailed lower and nuzzled her neck, then his tongue found her beating pulse and circled it lazily. Sam's quick intake of breath pleased him, as did her fingers still tangled in his hair. He nipped at her throat in soft love bites, thrilling as the sound of her whimpers escaped. He went back to her mouth and traced the outline of her lips several times with his tongue. Her hands now fisted in his hair and she opened to him.

They kissed for a long time, each one deeper and filled with emotion. He stroked her hair and her back but reined in his hands from other things they wanted to do to her. He wanted her to trust him. He needed her to open up to him about whatever secret from her past was buried. She might not tell him tonight—but she would tell him. Only then could he see how to help her heal.

The distant chiming of a clock sounded and he finally broke the kiss. Sam lay her head on his shoulder, curled in his arms. They sat without speaking. He would stay here all night this way if she would let them. The feel of her in his arms was how it was meant to be. Contentment poured through him. He wanted to spend every night this way.

They sat until the clock chimed the hour. Sam lifted her head and her hands cradled his face. She gave him a sweet, lingering kiss and then made to get up. George rose and placed her on her feet but kept his arms around her.

"You are a very good man, George," she said softly. "I'm sorry Frederica hurt you so. You're over that hurt now, though. You're the George I once knew. My friend."

"I want to be the man I know I can be. For me—and for you."

She shook her head sadly. "You must be who you want to be for you and you alone, George. The Duke of Colebourne will be kind to his tenants. A gentleman who marries and begets a large family with a wonderful woman who will love and treasure him." She paused. "I am not that woman, George. I will never be that woman."

Her words were as a slap in the face.

"Why?" he demanded. "I see how you respond to my kiss, Sam. I know you have feelings for me. They may not be love but I know they will grow into it. Our bodies fit together as if they were made to do so. I want you by my side, Sam. I want you as the mother of my children. No other woman will do."

Her mouth grew hard. "And I've told you I don't want children and never wish to wed again. It's a stalemate, George. Just as we used to come to years ago when we played chess against one another. You want to be a respectable duke with a wife and children. I want to be a merry widow who engages in brief but satisfying affairs."

"That's not you," he protested.

"It is," she said emphatically. "I appreciate how you have awakened within me a desire to make love. It is a sweet gift that I will always cherish. I plan to do what other widows of the *ton* do, though. Or actually what many wives do once they've provided their husbands with an heir and a spare. I am going to take as many lovers as I want. I want to enjoy myself thoroughly. I will neither be bound nor beholden to any man ever again," she said fiercely.

Sam pushed her hands against his chest as she stepped back, breaking contact with him.

"That won't make you happy. I know you. It won't."

She smiled sadly. "The girl I once was wouldn't have been happy under those circumstances. The woman I have become accepts and embraces it. I *will* be happy, George. Because I will be doing what I want to do. I don't want to hurt you. You mean too much to me. That is why I will ask you to make your excuses to the Windhams and leave the house party. You don't need to see me flirt with other men under your very nose. I plan to do more than flirt. I will take them to my bed."

"No. You won't," he told her, determination swelling within him.

She looked at him in exasperation. "George, you don't have any say over what I do. I'm not some puppet you can control."

He heard the underlying bitterness in her words. He couldn't lose her.

"Then I accept you on your terms."

Confusion filled her face. "I don't understand."

"You don't wish to wed me but you *will* have an affair with me," he said bluntly. "We will do so until you tire of me. You may flirt with as many men as you like during this house party but I am the one who will be in your bed every night until it is over. Give me that much of you, Sam." He paused and added what he thought might tempt her. "I have much to teach you about your body. How you and others can pleasure it. No obligation on either one of us. Just a casual but imminently satisfying affair—and then we can go our separate ways."

Doubt filled her eyes. "I don't know."

"The party only goes for another week," he said smoothly. "Actually, slightly less than that. Let me warm your bed for the next five nights," he offered and then gave her a blinding smile. "I promise . . . you won't regret it."

George watched her mull it over as Sam chewed on her bottom lip.

"No commitments beyond this week at Windowmere?" she asked warily.

"None." He gave her a devilish smile. "Other than to making each night memorable."

He held his breath, hoping she would take the bait. He needed to show her they couldn't live without one another. Convince her that she wasn't the woman she said she'd become. His Sam was still buried somewhere within this hard, brittle woman.

He would do whatever it took to call her out.

"All right," she agreed. "Haskett was miserable in our marriage bed. He made me feel like a failure. I will learn from you what I can. But I still intend to flirt with the other eligible men present. I am as sorely out of practice doing that as I am in playing the pianoforte."

George gave her a charming smile. "Flirt all you like, my lady. As long as I am the one in your bed when the day comes to an end."

"For only this week," Samantha said.

"For only this week." He paused. "Are you ready to begin?"

SAMANTHA HAD WANTED to cut all ties with George. Spare him from watching her reel in other men.

But his offer proved far too tempting to turn down.

He may not want to be known as the Duke of Charm in the future but he was all charm and smiles now, persuading her to embark on a clandestine affair with him during the remainder of the house party. She thought of his hands caressing her body. His mouth on hers. How could she say no to such an offer?

She doubted he meant what he said, even if he had pursued nothing but casual affairs for the last several years. He'd told her he loved her. She shouldn't give in. She should push him away and run as fast as she could. She couldn't, though.

Because she loved him, too.

And this would be the only time they would ever come together. In the end, she would move on. He would hate her for it. She would hate herself for giving in and spending the next week with him. But when faced with a choice, she would choose George every time. Even if this was the only time they would have together. She would make the most of it. Build a treasure trove of memories that would see her through until her days came to an end.

She gave him a coy look. "I am always ready, Your Grace. Are you ready for me?"

He gave her a wide smile and enfolded her in his arms, his strength and warmth surrounding her. His mouth came down on hers, hard and possessive. Samantha reveled in it. The kiss went on and on, causing her bones to melt. She leaned into him, knowing she would want each night to go on and on.

She was the one who broke the kiss. "I'm ready for you in my bed. Come."

Samantha took his hand and led him from the drawing room to the bedchamber Phoebe had loaned her.

"Our bargain must include you leaving before my maid comes every morning," she said. "Other than that, I am yours."

Oh, how she wished she could be his forever.

George's fingers nimbly undid the knot of her dressing gown. She supposed he had much experience doing so and forced the thought from her mind. While they were together, she wouldn't think about all the other women he'd been with and made love to over the years. She would live in the moment and relish whatever passed between them.

He parted the dressing gown and pushed it from her shoulders. It fell to the ground. His eyes roamed over her body and she saw satisfaction in them. He bent and his fingers captured the hem of her night rail, pulling it up and over her head quickly before he tossed it aside. Again, his eyes studied her.

"Such perfection," he murmured and then tossed aside his banyan.

He was bare now except for his slippers. She knelt and took them off and he clasped her elbows, helping her to rise. They embraced and kissed for a long time, his hands running up and down her back and finally cupping her buttocks, kneading them. As before, her core began a fierce drumming, knowing his fingers would soon pay attention to it.

George broke the kiss and wordlessly led her to the bed. Samantha lay down and he climbed next to her and kissed her. Thus began the long descent down her body, his lips and tongue lovingly covering from her mouth to beyond her belly. His tongue glided lower and she panicked a moment, thinking it might continue to her core. The thought enticed her.

He came to his knees and turned her until she lay diagonally across the bed. Then he clasped her ankles and pushed on them until her feet were flat on the mattress, resting just below her buttocks. Samantha felt exposed and a bit frightened—but she knew George would take care of her.

"Are you throbbing for me?" he asked, a wicked smile on his face as his thumbs began rubbing her ankles.

"You know I am," she said playfully, trying not to show her fear. "I did before. Your fingers took care of me, though. I have no doubt they will again."

His eyebrows arched. "You think only my fingers can satisfy you, Sam? It's time for your first lesson to begin."

Still holding her ankles, he moved his head between her legs. She stiffened, unsure of what he would do. Then his tongue licked along the seam of her sex and she almost shot off the bed, the only thing keeping her there his grasp on her ankles.

"George!" she cried, her head coming up.

He looked up, their gazes meeting. "Yes, Sam?"

She found herself breathing heavily. "Do that again," she said, not believing those words came out of her mouth.

"With pleasure, my lady."

He did it again and she moaned. He released her ankles and slowly moved his fingers along her calves and up to her thighs, where he parted her legs further. She fell somewhere between mortified and embarrassed, knowing what was exposed, but she kept her mouth closed. His fingers parted her and his tongue danced along, making the drumbeat rage out of control. Then as his fingers had done, his tongue did the same, coming in and out of her. Soon, she was writhing on the bed, making sounds that surprised her as she gripped his hair and pulled him closer to her.

George feasted on her as if she were a fine meal. She whimpered, begging him for release as he continued to taste and suck and nip at her. The feeling built and built as before, only wilder, and then it came in a rush, sweeping her away. She cried out his name and bucked and moaned as she rode wave after wave that went on until she almost screamed.

It finally subsided. George licked and kissed his way up her belly. Between the valley of her breasts. Along her throat. Then he reached her mouth and his tongue plunged inside just as it had her core. Samantha tasted herself and found it the most erotic thing she'd experienced.

They kissed and he caressed her curves, making her feel like a goddess. Then she felt something pressing against her and knew it was his cock. She opened her legs so he had better access and he thrust inside. Her arms were about his neck and they kissed deeply as he continued moving in and out of her. She picked up on his rhythm and began moving with and against him. The stirring within her built and she knew it would happen again.

George broke their kiss. "Take it, Sam. Take everything you've ever wanted. This climax is meant for you."

The heat and light filled her again and she felt her body spasm and move. She tightened around his cock, squeezing tightly as the waves of pleasure engulfed her. As her trembling subsided, he pulled away from her, once again spilling his seed against her belly. It rested warm atop her.

He kissed her and then left the bed, returning with a cloth and wiping her clean. Then he gathered her in his arms and brought her snuggly against him. Suddenly, she felt so very tired. He pressed his lips against her temple.

"Sleep, my darling."

Samantha allowed the dark abyss to swallow her up.

When she awoke, George was gone.

Chapter Twenty

SAMANTHA ALLOWED LUCY to dress her in her riding habit and went downstairs for breakfast. Lady Boyston was already there, sitting with Lady Burton. Samantha retrieved a plate from the buffet and, after filling it, joined the pair.

"I see you're dressed for riding," Lady Burton said. "I've never been overly fond of it."

"I grew up riding every day," she said. "I did very little of it during my marriage but I've found I missed it. I plan to ride as often as possible."

George sat next to her and she felt her heartbeat increase. "Samantha was a natural rider from the moment she was placed in the saddle."

"Have you known each other long?" Lady Burton asked.

He grinned. "I met her on the day she was born. Her brother and I are best friends. Our family estates lie next to one another."

"Weston and George allowed me to tag along with them," Samantha shared. "I learned how to ride, shoot, and swim, thanks to them."

"How interesting," Lady Boyston said. "I have no brothers and had to learn to ride from an instructor. Neither of my parents felt comfortable atop a horse."

"I think my brother was born riding," she said. "George, too. They were both wonderful teachers." She felt the color rise on her cheeks, thinking of other things George had taught her only last night.

"Are you riding after breakfast?" he asked.

"Lady Boyston, Lady Elizabeth, and I are," she replied carefully.

Baron Stilton and Lord Baywell placed their plates on the table and Stilton asked, "Would you care for some company?"

Lady Boyston said, "We'd be happy for you to come along, my lord." She looked to George. "Your Grace, you are also welcomed to join us."

George smiled. "I haven't been riding since I've been at Windowmere. I would love to do so, especially with three such lovely ladies."

Samantha braced herself inwardly. She would rather George have not agreed to go because she truly wanted to try out her flirting skills. It would be difficult doing so with him watching her every move. Still, he knew the bargain they'd struck and he would have to live with the consequences.

Lady Elizabeth joined them. "I've already eaten. I don't like much in the mornings so I had chocolate and toast points sent to my bedchamber. Are you ready?"

"Yes," Samantha said. "We've also gained a few others to accompany us."

All but Baywell went to the stables and suitable mounts were found for everyone. The earl arrived with a small cloth bag.

"I've brought biscuits for later, thanks to Cook. Riding always works up my appetite," he said, gazing at her. Samantha saw more than hunger for a sweet in his eyes.

They rode west and then eventually turned north. George was familiar with Windowmere because of his prior visits and was able to point out various things to them. He rode at the front with Lady Boyston, who proved to be an excellent horsewoman, while Samantha and Baywell brought up the rear. After an hour, they stopped at a scenic vista and Baywell distributed the biscuits, making sure she was the last served as he took her arm and led her away from the others.

"That was very thoughtful of you, my lord."

One eyebrow cocked up. "Bringing the biscuits or moving you away from the others so I could have you all to myself?"

"The biscuits, naturally," she replied coquettishly. "And I've told you I wish for us to be nothing more than friends."

"Then you shouldn't smile at me so. Your smile alone would tempt a monk to break his vows."

She chuckled. "I am certain *you* are no monk." Her words sounded flirtatious to her ears. While she had told the earl she wasn't interested, he was a decent kisser. Perhaps since he was taken with her, she should keep up their banter. It made for good practice. Fortunately, George was out of hearing range, though she sensed his eyes on them.

His eyes gleamed. "And my thought is that you're no nun, my lady."

She laughed. "I am far from being a pious good sister."

"Perhaps we could see more of the gardens this afternoon," he suggested. "We were interrupted before. I'm sure there are more plants and vegetation which I could point out to you."

She remembered what George had said to her and replied, "Would it be possible for me to see them with my eyes closed and your lips on mine?"

Baywell roared with laughter. "Oh, I do like you, my lady."

"If we have time, we might see a small portion of the gardens," she said primly.

"A small part may satisfy me for now. I hope we may see the entire gardens soon."

Samantha would allow a few kisses between them but she'd promised George he would be the only one in her bed this week. Perhaps when the Season came around next spring, she would extend her flirtation with Baywell. Until then, he would have to be satisfied with a few stolen kisses.

She turned and saw the others beginning to remount. Her gaze connected with George's and she saw mirth in his eyes.

"It looks as if everyone is ready to move on," she said. "We should join them."

"Or not."

Samantha ignored him and moved toward her horse. She allowed the earl to help her mount and then he swung into the saddle and the group continued their ride. When they returned to the stables, everyone thanked George for guiding them about the property. She saw Lady Boyston put her hand on George's forearm and a frisson of jealousy ran through her.

"Ridiculous," she murmured under her breath, knowing the woman would be an excellent match for him and angry that she resented seeing them together.

Her resentment grew as she saw George give the woman a charming smile and then laugh at something she said. Samantha turned toward the house and saw Elizabeth ahead of her. Before she could catch up with her friend, Baron Stilton spoke.

"Did you enjoy your ride, my lady?"

She calmed the tides raging within her and turned to him. "Very much, my lord. The Windhams are lucky to possess such a beautiful property. Where do you reside?"

His green eyes, filled with mischief, intrigued her. "I have a country estate in Surrey but I spend most of my time in London. I don't believe I've seen you during the Season."

"I haven't attended in several years. Not since shortly after my marriage."

"Oh." He frowned. "And will your husband be joining us sometime this week?"

"I am a widow," she said. "My husband has been dead several years now. I am ready to return to society and make new friends."

"Ah. I see. I hear His Grace will have archery and lawn tennis set up for us after luncheon. Would you care to play with me? Not to brag, but I am an expert at hitting a target. I'd be happy to teach you."

Samantha smiled at him. "That would be lovely, my lord. I look forward to it. For now, though, I must change from my riding habit."

"I'll look for you later," he promised, his eyes sparkling.

As she retreated to her bedchamber, she thought the baron had potential and wondered if he kissed as well as Baywell did. Perhaps he even kissed better than George. She didn't suppose that was possible. George had far more practice than most men of the *ton*. She also had some mystical connection with him, due to their long acquaintance, which made his kisses seem far better than those of other men. She would do well to remember that.

After changing, she returned to the drawing room and found Phoebe chatting with some of the female houseguests. She joined them until luncheon and, afterward, went outside to participate in the games set up. Immediately, she found Baron Stilton at one elbow and George at the other.

"Are you going to participate in archery?" George asked.

"Yes. Baron Stilton has promised to teach me his secrets on hitting a target."

George pursed his lips and Samantha knew he bit back a retort. George had been the one to teach her everything about archery years ago. Though she hadn't picked up a bow and arrow in ages, at one time she would have outshot most of those gathered here. She gave him a warning look and he merely shrugged.

Elizabeth came over. "I've never held a bow before," she exclaimed. "It looks as if it would be fun, though."

"The baron is already engaged to work with Samantha but I'd be happy to show you what I know, my lady," George said. "Here, Stilton, let's fetch some arrows and show these young ladies how it's done."

The pair retrieved a good number of arrows and two bows and brought them back to the women.

"Hold the bow thus," George modeled and handed his to Elizabeth.

The baron gave Samantha a bow and then stepped behind her, his body very close. So close she could smell the soap he had used at his bath.

"Let me guide the way you must hold your bow to achieve success, my lady."

His arms went about her and he helped her raise the bow, his hands atop hers as he demonstrated how to pull back and release. He did it several times. Samantha could have done what he showed her in her sleep.

Her attention was fixed on George and Elizabeth.

George did the same as the baron, stepping behind Elizabeth and showing her the proper way to hold the bow. He moved, taking her with him as he retrieved an arrow and slipped it against the bow. Envy rippled through Samantha. She wished it was George standing behind her, holding her in the circle of his arms as he guided her through the motions.

"Do you understand?" Stilton asked.

She realized he must have been speaking to her and replied, "Perfectly. It all makes sense the way you have put it."

"Let's try shooting a few arrows. I'm sure we'll hit the target."

The baron continued to hold her near and actually did all of the work in aiming and firing the arrow. As he predicted, it hit the center of the target.

"See? You are an excellent student, my lady," he praised.

"Oh, I think I have it!" Elizabeth exclaimed. "Shall we have a friendly little competition, Lady Samantha?"

"Certainly," she replied. Looking over her shoulder, she told Stilton, "I believe I can take it from here."

He stepped back. "May fortune smile upon you."

"Who should go first?" Elizabeth asked as George retreated several steps away.

"You issued the challenge," George told Elizabeth. "That means Samantha should go first. Shall we say best of three attempts? Or five?"

The baron spoke up. "I'd say three. Archery exercises and strains muscles delicate ladies aren't even aware they have. If you don't want to be too sore tomorrow, you'll limit your play this afternoon."

"Three it is," she said, picking up an arrow and resting it against her bow.

"Let me remove the arrows already fired," George said. As he raced to the target, he said over his shoulder, "Be careful, Samantha. I wouldn't want you to shoot me by mistake."

She lowered her bow and arrow, knowing if she wanted that she could hit him in the buttocks. That would show him for flirting with Elizabeth.

He pulled the arrows from the target and returned, standing a distance behind the two women.

"Remember what we talked about," Stilton reminded as Samantha raised her weapon again. "Locate where you want to shoot. Concentrate and aim carefully."

Exasperation filled her. She didn't need some silly man telling her what to do. If she wasn't so interested in seeing how the baron kissed, she would speak up and shoo him away. Instead, she focused on the target and released the arrow, which flew through the air and struck true.

"Excellent shot, my lady," praised Stilton. "You are a prized pupil."

"I'd say beginner's luck," George quipped, not looking at her when she turned to glare at him. "Go ahead, Lady Elizabeth. It's your turn."

Elizabeth loaded her arrow and lifted the bow, frowning deeply. She released her arrow and it flew through the air, landing on the lower third of the target.

"I hit it!" she declared. "I wasn't sure if I could or not."

Samantha realized that she shouldn't show any prowess, else the baron would think it was his tutelage that had led to her victory. She decided to boost the young woman's spirits by letting her win.

Stepping up once more, she chose an arrow and slipped it against the bow. She took her time and fired. The arrow struck what would be ten on a clockface, barely on the target.

"At least I've hit the target twice," she joked, "if not the bullseye."

Elizabeth stepped up and repeated the actions, this time striking close to the center. She squealed with joy. "See if you can match that, my lady," she challenged.

Samantha planned for her next shot to go wide. She lined up and aimed. The arrow whizzed by, missing the target entirely.

Attempting to look dejected, she turned. "I suppose it was beginner's luck. Let's see if you can beat me, Lady Elizabeth."

"She can," George assured them. "Take your time, my lady. Aim for the target and see in your mind's eye where you wish your arrowhead to go."

She watched the young woman follow George's instructions. When the arrow sailed through the air, it landed true, in the dead center, besting Samantha's first shot.

"I won!" Elizabeth cried. She turned and hugged George.

Samantha turned away, not wanting to see them together.

The baron stepped near her. "Don't be discouraged. Archery takes practice. Perhaps you will be better at lawn tennis."

She smiled. "I'm sure I will—if you promise to work with me."

Stilton caught her flirtatious tone and returned her smile. "Let's find you a racket."

She allowed him to show her how to hold the racket, even placing her fingers the wrong way so he would correct them. Again, he stood behind her and showed her different strokes, his body pressed against hers as he emphasized the importance of following through. After a while, she told him she was ready to play. He went opposite her.

"I'll go easy on you," he promised and sent the ball toward her.

Swinging with ease, she returned it and hid her grin at his surprise as it whizzed past him. He claimed the ball and sent it her way again. They continued volleying for some minutes. Others even stopped to watch and cheered them on, particularly the assembled females.

"Show him ladies can do it!" Phoebe cried.

"Keep it going," called Jon, taking her side over Stilton's.

She noticed her partner began sending the ball harder and faster toward her. Samantha returned every shot with glee. Then she began toying with him, knocking it so he had to run to hit it. Finally, she finished him off amidst cheers.

The baron came toward her. "I do believe you have played lawn tennis before, my lady," he said graciously.

"I have," she admitted and then quietly said, "but I certainly enjoyed you showing me how to hold my racket."

"Indeed." He looked pleased. "Perhaps I can retrieve a bit of lemonade for us and we can discuss our match as we stroll."

"An excellent idea, my lord."

Once again, she saw George noting the friendly banter between her and Stilton. He inclined his head to her and then turned to talk with Andrew.

Stilton returned with cups of lemonade and offered her his arm. They walked across the lawn and around the house, moving to the front, idly chatting about inconsequential things. He led her into a grove of trees that lined the lane leading up to Windowmere. When they were out of sight, he stopped and took the cup from her, tossing both of them aside.

His arms went around her. "Are you a minx, my lady?" he asked in a sly tone.

"I resent that implication," she said stiffly. "I'm no trollop, Lord Stilton."

"But you *are* a widow. The widows I am acquainted with in the *ton* are more than willing to play."

"It's true that I am a widow. What do you mean?"

"I thought it would mean you are amenable to kissing me," he said. "In fact, I recommend you do so."

"Why?" she asked boldly, not liking how overconfident he was.

"I think we would both enjoy it."

He pulled her closer. His mouth descended on hers. There was no teasing or getting to know one another. His kiss was insistent from the beginning. He forced his tongue into her mouth. Samantha let him do all the work. He was skilled but, as before with Lord Baywell, she felt absolutely nothing.

What if George had ruined her for any other man?

The baron sucked on her tongue and then stroked it with his. She found his kisses far too slobbery for her liking. She turned her head, breaking the kiss.

"Thank you, Lord Stilton."

He frowned. "Thank you? That's all I get? Especially after you embarrassed me in front of all of those guests? You are the one who has flirted ceaselessly with me. I'll decide when we're through."

His hands tightened on her. Panic filled her. He was much larger than she was. The only thing she could do is stand her ground and hope he would be gentleman enough to respect her wishes.

"No, I want to stop," she said firmly. "You have had your kiss. That is enough."

His eyes turned hard. "It's far from enough. Whether you know it or not, you want more. I'm ready to give it to you."

"I do *not* want more, sir," she said, enunciating her words carefully. "I expect you to behave as a gentleman would and release me. Now."

"Or what?" His eyes narrowed. His gripped tightened until she couldn't breathe.

"Or you will have me to deal with."

Samantha glanced over her shoulder, sagging in relief.

George stood there, anger darkening his handsome face.

Chapter Twenty-One

George hadn't liked Stilton when they were at school. He was surprised when the baron had turned up as a guest for the house party. George had thought Stilton to be somewhat of a bully. He watched carefully as the baron escorted Sam away from the others.

"Andrew, why did you invite Stilton to Windowmere?"

"Phoebe asked me to. Or rather her brother-in-law wished him to be here."

"Viscount Burton is friends with Stilton?"

"Not exactly friends. They've had some business dealings together. He was at Burton's estate shortly before they were to leave to come to Windowmere. Burton must have mentioned where he and Lady Burton were going once their business concluded and Stilton said he was eager to renew his acquaintance with me. Phoebe received a note asking if we minded Stilton being invited. Since I doubted Weston would show up, I didn't think it would hurt to have another bachelor here for the week."

"I don't like him," George said flatly.

"I never have either though he hasn't given me any reason not to since we've become adults. I've seen him at White's occasionally and we've spoken briefly."

"He won't like that Sam beat him in lawn tennis," he pointed out.

Andrew grew thoughtful. "No. He won't."

George looked around and saw Stilton and Sam turning the corner, falling out of view.

"I'll go after them. Stay here with your guests."

He moved across the lawn. Lady Boyston stopped him for a moment and asked for help. Her bracelet had become entangled with the strings in her racket. He undid the clasp and removed it from her wrist and then worked it loose.

"Oh, thank you, Your Grace," she said, giving him an encouraging smile.

"I am happy to be of assistance," he replied. "Please, excuse me."

As he rounded the house, he thought how much he liked Lady Boyston. The old George wouldn't have. He would have thought her far too clever and only moderately attractive. If he hadn't been interested in winning Sam, though, he would very much like to pursue Lady Boyston. He hoped she would pair with another of Andrew and Phoebe's guests.

Glancing about, he saw no one in sight. Stilton must have led them into the trees, out of sight, seeking a kiss. Or more.

He glanced at the dirt in the lane and saw two sets of footprints and followed them until they veered into the grass. From there, he moved straight toward the trees, hoping he would find Sam soon. George didn't want to spy on her but he certainly didn't trust Stilton.

Then he caught sight of them. They were kissing—until Sam turned her head and they had words. He could tell Stilton wasn't pleased with the kiss ending. He looked to be holding Sam possessively, almost against her will.

George rushed toward them and caught Sam's words.

"I expect you to behave as a gentleman would and release me. Now."

"Or what?" the baron asked, causing George's anger to bloom.

"Or you will have me to deal with," he said, his eyes locked on Stilton's. He knew Sam looked at him but he avoided her gaze. "Release her immediately."

The baron did so reluctantly and Sam stepped away. "It was nothing, Your Grace. A mere misunderstanding."

"Understand this," he said, his gaze directed at Stilton. "You will return to the house and have your valet pack your things. Then you will find the Windhams and apologize profusely as you tell them a messenger arrived with news. You must leave at once in order to settle an urgent business matter."

"See here—"

"I did see what occurred, Stilton. Lady Samantha kissed you and you pressed for more. She didn't agree and you would have forced her hand. Forced yourself on her." He paused. "And I won't allow that to happen."

The baron's face grew red. "You think—"

"I don't think. I know that you were a bully at school and you haven't changed your ways. You've gone from bullying younger boys to ladies. If you don't wish me to issue a challenge to you, you will drop the matter and do as I suggest." George paused. "And may I remind you that I'm an excellent shot, Stilton. By the way, so is this woman. I taught her to shoot myself—and she doesn't miss. Perhaps I should give her the chance to teach you a lesson."

His words hung in the air.

The baron's face grew red. "Good day," he ground out, storming off without a backward glance.

George turned and watched until he disappeared from sight. Then he looked back to Sam. She chewed nervously on her bottom lip.

"I suppose you think I deserved that. For flirting with him," she said.

"No woman deserves to be ill-treated. Least of all you," he said softly.

He held his arms open and she came to him. He enfolded her, holding her close. He thought she would cry or even tear up but she remained stoic—though she did rest her head against his chest.

"I knew Stilton at school. He wasn't nice as a boy and hasn't changed as a man. Not everyone you flirt with will be so."

"I suppose I'm not a good judge of character. I married Haskett, after all."

He heard the bitterness hidden in her words. "Did he mistreat you?"

"Worse. I've told you how he ignored me. He was under his mother's thumb and was paralyzed unless she told him what to do. I had sought a friend. A companion I could talk over anything with, as well as a lover. Once we returned to Rockwell, he had little to do with me, before and after I lost the babe. Lady Rockaway tried to place me under her thumb, as well."

"I'm sure you didn't let her. You've got too much spirit for that."

Sam stilled in his arms. He noted the subtle shift. She pushed away and gave him a bright smile.

"At least I determined by Stilton's kiss that I did not want him in my bed. That's why he was so upset. Baywell is a much better kisser."

"Will you invite the earl to your bed after you leave Windowmere?" he asked carefully, afraid of her answer.

"I hadn't thought to. I won't see him again until next Season. I'll see if I've changed my mind by then. Hopefully, being in town, I'll have many more prospects."

He offered her his arm. "May I escort you back to the house?"

She took it. "Frankly, I think I'd like to play a little more lawn tennis if you're up for it." Her aquamarine eyes gleamed at him. "Or archery. And this time, I won't hold back."

SAMANTHA CURTAILED HER flirting after that. While she was cordial to all of the male houseguests and participated in the various activities Phoebe had planned for the group, she spent the rest of her time in the company of the females. Not only did her friendship with Phoebe deepen, but she found herself becoming firm friends with Elizabeth and Phoebe's sister, Letty, so much that both women issued invitations for her to visit them in their homes once the house party ended. She had no firms plans other than to return to Treadwell Manor once she left Windowmere and decided she would take up both women on their offers at some point.

She needed to go into town for the final fitting of the gowns she'd ordered from Mrs. Echols and Phoebe, Letty, and Elizabeth all accompanied her into Exeter. Letty and Elizabeth went next door to look at gloves and hats while she and Phoebe went to the dressmaker's shop. Mrs. Echols welcomed them warmly.

"I have all of your gowns completed, my lady. I hope you'll be pleased with my efforts."

"I cannot wait to see them," Samantha said. "Might Her Grace come back with me to see the final fittings?"

"Certainly," the dressmaker responded.

Every gown fit her perfectly, with no adjustments required. It pleased her to have some new gowns of her own, including a new riding habit. She would return Phoebe's once they arrived at Windowmere.

Mrs. Echols placed each gown in its own box and Samantha realized she would need to purchase a trunk to bring them and the gowns Phoebe had given her back to Treadwell Manor. She mentioned this to her friend.

"Oh, don't worry. I'm sure we have countless trunks at Windowmere and you are welcome to have one."

She looked at her friend. "Phoebe, you look a bit pale."

"No, I am fine. Let's go see what the others have bought."

Phoebe motioned to the footman as they left Mrs. Echol's shop and instructed him to bring the boxes to the carriage. They went to the milliner's and found both women had purchased two hats each.

"I believe you can never have enough hats," Letty proclaimed, showing off one of her purchases. "Burton will love me in this one."

"Burton would love you hatless," Phoebe proclaimed and the others chuckled, knowing how the viscount doted on his wife.

They returned to the carriage and arrived at Windowmere. Elizabeth and Letty both said they had letters to write and excused themselves.

Phoebe asked, "May I accompany you to your rooms?"

"Of course," Samantha replied, still worried about how wan Phoebe looked.

The footman brought up all the boxes containing the new gowns and Lucy began opening them, ooh-ing and aah-ing over how they had turned out.

"Shall we go to the sitting room?" Phoebe suggested and Samantha followed her friend there, noting Phoebe closed the door behind them before they went to sit by the window.

"I love this view," Phoebe said. "Windowmere is a lovely place to live."

"You and Andrew will have to come to Treadwell Manor once I've settled in. I'd love to have your company. The place hasn't had a woman's touch in many years. I'm thinking I'll need to make a few changes. I'm sure Weston won't mind. He's rarely there."

"I hope he will return to your home and stay a bit. I know you must have missed him."

"I have. Dreadfully," she admitted. "Yet I still am holding on to a bit of anger."

"You wanted your brother to rescue you from Rockwell."

"Yes. I knew it wasn't possible and yet I watched out the window every day, hoping he would make a surprise visit and learn of my circumstances. It was an unrealistic expectation on my part. We'd already drifted apart after my marriage and his broken engagement."

"Still, you wanted your big brother to save you."

Samantha nodded. "I did. And when that didn't happen, I had to save myself."

Phoebe reached out and took Samantha's hand. "You were very brave to have taken action in order to free yourself from such abominable circumstances."

"I have learned to depend only upon myself," she said firmly.

"What about George?" Phoebe asked.

"What about him?"

"He loves you. It's obvious."

She sighed. "He's told me as much. But I don't want to marry him. I want to be his friend and neighbor. No more than that."

"What about his late night visits?"

She gasped. "You know about those?"

Phoebe nodded. "Andrew saw George slip into your chamber a few nights ago."

"Blast!"

"I like George," Phoebe said. "I think he would be good for you. And you for him."

"George is charming," she admitted. "We've enjoyed our time together. I've told him, though, that it ends once the house party is over."

Suddenly, Phoebe's hand flew to her mouth. She stood quickly and dashed to the bedchamber, where she vomited in the chamber pot. Samantha dampened a cloth and brought it to her. Phoebe dabbed her mouth.

"I'm sorry. It came on quickly."

"Come, lie down," Samantha took Phoebe's hand and started to lead her to the bed. "I'll get Andrew. He can summon the doctor."

Phoebe resisted. "No, I'll sit."

They returned to where they'd been conversing and Phoebe said, "I'm with child so this is considered perfectly normal."

"Oh! That is marvelous news," Samantha said. "Does Andrew

know?"

"I told him last night. He is thrilled beyond words. We hope we will be blessed with several children."

Samantha took Phoebe's hand. "You will make wonderful parents."

"We have talked about making you and George the godparents. Would you consider it?" Phoebe asked.

She'd known she would be thrown together with George. They did live side-by-side and had many of the same friends. This would keep them in contact. Yet she couldn't say no, not after the great kindness Phoebe and Andrew had shown her.

"I'd be delighted to be godmother to your child," she declared. "Hopefully, I'll be Aunt Samantha to the baby."

"Thank you for accepting. For now, though, would you wait before speaking about it? It's still early and we know things can go wrong."

"I will keep quiet," Samantha promised. "What does Letty think of Basil having a cousin?"

Phoebe laughed. "I haven't told her yet. Letty isn't one to keep a secret, especially one of this kind. I will wait until she and Burton are climbing into their carriage to return home before I share with her our good news."

"Does George know?"

"I haven't told him. I don't know if Andrew has or not."

"I won't say a word to him—or anyone."

That night, George came to her bed. It would be the next to last time they would share it. Samantha had come to the realization that she didn't want to take lovers once she arrived in London next spring for the Season. None of them would be as considerate or skilled as George. Her heart warred with her mind, part of her wanting to make things more permanent with him and the other fighting against being bound to a man, whether by law or informally.

George slipped into her room without knocking and came to her as she gazed out the window, wrapping his arms around her and tenderly kissing her neck.

"Andrew and Phoebe know you've been visiting me," she told him.

"How?"

"Andrew saw you sneak into my chamber."

She felt his shrug. "They won't say anything to anyone else." He turned her to face him. "I have a few things to show you tonight, my lady. Things I think you will enjoy."

With that, he kissed her. She allowed all thoughts to flee as she gave in to the kiss.

Every time they came together, George did something to surprise her. He was a generous, thoughtful lover, always making sure she reached satisfaction. Tonight was no different.

"You can be rather bossy at times," he teased as he undressed her and swept her into his arms, carrying her to the bed. "I want you to be totally in control tonight."

She had no idea what he referred to—but quickly learned. Once they had touched one another, their caresses bringing them to a frenzy, George lay on his back and lifted her until she was atop him. Slowly, he brought her down, her body taking in his manhood.

"You are on top. You set the rhythm, my darling. Do whatever you wish."

Samantha found being in a position of power to her liking. It also allowed him to rest deep within her. She experimented, moving different ways and finding what they both liked. He brought her to her climax and then lifted her off him, turning away and rising from the bed to spill his seed in a handkerchief he withdrew from his banyan. She collapsed against the pillows, her breathing quick and uneven.

He returned and slipped his arms around her, her back pressing against his front. He kissed her hair.

"Go to sleep," he urged.

She found herself drifting off, secure in his arms.

And woke up screaming.

Chapter Twenty-Two

GEORGE BREATHED IN Sam's essence as she slept in his arms. He'd had plenty of warm women nestle against him but this would be the last one. Never again would the Duke of Charm run rampant among the boudoirs of London's ladies. He only wanted Sam, this amazing woman full of passion and compassion.

He only had one more night to convince her that they belonged together.

He'd noticed her change in behavior after the incident with Stilton. While Sam had remained friendly to all, she'd spent more time with the women houseguests. He didn't think she was afraid of the other men present, but perhaps she was more wary now in how she approached them. He'd noticed Baywell had halted his dogged pursuit of Sam and had turned his attention to other women present.

Did that mean she was forsaking other men and had decided to choose him?

George didn't know. He was afraid to ask her. Afraid of upsetting the delicate balance between them. By day, they were friendly toward one another. He'd been a part of the group that had gone riding several times and they'd even ridden next to one another twice. They'd partnered in several card games, usually winning. He'd even sat beside her one evening while a few of the ladies entertained in song.

At night, though, they had come together with an explosive passion unlike any he'd ever known. Making love with Sam had become an earthshattering, soul-bending experience. He didn't think he could live without her. It was as if she were the essence of life. She was the food for his soul. Together, sheltering in one another's arms, he was complete.

But was she?

He still longed to know whatever secrets she held close. She had shared with him how her husband was distant. That he didn't see her as a companion and had rarely come to her bed. She'd even mentioned her mother-in-law being overbearing. He could see where that had been difficult but it shouldn't have changed her fundamentally, as he suspected something had. Both Andrew and Phoebe had warned him she was in a fragile state of mind. Even Sam herself had not hinted at but rather came out and told him of a darkness within her. He wanted to soothe her. Steer her away from whatever troubled her and bring her into the light. He wanted to love her, now and for all time.

If she'd let him.

He wished he could wake her again and make love to her but she needed some sleep. Easing his arms away, he retreated from the bed and slipped into his banyan, belting it and then leaning over, dropping a kiss on her brow. George rose and simply gazed upon her. Love for this woman washed over him anew. Somehow, he had to convince her to be his. He was bright and creative. He would find the solution.

As he crossed the room, a sudden scream pierced the air. He wheeled and raced back to the bed. Sam was still asleep but her face was contorted in terror. As her scream died, he sat on the bed and grabbed her by the shoulders, raising her and shaking her. Her mouth opened to scream again and he kissed her to silence her, worried that others would rush in and find them together.

Sam began struggling, trying to push him away. His arms fastened about her, trying to show her she was safe. He continued to keep his mouth on hers and realized the moment she fully awoke. He waited a beat and then lifted his lips, hovering just above hers.

"You're all right. Nothing can harm you while I am here. You are safe, my sweetest Sam."

She began trembling and he brought her head to his chest. He stroked her back, moving his hand up and down it to reassure her. Her breathing finally calmed and she lifted her head, her beautiful eyes staring up at him.

"I'm sorry."

"No need to apologize. You were having a nightmare."

She shuddered. A dark shadow crossed her face. Her mouth hardened.

Whatever she'd dreamed of was what troubled her.

"Let's sit a while," he softly suggested as he released her and climbed into bed, his back braced against the wall. He settled her between his legs and she leaned into him, her head and back resting against his chest. His arms went around her. Deliberately, he kept quiet, hoping she would open up to him.

She didn't.

He fought the disappointment that filled him. More than anything, George had wanted Sam to trust him. Clearly, she didn't. He was good enough for a romp in bed but when it came to what was important, she held him at arm's length. It might never change. Still, he loved her. He would rather claim the miniscule scraps she threw him than be without her at all.

Sam stroked his forearm, which rested against her belly. Her breathing returned to normal. The trembling ceased. She leaned over and captured the bedclothes and pulled them up over their legs until they rested at her waist. Then she took his hand, her fingers entwining with his. He held his breath.

"I was very unhappy at Rockwell," she began.

He didn't dare speak. He squeezed her fingers to urge her on.

"Haskett wasn't a smooth talker or dancer as you and Weston

were. He was a bit awkward but it endeared him to me. Especially after you told me you would marry Frederica Martin."

"I remember you were shocked at my choice," he replied evenly. "You do understand I was running from my feelings for you."

She sighed. "I wish I would have known that. I was dogged enough back then that I would have pursued you relentlessly."

"I wish you would have. Our lives would be so different if either one of us had let the other know how we felt."

"You washed your hands of me. I believed I was only the pesky little sister to you. Haskett was your opposite in almost every way. We did get on. In the beginning. I thought he was slightly immature but I thought we could grow and mature as a couple. It surprised me when he insisted on marrying in London. His parents weren't even in attendance."

"I didn't remember that. I was drunk that day," he admitted. "It was hard to see you pledge yourself to another man and not me."

She waited a long moment and then said, "Everything changed when we arrived at Rockwell."

Sam fell silent again. This time, George let the silence blanket them. His gut told him she was ready to reveal to him what troubled her.

"My new husband had no backbone. Neither did his father. They kowtowed to Lady Rockaway, who ruled Rockwell with an iron fist. The earl hid in his study most days. My husband fawned over his mother and couldn't even turn a page of the newspaper unless she approved. He neglected me since she hadn't approved of our marriage, as if by punishing me all would be well again. We rarely spoke. I found people in the north weren't welcoming to an outsider such as me. I felt shut out by Haskett and his entire family, as well as the surrounding community."

Just hearing her words and thinking of her bleak existence made his heart heavy. "I'm sure you were lonely."

"I was," she admitted. "When I found myself with child, I thought the baby would make everything all right. Either it would bring my husband and me closer together or, if it didn't, I would at least have a child to lavish attention upon." Her fingers tightened on his. "I lost the baby and any chance at happiness. Haskett had nothing to do with me after that. We barely spoke. I was drowning in loneliness. And then he was murdered."

"I know little about that," George said.

She told him how Haskett had gone to help get his cousin settled at university and how after having too much to drink, they were set upon by thieves.

"He was stabbed. Percy, the cousin, brought the body home for burial."

Knowing there had to be more to her hurt than suffering the loss of a husband she cared little for, he waited patiently.

"I did my part. What I believed to be right. I stayed a year, wearing my mourning clothes, remaining respectful every time Lady Rockaway spoke about her son. Once the year had passed, I planned to return to Treadwell Manor."

Sam tensed in his arms. He waited anxiously, hoping she had the strength to keep speaking.

"Lady Rockaway wouldn't let me leave."

Her words confused him. "What do you mean?" he asked carefully.

She now gripped his hand so tightly that his fingers grew numb. "I was told I was a part of the family. That I would remain until Cousin Percy, who was now the heir apparent to the earldom, completed his studies at university. We would then wed and I would one day become the countess."

Anger filled him. "What did Lady Rockaway say when you told her you wouldn't wed Percy?"

"You know me well, George. I did my best to politely inform the countess that Percy and I would never suit. Her response was to lock me up."

"Lock you up?" he echoed, afraid to comprehend what Sam was saying.

"Yes. I was physically carried to my bedchamber. I railed at the top of my lungs for hours, beating against the door, demanding to be turned loose. No one ever went against Lady Rockaway, however."

Though he wanted to turn her so he could look her in the eyes, George realized that Sam was able to reveal what had happened only because she didn't have to look at him.

"You remained locked in your chamber for how long?" he asked carefully.

"Two years."

Two years?

Stunned, he had no words. He could only bring his free hand to cup her cheek. She leaned into it.

"Lady Rockaway did what she could to break my spirit. I was starved. Beaten. Ridiculed. Belittled. She didn't understand that I was a Wallace. We are notoriously stubborn. I vowed never to give in to her. I would remain strong, both physically and mentally."

Rage filled George yet he held it inside, wanting to comfort Sam in whatever way he could.

"I am so sorry you suffered in such a manner. That West and I didn't know."

She laughed harshly. "Oh, I was angry, more at him than you. I was his blood. His responsibility, whether I was married or not. I wanted him to come and save me. In the end, I knew I had to do whatever it took to save myself."

Sam now turned so that she faced him. He saw the raw pain mixed with determination on her lovely face.

"Occasionally, I have a nightmare. I dream I'm imprisoned at Rockwell again. It's not often but I realize it will probably happen the rest of my life."

He wanted to ask how she escaped and realized that wasn't important. The fact she had been able to flee the monsters who held her hostage was enough.

"You are the strongest person I know," he said. "My admiration for you knows no bounds. I can never understand what you endured during that time. I only want to see you happy and whole now."

Her face softened. "I was determined never to wed again. My marriage had proven to be such a disaster. I never wanted to be legally bound to a man and subject to his whims—or those of his family. I never wanted to give anyone control over me, as a husband would have. I fought hard to win my freedom and would never relinquish it willingly."

Sam's fingers stroked his cheek. "I understand now that I have a choice. I can choose to live my life beholden to no one. I am strong and stubborn and would ignore any gossip surrounding me. It would be a lonely existence, though."

Hope filled him.

She gazed into his eyes. "Especially when I have a good man who loves me. Who would treat me as his equal. Who would protect me and stand beside me. I would be a fool to ignore what is in my heart—and yours."

"I would be proud to stand at your side, Sam. As your husband. Your lover. Your friend. Your confidant. Your rock. I would kill for you. Die for you," he said fiercely.

She smiled tenderly. "And I would do the same for you, my love. Oh, George. I am sorry I have pushed you away as I have. I wallowed in a world of hurt, bitter and sad. I thought all I wanted to do was make merry and have no commitment to anyone." She paused. "I do want to have a little fun. It was denied to me for so long. But more than anything, I want to build a life with you, the man I love." She paused, tears brimming in her eyes. "The man I have always loved."

He cradled her face in his hands. "We still have the essence of being the same people we once were, Sam. True, our different experiences have changed us. Shaped us. But deep inside, there is that remnant of who we were—and who we can grow to be as we come together. You have suffered greatly. I have been a rake of the worst kind. Still, by standing together and sharing our lives and our love, we will mature together. I promise you this—we will have a good life because it will be one lived in love."

George tenderly kissed her. "Thank you for trusting me, my darling. For sharing what happened to you. I may never understand all of it but I am here for you. Always."

Her eyes glistened with tears and then they cascaded down her cheeks. "I love you, George. I have since I was a girl. I will love you even more as a woman. I want to grow old with you. Make a family with you. Have the life we both deserve."

Sam kissed him, the sweetest kiss they had ever shared.

The first of many more to come.

CHAPTER TWENTY-THREE

SAMANTHA WATCHED GEORGE leave her bed and shrug into his banyan. He had made love to her once more after their declarations to one another. The act had been filled with poignancy and tenderness. This time, he did not withdraw but filled her with his seed. Fully joining with George fulfilled a childhood dream, one in which she had worshipped him and longed for them to be together as man and wife. Though no longer a child, Samantha still held an abundance of love in her heart for this man, more so because of everything she had gone through. She chastised herself for having denied her feelings, both to herself and George.

It didn't matter. They knew they were soulmates, meant for one another. True, a few years had been wasted as they'd gone their separate ways. Coming together now, though, gave her a greater appreciation for what they would create in their marriage and family. She had proved far stronger than she'd ever imagined and she would always stand up for herself and speak out, knowing that she would never stand alone. She would always have her loving husband by her side.

He came and perched on the edge of the bed, her night rail in hand.

"Slip this back on," he said, helping place it over her head and smoothing it down. Grinning, he added, "We won't have to hide much longer from Lucy—or the world."

She beamed at him. "I would marry you today if we could." She took his hand and kissed his knuckles and then held his hand against her cheek.

He grew thoughtful. "When do you wish to wed? We have several options."

"I know we can return home and have the banns read in our local parish over the next three Sundays."

"True. I could also obtain a common license. Any clergyman in the Church of England can issue one for a small fee."

"How long does it remain valid?" she asked.

"I believe fifteen days. We would still have to hold the ceremony in a sanctified church in our home parish. But once we had the license, there would be no wait. Or I could ride to London and purchase a special license from the Archbishop of Canterbury."

Samantha frowned. "That's a long way to go. It wouldn't save us any time and you'd have to be granted an appointment with the archbishop to acquire it."

"I thought I could look for West if I went to London," George said. "I was hoping he would attend."

"By the time you went all the way to London and back, the banns could be called for at least two of the required Sundays," she pointed out. "While I would like for my brother to be at our wedding, I am not going to wait until he is roused from wherever he is hiding. If I did, we might not wed until next decade."

"Then why don't we go home and speak to Reverend Clements and secure the common license? I won't bother going to London. Truth be told, I'd like to marry you in the next few days. This way, we can do so."

She wound her arms around his neck and pulled him down for a long, delicious kiss.

He finally broke it. "I gather that's a yes on your part?"

"Most definitely."

"We should leave today and see Clements. Pick a date a few days from now."

"Can we tell a few people?" she asked. "I'd like for Phoebe and Andrew to be there. Jon and Elizabeth, too. And the Burtons, if that's all right with you."

"I'm agreeable to announcing our engagement to the entire house party and you may invite whomever you wish." He thought a moment. "Since it's been a good while since you've been at Treadwell Manor, they may not be ready to receive a number of guests. Why don't I leave after breakfast? I can stop by and see Clements and then go on to Colebourne Hall and have preparations made for our guests to stay there. I'll even choose the date with the good reverend if you don't mind."

"Let's say three days from now," Samantha suggested. "The house party ends tomorrow. Our guests can go straight from Windowmere to Colebourne Hall. That would give a day of rest between their arrival and our ceremony."

"Will you have Andrew drop you at Treadwell Manor?"

"I was thinking I would. Then he and the others could go on to you."

George kissed her soundly. "That sounds as if we have a plan, my darling. I'll have Cook work on a menu for the wedding breakfast and you can approve it or add to it if you'd like."

He rose. "I must go. The hallway will be full of servants and houseguests soon."

Samantha laughed. "If you are caught leaving my bedchamber, you'll have to marry me, Your Grace."

George left and she fell back against the pillows, grinning from ear to ear. She was going to marry George. They were to be husband and wife. And eventually, Mama and Papa. If she had to go through all the pain and misery again at Rockwell in order to reach this moment, she would do it all over again, knowing George becoming her husband would be her sweet reward.

Rising, she went to the wardrobe to see which of the dresses Phoebe had bestowed upon her might work as her wedding gown since none of the ones Mrs. Echols had sewn would be fancy enough. As she browsed, Lucy entered.

"Good morning, my lady," the girl said brightly. "The house party is almost over. Soon, we'll be back at Treadwell Manor."

"Are you looking forward to going home?"

"Yes, my lady. I'd rather be anywhere other than Rockwell." Lucy shuddered. "They weren't friendly there at all. Lady Rockaway's sharp tongue could cut a servant into tiny pieces. And that . . ." The servant's voice trailed off. "Well, let's just say I'm glad we'll not being seeing that place again."

Samantha sensed something was wrong. "Lucy, did something happen to you at Rockwell? While I was locked up?"

The maid's color rose, red blotches painting her neck and cheeks. "No, my lady. Not at all."

She caught Lucy's wrist as the girl made to turn away. "You know you can tell me," she said gently.

The servant burst into tears, waving her hands in the air, then turning in circles. "I'm sorry, my lady. You've been through enough. It's not right to tell you. I don't want it to be a burden, especially since it's over and done, with no looking back."

"Please," she pleaded. "Come and sit. Talk to me."

She went to a chair and seated herself, hoping Lucy would follow. Reluctantly, the maid came near and finally took a seat.

"Did Lady Rockaway do or say something hurtful? Spiteful? Because you were my maid?"

Lucy laughed harshly. "Oh, she was always right mean to me, my lady, but I knew it was because of you and her not liking you. I didn't take it personally. And when they wouldn't let me see you, I became a scullery maid so I never had to see the countess."

"Then what was it?"

Tears escaped Lucy's eyes and spilled down her cheeks. "It's that blasted cousin," she spit out. "Forgive me for cursing, my lady, but he's just awful."

A sick feeling filled her. "Percy? Are you referring to Percy Johnson?"

Lucy nodded. "Him. He's the one. He took a fancy to me and badgered me day and night. I wasn't about to give in to the likes of him." She hesitated. "But . . . he caught me alone one evening. It was long after the earl and countess retired. I was the only one in the kitchen. And he . . . well . . . he's something terrible, he is. That's all I'm saying."

"Oh, Lucy." Samantha reached for the girl's hand. "I'm so sorry he hurt you."

Lucy's mouth set in a grim line. "At least there wasn't any baby. I have to be grateful for that. Old Lady Rockaway would have turned me out into the cold without references if that had occurred."

"It was just the one time?"

"Yes, my lady. He's one who's all about the chase. Once he had me, he told me I hadn't even been worth his time." Lucy's tears fell onto the front of her uniform. "He never bothered me after that. I was so worried when I heard you were the one who would marry him."

She squeezed Lucy's fingers. "We made sure that didn't occur," Samantha said, causing Lucy to smile.

Samantha had never liked Percy and his sly looks in her direction while she'd been married to Haskett. To hear that he'd abused Lucy angered her to no end. If Percy Johnson ever showed his face during the Season, she would make sure he knew exactly how little she thought of him. The thought of telling him off in front of Polite Society made her smile.

"I must ask you something," she began, wanting to see if Lucy would rather stay in her employ or remain behind at Treadwell

Manor.

Panic filled Lucy's eyes. "Oh, I shouldn't have told you about it. You'll think less of me. You're going to sack me, aren't you?"

She gave the girl a stern look. "Knowing what I suffered at the hands of Lady Rockaway, you would think I would judge you?" Samantha shook her head. "Just think of what the *ton* would think of me if they knew all I'd been put through. No, Lucy, what happened at Rockwell will stay at Rockwell. We need never talk about our experiences there ever again."

On second thought, she would merely give Percy and the Rockaways the cut direct if their paths crossed in the future.

"Then . . . what?" Lucy asked, still suspicious.

"I won't be staying at Treadwell Manor for long," she began. "I will move to a new home and was hoping you might come along with me."

"Where?" the maid asked, bewildered.

"His Grace, the Duke of Colebourne, has asked me to be his wife. We would live at Colebourne Hall a good portion of the year, with time spent in London and his other estates."

Lucy sprang to her feet. "You're going to marry the Duke of Charm?"

"Yes," she said slowly and rose. "Is that a problem?"

The girl thought a moment. "If you would've asked me before, my lady, I'd have warned you off. I've heard things about the duke, you know. But seeing him here at Windowmere, he seems like a different person than what I've heard from others." She nodded sagely. "And he does seem to be sweet on you. All the servants have talked about the way he looks at you."

Samantha laughed. "Well, will you come with me? If not, I can find you a place at Treadwell Manor."

Lucy looked indignant. "Of course, I'll come. I'll be lady's maid to a duchess. There ain't many of them around. Besides, who could dress your hair as well as I can?" she boasted.

She hugged the girl. "I am glad you will remain in my employ. Now, let's finish getting me dressed so I can breakfast downstairs. I'm going to break my good news to our host and hostess."

While Lucy remained upstairs to decide which gown Samantha might wear to her wedding, she made her way to the breakfast buffet. George joined her.

"You're looking rather ravishing today," he said. "Even if you didn't get much sleep."

She pertly said, "I am glowing because I am in love, Your Grace. With Your Grace, I might add."

His smile caused her insides to flutter. "I will be leaving after breakfast. Briggs is packing for me now and my coachman has been notified to bring my carriage around. I had to see you one more time before I left."

"Then join me as I share news of our engagement."

Samantha led him to a table where Andrew and Phoebe sat with the Burtons. Lady Boyston and Lady Henrietta were also seated with them.

"Might we join you?" George asked.

"You're welcome to the last two places," Andrew said jovially. "You certainly look as if you're in a good mood."

Samantha took her seat and George slid into the one beside her. He reached for her hand under the table, their fingers lacing together.

"I believe I will be in a glorious mood today and the rest of my days," George proclaimed, glancing to her.

The table was quiet and she saw everyone leaning forward as her cheeks heated. She nodded to her fiancé.

"Samantha has accepted my offer of marriage," he announced, raising her hand and kissing her fingers.

"Oh, how romantic," Lady Henrietta proclaimed.

Everyone began offering their congratulations. Samantha found she couldn't stop beaming.

"When is the wedding?" Letty cried. "Oh, you two simply look as if you were made for one another."

"Very soon," George told the group. "In fact, I'm leaving now to see to the arrangements." He looked to Andrew. "Would you and Phoebe see Sam home tomorrow once your guests depart?"

"We'd be happy to do so," the duke said, winking at Samantha.

As they began eating, Lady Boyston leaned over and said, "I saw this coming. I know you were friends in childhood. You are lucky to have a second chance at marriage."

"I hope you, too, will have that opportunity, Lady Boyston," Samantha said. "And that you'll visit us at Colebourne Hall."

"Thank you for your gracious invitation. I may take you up on that."

Once the meal concluded, Andrew and Phoebe joined Samantha and George as they walked to his waiting carriage.

"We'll wed in a few days," George told the couple. "Once you see Samantha safely home, will you come to Colebourne Hall and stay for the wedding? We'd like for you to stand up with us."

"You aren't going to wait for Weston?" Andrew asked, his surprise obvious.

"No," Samantha said. "We are eager to wed and begin our lives together. Weston will find out in due time."

Phoebe said, "We'd be happy to do so."

George looked at her and Samantha's pulse raced. "I don't want to say goodbye but someone has to see to the arrangements."

He pulled her into his arms for a lingering kiss. "Hopefully, you won't forget me."

"Not after a kiss like that," Andrew teased.

George kissed her swiftly again and then hopped into his ducal carriage. She pressed two fingers to her lips and held them up to him.

"I love you," she said.

"I love you even more," he replied and rapped his cane on the vehicle's roof, causing the carriage to take off.

As she watched it drive away, Phoebe linked arms with her. "You are marrying a good man. Why, George is almost as good as my Andrew."

The duke chuckled and gave his wife a wicked grin. "Yes, I am good at several things. Making babies is one." He turned to Samantha. "Phoebe tells me you know."

"I do and am very excited for you, Andrew."

"You'll be next," he predicted.

Knowing George had emptied his seed in her this morning, Samantha wondered if she might already be carrying his child.

Chapter Twenty-Four

The good news spread quickly and all of the houseguests sought out Samantha to give her their good wishes on her upcoming nuptials.

"Are you certain you aren't too good for him?" asked Jon, a teasing light in his eyes.

Elizabeth swatted her brother. "Samantha and George are perfect for one another," she said fiercely. "I've thought so since we arrived. Any fool could see how besotted Colebourne is with her."

Jon shrugged. "I just thought I would ask. In case Sam might want to change her mind and think about marrying me instead."

She laughed. "Though I would love to be related to Elizabeth by marriage, I will merely keep her—and you—as my friend."

He grinned. "It never hurts to ask."

Letty squealed when she heard the news. "Oh, this is marvelous, Samantha. When you visit us, you'll be coming with your husband."

"You'd still like me to come? Or rather, us?"

"Of course. You are now one of my dearest friends and Burton and Colebourne seem to get along quite well. They can go off hunting and shooting while we pursue more ladylike things."

Andrew laughed. "You probably don't realize this, but Samantha can probably ride and shoot as well as your husband and George."

"I'm out of practice, Andrew," she said. "Give me time, though, and I'll see what I can accomplish."

Letty wasn't having it. "Enough talk of that, Your Grace. We need to discuss what you will wear for the ceremony. When will you wed?"

"In three days," Samantha shared. "George and I would like you and Burton to come, as well as Jon and Elizabeth. He's left to arrange for our license and have Colebourne Hall prepared for guests."

Elizabeth looked to her brother. "Can we go, Jon?"

"I wouldn't miss it," he declared. "The Duke of Charm setting aside his rakish ways and slipping a wedding ring on a woman's finger is a huge event. I need to witness the ceremony and confirm to Polite Society that our wild George will now be a steadfast, loving husband." Jon took Samantha's hand and kissed it. "You have tamed the mighty lion of London's jungle, Sam. Congratulations."

"Letty is right," Phoebe said. "We need to think of what gown you'll wear, Samantha." She turned to her sister. "Would you play hostess to our guests for a while, Letty? I want to have Samantha look at a few gowns of mine that might work."

"I'd be happy to," Letty said. "Come along, Burton. You, too, Your Grace and Lady Elizabeth. We will keep everyone occupied and happy."

After everyone left, Phoebe said, "Let's go to my dressing room. I have a few ideas."

Samantha accompanied her friend upstairs, wondering what she had in mind.

"It depends on what will look good on you. We have all of today in order for my maid and yours to do any alterations."

"I was thinking of wearing one of the dresses you've already given me."

"No, those won't do," Phoebe said, sifting through several gowns until she stopped. "Here. This is what I pictured you in."

The duchess held up a gown of the palest blue satin. It had an overdress in striped gauze and was trimmed with Brussels lace.

"It's perfect," Samantha exclaimed.

Phoebe brought the dress against Samantha. "Hold it up," she instructed and stepped back. She studied Samantha a moment and then smiled. "It looks lovely. Would you like to try it on?"

"Yes!" she cried.

"Let's summon our maids to help," Phoebe suggested and rang for them.

As they waited for the servants to arrive, she asked, "On what occasion did you wear this?"

"My wedding."

"Oh," Samantha said. "I can't borrow your wedding dress."

Phoebe shook her head. "You most certainly can. It obviously has brought me much happiness." Her hands rested against her still-flat belly. "I doubt I'll be able to wear it again. I've heard a woman's body changes after they give birth. Letty's certainly has."

"But surely the gown has sentimental value for you," she protested.

"I have everything I need in Andrew. Besides, I think it will look lovely on you."

The two maids arrived and soon had Samantha undressed and placed into Phoebe's wedding gown.

"Oh, my lady, you're beautiful," Lucy exclaimed, her eyes as round as saucers.

"Just a few nips and tucks and it will fit you like a dream," Phoebe's maid added.

She allowed the servants to make a few adjustments and then they removed the gown.

"It won't take long at all to make these alterations, my lady," promised Lucy.

"That's good to know. Once it's done, you'll need to pack for us, Lucy. We'll be leaving for Treadwell Manor tomorrow with His Grace and Her Grace."

"I'll see to it, my lady."

"You'll need gloves," Phoebe said. "White kid gloves would look best. And slippers."

"I actually have a few pairs of slippers that I left behind at Treadwell Manor," Samantha said. "I'm sure they'll still fit me. And I bought gloves in Exeter that will work."

"So the slippers will be something old. Your gloves will be new. The gown is something both borrowed and blue," the duchess said.

"It seems as if I'll be ready."

"You look not only ready but happy," Phoebe noted. "At peace with your decision to wed George."

Samantha felt her face soften. "I am. As a little girl, George was always there. He was an only child and his parents were quite sedate. We Wallaces are loud and rowdy and George spent more time at Treadwell Manor than he did at Colebourne Hall. I grew up with him being a constant presence. In my mind, I always assumed we would be together one day."

"When did you know you loved him?" asked Phoebe.

"I think it was always there. He broke my heart when he told me he was engaged to Frederica Martin. It's what pushed me to quickly find a husband. And then I wed and shortly afterward, George was jilted in front of the entire *ton*. If only I'd known."

"You can't recapture those lost years apart but you can fully live the ones that come," her friend declared.

"Exactly. I think I love George even more, going through what I have. Becoming his wife now will be even sweeter. I do love him, Phoebe. Madly. Passionately. Completely."

"He feels the same way about you. It's obvious. Jon is right. The lamb has tamed the lion." Phoebe chuckled. "Well, I don't think I would call you a lamb. You are sweet but you are fearless and confident. It took a strong woman to bring the Duke of Charm to heel."

Samantha smiled. "And I plan to be the only woman he charms in the future."

⋙⋘

GEORGE GLANCED AROUND those gathered at his dining table and raised a glass. He looked to Sam and saw love for him shining in her eyes.

"To the woman who has made all the difference in my life. I look forward to spending the rest of my days with you. I love you, my darling. To Samantha!"

Those gathered around the table echoed, "To Samantha," and drank the very fine Madeira in their glasses.

Tomorrow, they would wed. Begin their new life in this very house. He hoped by this time next year they would already have added a baby to what he hoped would become a very large family. He had hated being an only child and longed to fill Colebourne Hall with the sound of little feet pattering through the halls.

He was also ready to begin anew in making that baby. With Sam staying at Treadwell Manor, he didn't have the convenience of slipping down the corridor and climbing into her bed. Although it had only been two days since they had made love, he felt as if he were suffering through a drought. Only this woman would quench his thirst. She was a balm to his soul.

His only regret was that West would miss their wedding. He'd sent a note, as had Sam, to London, hoping West would read it at some point and come to visit them. George wondered what his dearest friend would think about his sister being married to his best friend.

"We should all turn in early," Phoebe suggested. "Tomorrow is a big day. Are you sure you don't need me to come and help you dress in the morning, Samantha?"

"No," said George's bride-to-be. "Lucy will handle everything. I will see you at the village church at nine."

"I hope you'll like how we decorated it," Elizabeth said. "Mrs.

Clements was a little overwhelmed with all the flowers Letty and I had brought in this afternoon."

George laughed. "Mrs. Clements is a mouse of a woman. In fact, a mouse would overwhelm her."

"She is very kind, George," Sam chided.

"True. Kind to have married a stuffed shirt such as the good reverend," he quipped.

"George," she warned and everyone at the table laughed.

He rose. "Why I don't see my fiancée home? I'll say my goodnights to you all now."

"Be sure and come home," joked Jon. "Perhaps I should check your bed to see if you make it there."

His sister elbowed him in the ribs.

George went and pulled Sam's chair out so she could rise. "Goodnight, everyone," she called. "I will see you bright and early tomorrow morning."

He took her arm and led her from the dining room. The butler handed him her cloak. October had turned chilly and he wrapped Sam up in it and escorted her outside, where her carriage awaited.

Opening the door, he helped her inside and then climbed in himself.

"What are you doing?" she asked, her mouth twitching in amusement.

He sat next to her and took her hand. "I find I have a great need to escort you all the way home. We haven't been alone since we left Windowmere." He rapped on the ceiling and the coach took off.

"We are going to be alone every night after this one," she reminded him.

"Then I need a small preview of what that might be like," he replied and pressed his lips to hers.

They kissed the entire way to Treadwell Manor, which in his mind wasn't nearly long enough. The vehicle halted and a footman opened the door. George bounded out and lifted Sam to the ground.

"I will now see you safely inside."

"Wait for His Grace," she called to the driver. "You will be taking him home shortly."

"Yes, my lady."

As they walked to the front door, he asked, "Shortly?"

Sam blushed. "Well, I didn't think you'd be staying the night."

"Think again."

"George! You will kiss me goodnight and then go home," she ordered.

"You will let me come inside and give you a present," he corrected. "Then I will kiss you goodnight and go home."

The door opened and they hurried inside. She gave her cloak to the butler and George took her arm, leading her upstairs to the library.

"Let me pour us a brandy. That will take the chill away."

He did so and they tapped their snifters together and began sipping.

"It certainly burns a fire down my throat to my belly," she declared.

He lifted the snifter from her hand and placed it down. "You light a fire within me," he said and kissed her.

She entwined her arms about his neck and pressed her body against his. After some minutes, he broke the kiss.

"Is it time for my present?" she asked playfully.

"Yes." He reached inside his coat pocket and slowly withdrew a diamond necklace.

"Oh!"

"Turn around," he ordered and she spun around so he could place the necklace about her throat and fasten the clasp.

Sam touched it reverently. "It has been a long time since anyone gave me a present. Thank you, George."

"There's more."

He slipped his hand into another pocket and extracted a pair of matching earrings. She squealed and put them on.

"My mother wore them on her wedding day," he said. "As had her mother. I thought it would be appropriate for you to wear the set on ours."

She threw her arms about his neck. "I love them. I love you." She kissed him. "I love that we're getting married."

He kissed her back. "And I can't help but think in twenty years or so that we will give these to our oldest daughter so that she, too, can wear them on her wedding day."

Sam smiled. "That's a lovely thought. But what if I only give you sons?"

He cradled her cheek. "Certainly, I want sons. Yet in my mind's eye, I see a beautiful young woman. Her hair is dark like her mother's and her eyes are your wonderful mix of blue and green. She will have wrapped me around her littlest finger from the time she arrives. We will be doting parents and watch her as she puts on this jewelry. I will slip my arm about your waist and we will be happier than we've ever been because our little girl is in love and marrying a wonderful man." He smiled. "That is but a glimpse into our future."

Sam's eyes misted with tears. "I can't wait to live these years with you, George. I already love you so much and yet I know that with each passing day, somehow I'll love you even more."

They kissed again and feelings of tenderness filled him.

"Sweet dreams, my darling," he said. "The next time I see you, I will vow to love and honor you in front of our friends."

She walked him to the door and he gave her a last, soft kiss.

"Tomorrow," he said.

"Tomorrow," she agreed.

Chapter Twenty-Five

"THERE YOU GO, my lady. You look ever so nice. His Grace will swoon when he sees you," said Lucy.

Samantha stared at her image in the mirror, seeing the smooth chignon her maid had arranged, the perfect complement to her simple but elegant wedding gown. Her new jewelry sparkled in the light.

"I doubt His Grace has ever swooned in his life," she commented. "Most likely, I'll be the one doing the swooning when I see him."

Lucy smiled brightly. "It's so wonderful, seeing how you and His Grace are a love match." She giggled. "I suppose I better start calling *you* Your Grace."

Samantha stood. "I am not the Duchess of Colebourne yet," she reminded the servant.

"Well, you will be in an hour or so."

Suddenly, Lucy captured Samantha's hands and kissed them fervently. "Thank you again for being clever and brave and bold enough to help us escape that horrible place. And now you're going to be a duchess and you and His Grace will make the prettiest babies ever."

She blushed at the thought of what would go into the making of those babies and then embraced Lucy.

"I couldn't have done it without you, Lucy. We survived and will now thrive at Colebourne Hall."

The two women went downstairs and the butler wished Samantha well. None of the servants would be attending today's wedding. It was to be a very small affair, with only the select few they had invited. Lucy would ride with her and be dropped off at Treadwell Manor and then the driver would take his mistress to the village church, where Reverend Clements and her groom would be waiting.

Lucy called out to the driver, "You can let me off in the road when we reach Treadwell Manor. I've a mind to walk a bit."

"Are you sure?" Samantha asked. "It will probably take you a good twenty minutes to reach the house."

"I don't mind. It's a cool, crisp autumn day. It'll do me good to be out of the house. Don't worry, Your Grace. Everything will be laid out for you."

"I know. You are always efficient and take such good care of me."

Lucy had supervised taking Samantha's things to her new home yesterday and had already put away all of her clothing in the dressing room.

The driver handed her and then Lucy into the carriage. She'd discovered when she'd arrived home that only a skeleton staff was in place with a butler, cook, two maids, and the driver, who functioned also as a groom. Their butler had explained that her brother was so rarely in residence that only a handful of servants was needed. It made her glad that she and George had decided to have their guests stay at Colebourne Hall.

She glanced out the window and saw the colors of autumn passing by. George had asked where she wanted to go for a honeymoon but Samantha only wanted to stay in Devon. She thought it at its best this time of year and she was also eager to put down roots after feeling adrift for so long. Today was perfect—except for the fact that Weston was missing. She said a quick prayer as she did every day, hoping that wherever he was he was safe and would decide to wake up and become the man he was destined to be.

The carriage began slowing and came to a halt. Lucy reached over and opened the door. The coachman helped her out.

She looked back inside and with a mischievous grin said, "Enjoy your wedding, Your Grace."

The door closed and Lucy started up the lane to Colebourne Hall. As the carriage began to move, Lucy looked over her shoulder and gave a wave, which Samantha returned.

It surprised her when the vehicle came to a halt less than a minute later. She heard voices and wondered why they had stopped again. Glancing out the window, she couldn't see anyone. She hoped nothing was blocking the road because she certainly didn't want to be late to her own wedding.

Suddenly, a loud noise rang out, startling her. A moment later, a thud sounded, as if something heavy had dropped to the ground. She saw nothing from her side of the coach and started to move toward the door to see the other side when it swung open. Samantha gasped.

Percy Johnson appeared in the doorway.

Quickly, she scrambled back to the far side of the coach as he climbed in and sat.

"Surprised to see me?" he asked. "I'm delighted to finally have caught up with my runaway fiancée."

"I was never your fiancée," she said emphatically. "No offer was made. No settlements were drawn up."

"It wasn't necessary," he said nonchalantly. "As the Countess of Rockaway, you will have all you need."

His words caused fear to pool in her belly. "Are you the earl?"

"I am," he said jovially. "It only took ridding me of my cousin and uncle but at last I hold the title."

"You what?"

"I had to clear the path, my dear. It would have been next to impossible to dispose of Haskett at Rockwell. I convinced him how much I needed him to help establish me at university. That his doting mama would think highly of him for helping out his poor, orphaned cousin."

Fear spread through her in an instant. "You killed him."

Percy nodded, his eyes bright. "I did. It was incredibly easy—and fun. Haskett never could hold his drink. I plied him with enough liquor to make him a total mess then led him back through a dark alley. Thrusting the blade in him several times was one of the most fascinating moments of my life."

Nausea filled her. "You murdered your cousin. For his title?"

"And you."

Panic rippled through her. "What?"

"Oh, I was taken with you the moment you appeared at Rockwell, Samantha. I knew I would do whatever it took to have you."

"You were only a boy when I arrived."

"No, a young man. One who was eager to fulfill his destiny. Haskett stood in my way."

"He loved you," she cried. "He thought of you as a brother."

Percy shrugged. "He was a supercilious boor. He couldn't make a decision on his own without looking to his dear mama. I will make for an excellent earl, with a lovely countess by my side."

He grabbed her wrist and she shrank back as he laughed. No, she couldn't be cowed. He would enjoy that too much. Samantha sat up and glared at him.

"Release me," she commanded.

He did, which surprised her.

"How did Rockaway die?" she asked.

"I am Rockaway," he reminded her. "My uncle was in ill health for some time. Oh, that's right. You wouldn't have known because you kept to your rooms." He flicked a piece of lint from his trousers. "Arsenic will do that. Ingested in small amounts over time, it can make one very sick. And then when a larger dose is given and the person is gone, no one questions it, not even the fool doctor who attended him. Rockaway went into the ground three days after you decided to leave."

Horror filled her. "You are mad."

"Mad? I prefer to use the word determined. I wanted to be the earl. I wanted you as my wife. I went after both—although you have made things very inconvenient for me, Samantha."

He latched on to her wrist again, his grip firm. "I went to London first, thinking you would go there. It surprised me when I couldn't find you or that wastrel brother of yours anywhere in the city. I figured you must have gone back to Treadwell Manor instead. You weren't there, either. Fortunately, gossip abounds and I heard you would be arriving soon. For your wedding, of all things."

He clucked his tongue, his grip tightening on her. She was afraid her bones would shatter from the pressure but she refused to cry out and give him satisfaction.

"How could you have another groom when we are destined to wed and spend our lives together?"

Percy released her and she moved as far away as she could, her back pressed against the coach as she rubbed her aching wrist.

"Ah, you look at me with mistrust now, my dear. Soon, you will award me with adoring gazes."

"You are madder than I thought if you think I would ever wed you."

"Oh, I have everything planned. We'll go several villages away. Not too far because I want to marry you today and consummate the marriage, especially if your groom decides to give chase. If he does, we'll already be wed and I'll have dipped my wick into you before he arrives."

"No," she said resolutely.

"No?" Percy laughed. "You act as if you have a choice in the matter, you silly bitch."

"You are the last person I would wed. I would rather be dead than wed to you."

He struck her without warning. She took the full blow, out of practice of trying to avoid those from her time locked up at Rockwell.

A myriad of stars blazed across her horizon as the pain exploded along her cheek and eye. She brought her hands up protectively. Slowly, a grinning Percy came back into view.

"Don't trifle with me, Samantha. If you thought Lady Rockaway was your worst nightmare, think again. You will do everything I say without hesitation. You'll be like a well-trained dog that I will command, one who will never think of biting its master's hand."

Cradling her face, she looked at him in hate. "Why would you believe I would ever be your slave?"

"Because if you don't conform to my wishes, I will kill the Duke of Colebourne."

"No!" she cried.

"Yes," he said cheerfully. "I find I have quite a taste for it now. Of course, I would make you watch as I did so. I wonder how long I could draw it out?" he mused.

"You are a monster!"

"No. I am an earl. A peer of the realm. I have a marvelous estate and will have a beautiful, submissive wife who hangs on my every word." His eyes grew hard. "If you love this duke of yours, Samantha, then you will spare him my rage. I will gladly kill him—and you will still be mine. It's your choice whether Colebourne lives or dies."

This was worse than any nightmare she could have imagined. She knew Percy was insane and should be locked away from society so he could do no harm. Even if she somehow escaped this carriage, he would come for her.

And kill George.

She couldn't risk it.

"I'll marry you," she said quietly, defeat blanketing her.

Percy smiled benignly. "I knew you would see reason."

GEORGE WAITED IN a small room inside the chapel.

Today was his wedding day. Sam would be his bride. His wife. The mother of their children. Nothing could ever match the love he felt for her. His life had changed in such a short amount of time. Where once he had dreaded the emptiness and sameness of every day, from now on, each one would be full of joy—and love.

He did regret that West and Sebastian, who rounded out their group of five, wouldn't be present today. At some point, West would finally show up. As for Sebastian, he was still at war against Bonaparte. George hoped he could reunite with all his friends in the near future.

"Any nerves?" Andrew asked.

"None," he said firmly, knowing he and Sam had a bright future ahead of them.

"Good," his friend replied. "I know what having Phoebe in my life has been like. Every day is a precious one, filled with joy." He paused. "And soon, there will be three of us."

George grinned and slapped Andrew on the back. "Well done, Your Grace."

"We've talked it over and would like you and Samantha to be godparents."

"We'll happily accept that role. It will be good practice for us. I hope we'll provide a playmate for your child in the very near future."

The church bells sounded the hour. Andrew glanced out the window. "I don't see the carriage yet."

"Don't worry. She'll be here."

He'd never known Sam to be late, however. For a moment, a sliver of doubt wedged its way inside him. He thought of his first wedding. How West had showed up looking like death warmed over and told George he would be the only man marrying at St. George's Chapel that day. Then he'd gone out in front of hundreds of wedding guests and watched Frederica come down the aisle. She'd told him she couldn't marry him because she was in love with Viscount Richmond and jilted him at the altar.

That day had started his downward spiral.

Today, though, he climbed from the abyss. To begin a life with the woman he loved. Worshipped. Adored.

If she ever showed up.

Another quarter-hour passed and the bells chimed again.

"I'll go see if—"

"No. We'll both go, Andrew."

The two men left the room and went to the chapel. George glanced out and saw Jon and Elizabeth sitting with the Burtons. Mrs. Clements stood at the rear with Phoebe, who held a small bouquet and wore a puzzled look on her face.

Reverend Clements stepped toward him. "The bride has not arrived yet. No word has been sent. I am certain it's but a small delay."

George's heart sank.

Sam wasn't coming . . .

Once again, he'd been left at the altar.

Bitterness filled him. All his hopes came crashing down. His plans to be a better man than he'd been now seemed like a pipe dream. Samantha had decided he was lacking in some way and refused to bind herself to him. Hurt. Disappointment. Anger. They all raged within him.

He turned to the few gathered. "It seems this bride—like my last one—has had a change of heart. I'm sorry to have inconvenienced you."

With that, George marched up the aisle and out the doors of the chapel.

CHAPTER TWENTY-SIX

GEORGE WOULDN'T LET despair rule the day. He would return to London at once, where he would work his way through as many women as he could. He had the rules he and West had drawn up. He would be certain to stick to them in the future in order to protect his shattered heart.

"Your Grace! Your Grace!" a voice called.

He looked up to see Lucy, Sam's maid, running toward him. She held her skirts in her hands as she hurried toward him. For a moment, he held his breath, hope filling him that Sam hadn't abandoned him after all.

"Where is she?" he cried, sensing the others spilling from the chapel and pausing behind him.

Lucy halted in front of him, breathing hard. Her cheeks were flushed and her hair askew.

"He has her," she spit out and then took several more breaths.

George grabbed her shoulders. "Who?"

"That bastard. Percy. Percy Johnson."

For a moment, he had no idea who the girl meant. Then a chill rippled through him as he remembered the name.

"Haskett's cousin?" he asked, knowing Johnson was the man Samantha was supposed to have married.

"Yes," she said fiercely. "He's a horrible man."

His fingers tightened. "Tell me," he ordered.

Lucy explained how the coach dropped her off at Treadwell Manor and then headed toward the village.

"I heard it stop again and didn't understand why it did so. Then a shot rang out." She paused. "I cut through the trees and ran to the road. I saw Percy Johnson open the carriage door and get in. And that awful Steele, the one who always guarded Lady Samantha, climbed into the driver's seat and took off."

Tears now streamed down Lucy's face. "I couldn't stop them. I tried to help our driver. He was lying in the dust, a bullet in his shoulder. He'd been shot by Steele."

"I'll see to the coachman" Jon quickly volunteered. "I'll fetch a doctor and take one of the coaches and bring him to Treadwell Manor."

"I'll go with you, George," Andrew said. "There are two of them."

"I'll kill them both with my bare hands," he growled, seeing red even as relief poured through him.

Sam hadn't deserted him. She needed him. He would do whatever it took to get to her.

Moving as one, he and Andrew raced to the remaining coach. Jon had already seized the first one and it pulled away.

George shouted to Lucy, "Which way did they head?"

"North, Your Grace."

He signaled the driver to come down from his perch, knowing the man had heard everything and not wanting to endanger him. The servant shook his head. "No, Your Grace. I'm used to the vehicle and the horses. I can get the most out of them."

"All right," he said as he climbed to sit by the coachman. Glancing back, he saw Andrew leap onto the back, the footman he replaced standing there dazed. "Go!" Andrew cried.

The carriage took off, turning away from the church and toward the road. George wanted to pray and found that words evaded him. All he could mutter was a soft, "Please, God. Please," as they sped down the road. He tried to calculate how much of a head start Johnson had on them. Colebourne Hall was about three miles from the village church. Lucy would have had to run from there to the chapel and then it had taken a couple of minutes to explain the situation. Hopefully, Sam was less than an hour ahead of them. He must guess where Johnson was headed, else they would miss him and Sam might be lost to him for hours. Days. Who knew what might happen to her in that time?

If Johnson were desperate enough to come this far to claim her, he would want to make her his bride as soon as possible—though how he would force Sam to say her vows puzzled him. Would Johnson stop in the first village he crossed? If so, he would have to seek out the local clergyman and purchase an ordinary license and convince the man to marry them immediately.

George didn't think Johnson would pause at the first town he crossed. He would want to put a little distance between him and those who might come to Sam's rescue. He gambled on that now and had the driver pass through the first village they came upon. Turning, he saw Andrew give him a questioning glance. George shook his head and shouted, "Not here."

They drove for another half-hour before coming to the next village and he had the driver swing by the church. No carriage stood in front of the vicarage or church and he told the driver to continue. They would stop at every church and search for the Treadwell carriage.

He spied a gardener clearing weeds in the cemetery and motioned the driver to slow down. Leaping off the seat, he ran to the man.

"Has a ducal carriage passed by recently?" he asked frantically.

"Aye, my lord. About a quarter-hour ago. Maybe a bit longer."

"Thank you!"

George raced back and shouted, "They came through here not long ago. We've still time."

As he vaulted onto the bench and the driver flicked the reins, he said under his breath, "I'm coming, Sam. I'm coming."

SAMANTHA WARILY WATCHED as they came to another village. Would this be the one where they stopped? They'd already driven through four. Percy had said he wouldn't let too many go by before he would seek a clergyman to marry them.

Sure enough, as they approached, the vehicle slowed from the maddening pace it had kept.

"Ah, good. I'd told Steele to bypass five or six villages before he stopped."

Percy slipped his hand into his pocket and produced a length of cord. He grasped the ends with both hands, stretching it to its full length.

"Put your wrists together," he commanded.

"I will not," she said, her loathing for him obvious.

"Shall I strike you again, Samantha? I could do so from the other side this time, so you'd have matching bruises. Now, do as I say. Remember, you want to keep your handsome duke alive."

Reluctantly, she held out her hands, the palms facing one another. Percy wrapped the cord about her wrists several times and tied it off.

"There. See what a good girl you can be?"

She wanted to kill him. She thought she had hated her mother-in-law for everything she had been subjected to but the fury and enmity within her now far outweighed anything she'd felt for Lady Rockaway.

The coach rolled to a halt and, shortly after, the door swung open. Samantha caught a glimpse of the hefty man who had been her guard at Rockwell. He looked at her with hatred in his narrowed eyes and spat.

"I'll be back shortly, my dear," Percy said. "I'll explain to the good reverend that we need to be wed immediately and offer a healthy donation to his coffers to perform the ceremony."

"Do you think he'll do so even if the bride is bound and unwilling?"

His eyes gleamed at her, more than a hint of madness in them. "Oh, I thought we established that you were willing. That you adore me and can't wait to be in my bed. Remember, my lady, that once we are wed and our union is consummated, I can always turn back and kill your beloved duke."

"Then why should I bother to marry you," she challenged. "if you are going to kill George anyway?"

He looked at her solemnly. "I give you my word that if you go along with our bargain, I'll keep my word. I'll leave the Duke of Charm alone as long as you remain docile."

She couldn't trust his word. She couldn't marry him. Yet could she take the chance and risk George's life?

"Stay here. Steele will be outside the carriage. With your hands restrained, it would be difficult for you to exit the carriage, much less outrun him. Steele has been very, very upset that you escaped from his care before. If you try to flee, he has my permission to do whatever it takes to subdue you and bring you back."

Her eyes cut to her former captor. An evil smile played about his cruel lips. Terror filled her that Steele would claim she'd tried to escape—so he could do whatever he wanted to her.

"Close the door," she said to Percy. "I won't run. I'll be waiting here for you."

Samantha hoped with the door closed that the guard wouldn't open it and seek her out.

"Very well, my lady. I shall return shortly."

Percy slammed the carriage door. Samantha blinked back the tears that formed. She told herself that crying had done no good in the past and that she'd given it up. It didn't matter. Slowly, the tears cascaded down her cheeks. In all the awful times she'd lived through, she'd never felt such a feeling of hopelessness.

Fortunately, the door never opened. She wondered if Steele might be afraid of the new earl. She also wondered if Lady Rockaway was still alive. The countess wouldn't have cared one way or the other about her husband being poisoned but she would have taken exception to Percy murdering Haskett. She thought of how young Percy had been when she arrived at Rockwell. The fact that he'd become obsessed with her, so much that he'd planned for years and then murdered her husband to claim her, told her how deeply disturbed he was. She could never have his child and see such madness passed on.

In that moment, Samantha determined that she would have to kill Percy. To save George. And to save herself. The question was how to accomplish it before Steele could stop her.

Lost in her thoughts, it surprised her when the carriage door flew open. A grinning Percy popped his head inside.

"We have found a most willing man of the cloth to perform our wedding," he said brightly.

"Even with my hands tied?" she asked lightly, knowing she needed them free if she were to have any chance of ending her kidnapper's life.

"Come along," he encouraged and she rose, stepping to the entrance.

Percy took her waist and brought her to the ground. "He understands why they are tied. You are my betrothed. Our fathers were fast friends and we have known one another all our lives. Unfortunately, you got it into your head that you're in love with the handsome gardener. Your father dismissed him and the two of you ran away together last night.

"Fortunately, I caught up with you and convinced the gardener—by giving him a healthy amount of coin and a glowing recommendation—that he would be better off without you. Your lover handed you over to me and I have had to restrain you since you've had a tendency to lash out at me physically."

She couldn't believe the tale he'd spun, much less that a clergyman believed it. Then she saw the roof of the church and knew exactly why the man would overlook her distress. Percy had said he would give a hefty donation to the parish and Samantha knew the reverend would exchange performing the ceremony for a new roof.

He took her elbow. "Come along, my sweet. Steele," he called. "Remain here."

"Shouldn't Steele engage a room for us at the local inn?" she asked, hoping once they were alone that she would have the courage to bash in Percy's head. "I thought you wanted us to consummate our marriage as soon as possible."

"We can do that in the carriage afterward," Percy said, having an answer for everything.

Disgust filled her yet Samantha knew she had no choice. To protect George, she must sacrifice herself to this lunatic.

She allowed him to lead her into the dimly lit chapel. The only light came from the stained glass windows. Near the altar, a man and woman stood. She assumed them to be the clergyman and his wife.

"Good day," the man said sternly, glancing at Samantha's bound wrists and back up. "I am Reverend White. This is Mrs. White."

The woman nodded timidly but didn't speak.

"Shall we begin?" the groom asked pleasantly.

Reverend White frowned. "My wife counts as one witness but we'll need another. Could you ask your driver to step inside, my lord?"

Percy frowned. "I don't want a servant as our witness," he said haughtily. "Have you a curate?"

"I do."

"Fetch him," Percy said dismissively.

The clergyman looked to his wife and she left. Minutes went by without a word being spoken. Then the woman appeared with a young man in his early twenties.

"This is Mr. Gaddy, my curate," Reverend White said. "He will serve as your second witness." White went to the altar and faced them. "Come stand before me."

With a heavy heart, Samantha moved her feet. Percy stood to her right. She forced herself to remain rooted to the spot when every instinct told her to flee.

The vicar began and she retreated within herself. Just because she was standing there didn't mean she had to listen to his platitudes. When prompted, she would repeat the vows. It saddened her to think that, by now, she should have been married to George. Their wedding breakfast would have been over and he would have hustled her up to their suite of rooms and spent the rest of the day making long, slow love to her.

A thought hit her.

What if she carried George's child now?

It was certainly a possibility. The last time they had been together, he hadn't withdrawn. That had occurred less than a week ago. If she turned up with child, she wouldn't know if it was George's baby or Percy's. Anguish filled her.

She glanced at Reverend White, who asked if anyone objected to the union. Samantha thought it absurd to ask with no one there other than Mrs. White and a curate whose name she'd already forgotten.

"I object. Most strenuously."

Wheeling around, she saw George marching up the aisle.

Chapter Twenty-Seven

RELIEF FILLED GEORGE, knowing he was in time to stop the farce before him, but his rage soared as he saw Sam's swollen face. His eyes fell and he noted her wrists tied together.

"How could you even think to marry this couple?" he roared at the mouse of a man who shrank as George rushed toward the trio. "Johnson has beaten and bound her, forcing her to the altar. How dare you call yourself a man of God?"

"But he's an earl," the clergyman protested.

"And I . . . am a duke," George shouted, causing the vicar to stumble back in fear. "This man kidnapped *my* fiancée. I'll have her back."

He faced Johnson, who grabbed Samantha by the throat with one hand and wrapped an arm around her waist, pinning her to him. "Stand back. Else I'll choke her to death in front of you."

"George will crush you before you can do that," Sam said resolutely, even as her captor's fingers tightened against her throat.

"Stay where you are," he warned George.

"Or what? You have nowhere to go, Johnson."

"Rockaway," the man hissed. "I am Rockaway. I earned my title and you will use it, you filthy scoundrel."

Sam squirmed, bringing her hands up and trying to pry the earl's fingers away as George took another two steps forward.

"Release her," he ordered, his fists balling as he readied himself to attack.

"Maggot pie," wheezed Sam as she raised her knee and slammed her heel down on her captor's toes.

He shrieked and stumbled back as Sam sucked in a huge breath. George moved toward her but Sam was a woman on a mission. She rushed toward Johnson, her wrists raised, and swung them at his face, knocking him off his feet. The earl fell hard against the bare wooden floor and lay stunned, flat on his back. Sam raised her foot and slammed it down on his bollocks. He yelped like a kicked puppy, curling on his side, his hands protecting his private parts.

"Get her off me," he whined.

George clasped her elbow. "Are you through with him?"

"Almost," she said, determination shining in her beautiful aquamarine eyes.

With that, she kicked Johnson in the nose. The loud crunch and spurt of blood guaranteed that she'd broken it.

Turning back to George, she said sweetly, "I'm through now, Your Grace."

He roared with laughter and wrapped her in his arms, kissing her soundly.

"Who is your magistrate?" a voice said.

George broke the kiss and saw Andrew had entered the church with the large, brutish man they'd seen next to the carriage in tow.

When no one answered, Mrs. White finally sputtered, "Lord Wimbley."

Andrew forced the bloodied man down onto a pew. "Stay," he commanded and to Mrs. White, he said, "See that Lord Wimbley comes at once."

The woman blinked several times. "Who might I say needs him?"

"The Dukes of Colebourne and Windham," George replied.

The curate spoke up. "I'll go for Lord Wimbley." He fled, obviously eager to escape the church.

"We could do with a spot of tea," Sam told the couple standing at the altar, both their jaws still slack. "And I would like a cold compress for my face, please."

"Of course," the woman said, dragging her husband with her.

"Do you still carry a dagger, Andrew?" George asked. "Sam is in need of one."

His friend reached into his boot and produced the blade. Handing it to George, he said, "You may do the honors."

George went to his fiancée, who held out her hands. He sliced through the cord and tossed the blade back to Andrew then massaged her wrists with his fingers.

"That feels so good," she murmured.

By now, Johnson had rolled to his feet. George ordered him to join the other man on the pew.

"How did he get his bloody nose?" Andrew asked.

George slipped an arm about Sam. "Courtesy of my bride-to-be," he said with pride.

"Jolly good, Samantha," Andrew praised.

"Watch these two," he said.

"Oh, they aren't going anywhere, are you gentlemen?" Andrew asked.

George led Sam away from the pair, down the aisle, until they reached the last row. He had her sit and brought his arm about her shoulder. She lay her head against his chest and their fingers laced together.

"I'm sorry," he said.

"For what?" She raised her head. "Percy was lying in wait for me. He followed me all the way from Rockwell. He went to London first and then came to Devon. You couldn't have known that."

"Still, I wasn't there to protect you." He tenderly stroked her bruised face. "I suppose this means I can't ever let you out of my sight again."

"Ever?" she asked playfully.

"Never," he said firmly. "I shall have to accompany you at all times. I'll need to share your bath. Your bed. I will be your shadow."

She placed her head back against his beating heart. "Oh, George. I do love you. So very, very much."

Mrs. White appeared with a tea tray and the requested cold compress. Sam held it to her face as she sipped her tea. Lord Wimbley showed up soon after.

"What is going on?" the elderly man demanded. "Mr. Gaddy told me it was an emergency but I couldn't get much else out of him."

"I am the Duke of Colebourne," George informed him. "This is my fiancée, Lady Haskett, who was abducted on her way to our wedding this morning."

The magistrate stared. "I say. By whom?"

"By the man who murdered my husband and father-in-law," Sam said quietly.

George looked at her, stunned. He listened as she recounted to the magistrate what had happened from the moment her carriage had been stopped and her driver shot. Lord Wimbley listened to her entire account, asking a question here and there for clarification.

"I can take this Steele fellow into custody for shooting your coachman," Wimbley explained. "If the man dies, Steele will hang. If not, he will go to prison. It is much harder to accuse a peer of the realm of murder, my lady, especially with no proof other than his supposed confession. Justice can be finicky when it involves a lord."

"Percy admitted killing Haskett and Lord Rockaway," Sam protested. "He threatened to kill His Grace unless I married him."

The magistrate gave them a canny look. "An earl who admits to committing a double murder and plotting to kill a duke sounds mad to me. Don't you think so, Your Grace?"

George wondered where this was going. "What do you think should happen to someone in this situation?"

"It is a sticky situation, Your Grace. I alone do not have the authority to declare a peer insane and sent to an asylum for life. It would take a lunacy commission to do so. Unfortunately, they rarely meet and it can take months before they render a decision once they have been presented with evidence."

He shook his head. "I won't have this man free to terrorize us, Lord Wimbley."

The magistrate grew thoughtful. "I can—if I receive a formal statement from you and Lady Haskett, as well as the Duke of Windham—hold Lord Rockaway in custody while I see about arranging an appearance before the commission for him. Would that be agreeable?"

George nodded his approval. "As long as he remains locked away until this commission meets. And I insist upon providing testimony to this body."

"I can see that happens. Might the three of you be willing to sit for your statements at this time?."

"Can we give those at a later date?" George asked, eager to remove Sam from the situation.

"No. Now," Sam urged. "I want this affair over and done with."

"Certainly, my lady," Lord Wimbley said. "I have two men outside who will take the earl and his man into custody. Let me fetch them."

Moments later, two large burly men entered the church, immediately going to the front. They placed handcuffs on both prisoners and led them by their elbows down the aisle.

"Strumpet!" shouted Rockaway as he passed them. "Whore!"

Neither George nor Sam said a word. Andrew joined them.

"We're to go with Lord Wimbley and give a statement," he told his friend. "Then we can go home and put this incident behind us for a while."

He caught movement from the corner of his eye and turned to face Rockaway. The earl broke free from his captor and bent, quickly pulling a blade from his boot. With madness in his eyes, Rockaway charged toward Sam.

"I'll kill you, you filthy trollop!"

George jerked Sam behind him, ready to take the blow meant for her, when a loud explosion filled the church. He winced at the noise and watched as Rockaway came to an abrupt halt, an odd expression upon his face.

The earl looked down and George saw a red stain growing on Rockaway's shirt. Then the earl's knees gave way and he fell to the ground.

Andrew was the first to reach him. Feeling for a pulse, his friend looked up, shaking his head. "Dead," he proclaimed.

George slipped an arm about Sam's waist and turned to Lord Wimbley. Seeing the pistol in the magistrate's hand, he realized it was Wimbley who had fired upon Rockaway.

"Are you all right, my lady?" Wimbley asked.

"Yes," she said, her voice firm. "Thank you, my lord. For saving the duke's life."

The magistrate looked grim as he said, "There was no other way to stop him in time." He turned to the men he'd brought with him and gave them instructions to secure their prisoner before they returned to handle the dead body. Then Wimbley looked back and said, "Though Lord Rockaway is now deceased, it will be of utmost importance for me to obtain your statements. Including what you just witnessed and if you believed deadly force was necessary."

"There is no doubt of that, Lord Wimbley," George assured him. "The three of us are more than happy to provide those statements to you."

He watched as Wimbley left the church and the two men returned to retrieve the body. Turning to Sam, he brushed a kiss upon her brow, wanting to reassure her after the horror she had gone through.

"Are we going to wed today, George?" Sam asked quietly.

He looked at her in surprise. "Is that what you wish? You have been through so much."

She gave him a radiant smile. "I'd rather go to bed tonight and have the comforting arms of my husband around me."

He returned her smile, warmth spreading through him. "I am happy to accommodate your wishes."

George pressed a soft kiss against her lips.

They went with Lord Wimbley and made their statements. Sam's was much longer than his or Andrew's since she had spent more time in Rockaway's company. George promised the magistrate that he would send word regarding the condition of the driver so Wimbley would know what charges to bring against Steele.

They returned to the carriage and were warmly welcomed by his driver. Andrew offered to drive the Treadwell carriage, which would give them privacy. Sam curled up against George and quickly fell asleep, not waking up until they arrived at Colebourne Hall. Andrew opened the door and saw her asleep and said, "Head to the church. I'll gather everyone here and meet you there."

Andrew closed the door and must have told the driver where to go because the carriage started up again. It arrived at the village church. Sam stirred and opened her eyes.

"Are we home?"

"We're at the church. Andrew is seeing that our wedding guests will arrive shortly."

"Let's go inside the vicarage. I must look a mess. Perhaps Mrs. Clements can loan me a brush."

George didn't have to knock at the door. It was already open and the Reverend and Mrs. Clements stood anxiously outside.

"Lady Haskett would like to freshen up with your help, Mrs. Clements," he said. "Our guests will be arriving again in the next few minutes. Are you up to try the ceremony again?" he asked the clergyman.

Reverend Clements' eyes grew wide but he said, "Of course, Your Grace. I'll need to see to lighting the chapel."

Half an hour later, everyone was in place. The few guests held candles. Andrew escorted Sam down the aisle in case she felt unsteady. As she walked toward George, love soared within him. Despite her rumpled gown and swollen face, she was the most beautiful creature who'd ever walked the earth.

Andrew placed her hand in George's and went to stand by his friend. Phoebe stood next to Sam. As Reverend Clements' soothing tones filled the chapel, George clasped his bride's hand and smiled down at her.

"I love you," he mouthed silently.

"I love you," she responded, just as quietly.

As they pledged their hearts to one another, George knew theirs would be a life filled with love. He poured all his love into the tender kiss at the end of the ceremony, knowing how this special woman had changed the course of his life.

When he broke the kiss, Sam said, "We certainly will have quite the wedding story to tell our children."

George laughed heartily, knowing laughter would always be a key part of their lives.

EPILOGUE

London—1835

SAMANTHA AWOKE TO George pressing tender kisses along her nape. Her back was pressed against his chest, his arms wrapped around her.

"Good morning, my love," she said softly.

"It is a good morning, indeed," he agreed. "It's not every day that our firstborn child marries."

She wriggled until she faced him and lovingly stroked his face. At fifty, George still was a very handsome man. His mane of tawny hair showed a few streaks of light in it but other than that, he looked very much like the man she had wed over twenty years ago.

"I thought we should celebrate privately," he said, a wicked gleam coming into his eyes.

She pretended she didn't understand and looked about the room. "I don't see any champagne."

"When have we ever needed champagne to celebrate?" he asked, his voice low and rough at her ear.

He nibbled on her lobe and then bit into it. A frisson of desire raced through her as she moaned and pushed her fingers into his thick hair. His lips found hers and the searing kiss led to a full session of lovemaking.

Nestled in his arms in the aftermath, Samantha thought she would never tire of this man and the way he loved her completely. George was her world. He would go on being her everything as each of their children slowly left the nest, as Sophie would today at St. George's Chapel.

"Shall we go down to breakfast?" he asked. "Or would you rather have something sent up to us?"

She chuckled. "It will probably be chaotic downstairs. I say we enjoy the last bit of peace and quiet together before the day erupts in noise."

He rang and had breakfast trays sent up to them. As she sipped her hot chocolate, she savored every swallow, recalling when the simple treat was denied to her by her mother-in-law. Those times were far in her past, though. She lived for her present—and her future.

"When would you like to give Sophie her gift?" George asked.

"Let's wait until she's dressed and it's almost time to go," she suggested.

He kissed her. "Then I will see you in a little while."

Returning to her bedchamber, Samantha had Lucy help her dress. The maid had been with her from the terrible times until now and she appreciated Lucy's loyalty and friendship throughout the years.

"You look splendid, Your Grace," the servant said. "A perfect mother of the bride."

She glanced into the mirror. Though Samantha saw small signs of aging, George continued to tell her she was the most beautiful woman in England. She might be prejudiced but she thought her daughter would hold that honor today. Sophie had made a love match with Lord Ainsford and walked about with the glow of love embracing her these days.

"Thank you, Lucy. Let's go to Sophie's room and help, shall we?"

The two women went down the corridor and slipped inside the bedchamber, where Sophie stood in cream silk satin. The gown's bateau neck was trimmed with cream fringe and had attached capelets extending from her shoulders. The bodice had a satin lattice and twisted satin braid that went to her waist. Though Samantha had seen her firstborn in her wedding gown over numerous fittings, the realization that Sophie would be a wife in less than two hours caused her eyes to brim with tears. Quickly, she dabbed a handkerchief to them and slipped it inside her bodice again, knowing she would use it several times today.

"Mama! What do you think?" Sophie asked, twirling about, a radiant smile on her face.

She crossed to her and embraced her daughter. "You look lovely."

"Would Lucy do my hair?" Sophie begged. "She's so good with it."

"Of course, my lady."

Sophie sat and Samantha watched as the maid's deft fingers created a simple yet elegant coiffure. George slipped in just as Lucy finished.

Sophie saw him and came to her feet. "What do you think, Papa?"

"It's almost like going back in time," he replied. "You remind me so much of your mother at that age."

"I may have Mama's looks and her raven hair but I do have your green eyes," she said.

Samantha bit back a smile. Sophie had always been close to her father and Samantha thought it sweet of her to remark upon their shared eye color.

"Your mother and I have something for you," he said.

Sophie's eyes grew large. "What? Let me see," she said insistently.

George laughed. "Patience has never been one of your virtues," he teased and then pulled out the box from behind his back.

Sophie took it and opened it, gasping. "It's Mama's diamond necklace and earrings!" she exclaimed. "Oh, Papa, I cannot take them."

They both said, "You must," and George added, "They first belonged to my grandmother. She wore them on her wedding day and gifted them to my mother on her special day."

Samantha lightly touched her daughter's cheek. "And your father gave them to me to wear on our wedding day." She sighed. "He even said as he did so that we would give them to our oldest daughter on her wedding day one day in the future."

Tears filled Sophie's eyes. "Thank you."

She embraced them both and then grinned. "I suppose it's good I am your only daughter and all the rest of your children turned out to be boys." She fingered the necklace and then looked to Samantha. "Mama, would you help me put it on?"

"Of course, my darling."

She lifted the necklace from its resting place and brought it over Sophie's head. Fastening the clasp, she said, "Turn around and let me see. Oh, yes, it looks marvelous with your dress."

Sophie beamed and then put on the earrings. "Ainsford will love me in these," she proclaimed.

"Ainsford would love you if you showed up in rags," George said gruffly and turned away.

Samantha saw he wiped a tear away. She reached and took his hand, her fingers lacing through his. He smiled at her and then looked to their daughter.

"Shall we leave for St. George's Chapel?" he asked.

"Yes, Papa." Sophie stood on tiptoe and kissed his cheek and then Samantha's and said, "You have been a shining example to me. I hope Ainsford and I will be as happy as the pair of you."

Samantha looked to the man she called husband. Lover. Friend. Confidant.

"You will be," she assured her daughter.

Sophie crossed the room, Lucy following, leaving them alone for a moment.

"We have been happy, haven't we?" George asked.

"We have. And the best is yet to be," Samantha promised as his lips touched hers.

About the Author

Award-winning and internationally bestselling author Alexa Aston's historical romances use history as a backdrop to place her characters in extraordinary circumstances, where their intense desire for one another grows into the treasured gift of love.

She is the author of Regency and Medieval romance, including: Dukes of Distinction; Soldiers & Soulmates; The St. Clairs; The King's Cousins; and The Knights of Honor.

A native Texan, Alexa lives with her husband in a Dallas suburb, where she eats her fair share of dark chocolate and plots out stories while she walks every morning. She enjoys a good Netflix binge; travel; seafood; and can't get enough of *Survivor* or *The Crown*.